Unveiled
The Seelie Court Chronicles
Part One

J.B May

Dedication

Like most people, I struggle with a nemesis greater than any bully and it's a villain that can never entirely be defeated.

It's the voice that lingers in the back of my mind. It's different for everyone, some voices scream louder than others, some voices have less to say and sometimes people are just better at ignoring it, but it's there all the same.

I'm luckier than most. I'm blessed with wonderful people in my life that love me enough to help me drown it out.

I dedicate this book to the voice of doubt… You are finally nothing more than a whisper.

Acknowledgements

I want to thank my family, both blood and choice. Each of you have always believed that I am better than I am and have allowed me to see myself through your eyes, on more than one occasion, which I'm grateful for.

To my husband David, thanks for always making me wear my reading glasses and not letting me get too distracted from my dreams. Your push to make me take a chance on myself has made all of this possible.

My mum Kim who encouraged me to pursue my love of writing and made sure I never had another 'tentacles vs testicles' auto correct moment, like in that unfortunate assignment.

To Sue Kennedy and Lou Reed thank you both for seeing potential in my abilities and bringing this book to print. Without you, this book would have spent the rest of its days trapped inside my tiny pink laptop, where no one would have known of its existence.

Last but not least I want to thank my brothers. Ben, Jake, Patrick, Daniel and Michael there is a piece of each of you written in the pages of this book. Thank you for your inspiration.

Table of Contents

Introduction

Daydreams and imagination are things that shouldn't be contained. Left imprisoned in the confines of your mind they can become ravenous things. At times the only way to appease them is to unlock the shackles and set them free. This is why I wrote this book; because the untamed thoughts wouldn't allow themselves to remain caged any longer.

In a secret world filled with magic, monarchs and betrayal what would be your greatest asset? Is it the power you obtain, the fear you instil or the secrets you keep? Life is never just the choices you make; it is the actions and reactions of the people around you and no one mind ever has the full story.

'His pulse quickens as it fights to slip between the tautness of my fingers. I feel the final thread of his heartbeat; a gentle release of breath escapes his lips and his life is no more. I release my hold and let his body plummet into the icy waters below.' Seth has lived an eternity, where death, violence and depravity are just a normal Monday and that's the way he likes it. In his world of secrets and sin, he would never give a human a second glance. That is unless they had the unfortunate fate of becoming his next meal. But one girl is going to challenge everything he thought he knew…

Adaline Thomas has just survived the un-survivable. Keeping her life should be a blessing, but losing her mother is another thing entirely. Being a teenager is hard enough and doing it all without the unconditional love of a parent is almost unthinkable. If only grief was the only thing Adaline had to worry about. With her mother dead, the spell has been broken and the secrets of Adaline's past are coming back to haunt her. Is she strong enough to embrace the life she's destined for?

In a world of intrigue, betrayal and enchantment can a forbidden love save them both?

- 1 -

SETH

Look at them, the oblivious human race, they might as well be vermin the way they scurry around with their meaningless lives. If they took one single second to look outside themselves, perhaps their mortal eyes might be able to peer through the veil that separates our worlds. Maybe then they could see what's right in front of them. At this very moment, one of their fallen brothers is teetering just above their heads, inches from death. I am not referring to myself of cause; I haven't been human for a very long time.

The limp figure that cowers under my grasp lingers over the edge of the bridge. His wasted life amounting to nothing more than this, a faceless man who will soon be forgotten. I consider the trouble my bite marks on his neck might cause if they were discovered, but the marine life below will make short work of that. I look at the swine's neck once more and see no reason I shouldn't indulge myself.

As I sink my teeth through the thin layer of skin and into the connective tissues I can taste the bitterness of the methamphetamines pulsing through his system. The low-grade human chemicals begin seeping through his pores as he shudders under my bite. I'll admit it, I like the euphoric buzz that the drugs add to his blood, but I disdain the vile aftertaste they leave behind. I withdraw my teeth from the flow of his wound and clench my hand a little tighter around his neck. His pulse quickens as it fights to slip between the tautness of my fingers. I feel the final thread of his heartbeat; a gentle release of breath escapes his lips and his life is no more. I release my hold and let his body plummet into the icy waters below. Even as his corpse descends, no one notices, no one even blinks an eye in my direction.

I dance between the rafters of the bridge, watching the humans passing below. I'm invisible, a ghost drifting between shadows as they walk around blindly. I could almost pity them and their ignorance. I watch as drunken youths drag themselves out of the local watering hole, staggering with each step, each one of them easy prey for the taking. A couple in a car slow down to park at the shoreline, the man whispers sweet nothings into his lover's ear while she giggles and casts her gaze innocently towards the ocean view.

If any of them knew of my existence they wouldn't be so light-hearted. They would cling to their mother's breast as they trembled in fear, terrified of the monster lurking in the darkness. I envy the delusions of mortals, fooling themselves into believing they are decent species, but in secret, they are as corrupt as I am. The only thing that keeps most of their immoral desires at bay is their humanity. A switch they can turn off or on as they so desire. Humanity is a luxury I no longer have, and most days I'm thankful for it.

If I'm being honest there was something within me from the beginning, a wickedness that hid inside of me. It craved darkness and sin, but it continued to lay dormant beneath an illusion of humanity and kindness, at least until the night when I slithered from this world into the next. My rebirth was excruciating, I remember the piercing sound of my bones splintering as they manipulated themselves into something else, something strong.

My skin turned acidic, burning away everything that made me who

I once was. I desperately tried ripping the repugnant flesh from my body, but I was immobilized. Frozen in a state of torment, unable to make my limbs obey. I feared my body wasn't my own anymore, it had abandoned me and left me for dead. That's when all the darkness that had been simmering inside me floated to the surface, revealing a creature of darkness and iniquity.

When I awoke, I found my new life boiled down to nothing more than my basic instincts. My greatest and most unpleasant desires were unshackled from their chains and released into the world. I don't remember exactly how much time I lost inside the crimson veil, but the blood of my victims painted more than my hands, it numbered my days. I had become a creature of savage survival. It was years before my skin started to cool and my muscles ceased to quiver at the scent of blood. In time, I regained a fraction of self-control, little did it matter. Becoming one of the undead was never something I had planned on, but we don't always get what we want, do we?

I hear the soothing uproar of waves crashing below and despite their riot, I also hear the shuffle of feet knocking into rocks and breaking twigs under their weight. Somebody has stepped into my hunting grounds. I outstretch my arms and leap from the bridge; the wind beats against my face, the freedom of fallings surreal. It's one of the few things that still gives me pleasure anymore. I land silently next to Jason. The pleasure of the fall over before it even begun.

"You're still too loud," I say.

"I'll work on it," Jason replies.

"It's been fifty years. If you haven't gotten it by now I doubt you ever will," I tell him.

"Are you ready for the meeting?" Jason asks.

"I suppose. Run along and tell my brother I will be there soon," I order. Jason obeys with a small salute, vanishing before I can laugh at his gesture.

The only evidence he stood by my side is the small remnants of unsettled sand forming a cloud in his wake. I turn and look once more upon the figure as he drifts out to sea. I pine for the days when I didn't have to hide my true nature, but there's no room left in this modern world for ungoverned vampires.

- 2 -
Deklan

Twice a year for the last eighteen years I have had to leave the safety of the Vale and travel to the mortal realm. I have my reservations about the outside world, but business is business and I'll admit seeing Sarah is never a task I regret. During the six hours that I spend with Sarah, I have enough time to ensure the stability of the protection wards, arrange transportation and organise proper documentation for her and the child's next move. But with the child's powers growing stronger each day it's becoming increasingly difficult to shield their location and I worry relocating twice a year isn't frequent enough.

When Sarah wrote to me a month ago and asked to delay our meeting I admit I was hesitant to change our routine. But it had been two years since Sarah has seen her brother and I know too well the sacrifice she has made to keep the child safe. It's the same decision I made all those years ago. It's not easy keeping everyone I love at arm's length, but we do what we must for the greater good.

It's nearly five o'clock in the evening and I'm currently sitting between two unsightly humans, both of whom have bathed themselves in offensive sprays and oils. I'm almost thankful for their overpowering odour as it masks the stale sourness that's embedded in the seats and carpet of the rusty tin can. As I struggle with the numerous offending odours, a distressing thought drifts through my mind. I realise agreeing to postpone our meeting is turning out to be the biggest mistake of my life.

Sarah should have called me twelve hours ago when I arrived through the portal and she's never missed a deadline before. I've been calling her cell phone incessantly since the plane took off, only to be greeted each time by her sweet voice asking me to leave a message. I have the child's cell phone memorised, but I have never intended to use it. She's not meant to know about me, but I'm running out of options.

The flight has almost arrived at Portland International Airport when the captain announces phone restrictions will be enforced in the next ten minutes. I dial the number I promised I never would; I almost give up hope of an answer when a male voice responds on the other end. I ask to speak with Sarah; maybe the child never needs to know I called. The man begins to cry. Between muffled breaths, I hear the words I've dreaded hearing for the last eighteen years.

"She's dead," he says.

Sarah's loving face flashes into my mind, I remember the affectionate way she cradled the baby all those years ago. I recall how she took the burden in her stride and built a life for herself and the baby. Now I've failed them both. Everything we have sacrificed has been for nothing. The man regains his composure and begins to rehash the details of the plane crash and the loss of Sarah. My minds too preoccupied to focus, and I don't really give the man the attention he deserves. Every so often my voice switches to autopilot and offers my apologies.

"I don't know what I would have done if I had lost them both," the man admits, his voice softening with fondness.

"What do you mean both? Did the girl survive?" I ask.

"I'm sorry, I thought you knew. I figured that's why you called her cell phone. Who is this?" The man asks.

I disconnect the call and crush the cell phone between my fingers. The gawky woman next to me raises her eyebrows at the crumpled phone in my hands. I discard the phone to the floor and return my emergency bag to the overhead locker as people start settling into the planes decent. I may have failed Sarah, but it's not too late for me to save the child.

- 3 -

SETH

My foot touches the antique floorboards and regardless of their age, they don't creak under my weight. I climb the narrow staircase and make my way to the south wing, towards the great hall that once housed kings and queens. The walls of the castle hold the secrets of history; battle plans, affairs and more royal assassinations than I can count on one hand. I'm assured it will safeguard a few more secrets before my time here is through.

Every time I enter the hall I'm saddened by the contemporary enhancements that have besieged its classic beauty. Heavy green velvet drapes curtain the windows, attempting to hide the blackout retractable blinds beneath. Embellished silken rugs take the place of handwoven floor coverings that were built for warmth, not just aesthetic appeal. My brother Aedan insisted on installing tall electric candelabras, which still feel out of place to me.

I think real candles would have given the room the authenticity it deserves. A generous oak table with a shine that could rival any mirror holds the room captive in its glory. Accompanying the pretentious table are four regal chairs that surround it like guards. Usually, the table sits cold and empty but tonight three figures claim its attention.

Aedan sits with his back to the open window. He is dressed in a clean double button silk shirt and expertly ironed black pants. On his right is a sleek blonde-haired woman with a thick coating of black eye makeup and heavyset gold earrings. She's wearing a long black gown with a neckline that drapes down to her navel revealing more of her flesh than necessary. If her sullenness didn't ooze from her pores like bad body odor you could almost consider her attractive. The last inhabitant is older looking than the rest. He was in his late forties when he became one of us. His creamy milk chocolate complexion and glossy bald head set him apart more than his age does. Just like my brother Samuel is expertly groomed in a tailored Gucci navy suit that screams style and sophistication. As Aedan's eye's fall to me, I can see that he's unimpressed with my torn jeans and faded t-shirt.

"Seth, I'm so pleased you decided to grace us with your presence. You even dressed up for the occasion," says Aedan.

"Well I do like to live in this century," I joke gesturing to Maura's attire. The concerned look on Aedan's face warns me to watch my tone. "Excuse my rudeness, I forget my manners when I'm surrounded by such beauty," I say and offer her a respectful bow. She nods her head in response, waving me off like a child.

"Thank you for welcoming Maura and I into your home, it's been far too long," Samuel says.

Samuel reaches into his inner jacket pocket and reveals a small piece of parchment that's seen better days and places it on the table before us. I feel Maura's shoulders tighten and my brother's sharp release of breath. I'm confused by their intense response to a mangled piece of paper. I reach forward, closing my fingers around the brittle scroll and unfurl the parchment. Years spent signing one fae peace treaty or another has forced me to learn the lost language and I recognise it instantly. I read the fae passage aloud.

'In the darkest hours, man must fall,

Both magic and mortal will forfeit their all,

The child born with the power of change,

Redemption or ruin rests solely in the child's claim.'

"It's a nursery rhyme," I say blankly.

"It's more than a child's song, it's a prophecy. The fates have foretold it from the beginning," Samuel says.

Samuel withdraws a clipping from a newspaper article. In the centre below the title, 'Sole survivor' is a picture of a small plane smoking between rocky mountain ridges. Next to the article is another photo, this time of a girl in her late teens. In the picture, her eyes are bright and happy. She has generous auburn hair flowing down her back. Her figure is womanly, but her face still has the soft roundness of childhood. Her rosy cheeks and sweet coloured lips highlight her innocence and bring a warmth to her radiating smile. My fire element sparks a response, taking me by surprise. It's hard to articulate the right emotion that's stirring the fire inside me. I ignore the irrational sentiments and shove them deep down inside myself before they can take hold of my focus.

"We had to wait until the human media moved on to the next tragedy, but my witch was able to track her back to Texas. We need to contain her before others become aware of her existence. The last thing any of us need is for the treaty to fail, a war between the sides could destroy everything we have worked so hard to build," Samuel says.

"Just send one of the enforcers. I'll send one of my own if you wish," Maura adds with the wave of her hand. "We're not killing an innocent child," I say, surprised by the force in my voice.

"Since when did you grow a conscience?" Maura scoffs.

"No, he's right. We have no idea what kind of chain reaction killing her could cause. We could cause a natural disaster that could kill millions of people," Aedan says. I watch as the lines on Maura's face tighten and her mouth turns into a venomous snarl.

"Maura please adjust your mood or you're going to freeze us to death," Samuel says as I feel the chill in the air lessen. "This child has been destined since the end of the war. If the girl has arrived, I fear for us all," Samuel says softly.

"I don't understand. Why are you all so concerned, she's just a girl?" I ask.

"Because if she's here then the next great war isn't far behind," Samuel replies.

"Very well, Seth and I will fly out first thing in the morning," Aedan says.

Maura and Samuel excuse themselves and make their way to their bedchambers, leaving me alone with my brother. I sit idly as Aedan barks orders out to our men. He sends Jason to ready the jet while a select few are sent to the armory. My eyes find their way back to the article resting on the great table. My stomach flutters again at the sight of her, perhaps my midnight snack on the bridge had been ill-advised.

"Do you really think this girl is the one? She hardly seems like the bringer of death and destruction," I ask.

Aedan follows my gaze to the photo of the girl. His eyes widen in fascination, making my stomach lurch once more. I raise my eyebrows at his lingering stare, he catches my reaction and corrects his wandering eyes.

"I guess we will soon find out. We had better get ourselves ready to leave. Do try to pack something appropriate for the weather Seth we don't need any unwanted attention," he says. I nod in agreeance.

I cross the table towards the open window; a calm breeze climbs the castle walls and washes over me. The scent of the moss-covered stones tickles my nose; it's the smell of home, a smell I never thought I would become fond of, but here I am missing it before I have even left.

I can see frenzied storm clouds rolling in on the horizon, making their way down the mountainside. I just hope this hostile weather isn't a warning sign of things to come.

- 4 -

Adaline

The air is heavy in my lungs as I struggle to breathe. It's colder than I imagined, and the harsh movements rattle me. Suddenly I'm floating. I feel like a piece of me is being dragged from my body, like I'm losing an invisible limb. I float aimlessly wondering if I'll ever feel whole again. The lost part of me is clawing at my body, trying desperately to slip back inside. I can't hold on any longer, I think I'm dying. I should feel frightened, but I'm not. I release my grip on the blue haze that surrounds me and I'm comforted in the darkness. I feel at peace. That's when the bliss of oblivion is abruptly disturbed by a glowing warmth. It reaches out to me, soothing my body with its tender touch. The light begins to fade, receding into the darkness. I reach for it, but I'm not fast enough. The ecstasy of the memory dies. My body jerks in spasms and in the distance, I can hear a voice screaming, but I can't recognise it.

I scream, this time recognising the sound of my voice as it's floating between the world of sleep and wakefulness. Through sleep-deprived eyes and pale moonlight, I can see my body is glazed with a cold sweat that's sticky to the touch. I move my legs as they quiver under the thick blankets. I shake myself free from the bedding restraints and try to banish the awful dream with them. I sit up in the puddle of sweat and rub myself for reassurance, but the painful memory plays in the back of my mind like a song stuck in my head.

"Adaline are you okay?" Jerry calls out to me through the darkness. My poor uncle, he's suffering as much sleep deprivation as I am lately.

The details of the memory are starting to fade leaving behind a lingering agony that's hiding just beneath the surface of my skin. I draw the covers in tightly, trying to hide the evidence of my unbearable nightmares.

"It's just a bad dream. I'm fine, go back to bed," I assure him.

He hesitates for a moment, like he has almost every night since my arrival. He smiles sweetly before retreating to his room. I know he's unsure how to comfort me. Having no children of his own and a carefree bachelor lifestyle only a few short months ago, he was grossly unprepared for instant parenthood. Nevertheless, he has been my saviour through this hellish ordeal and I don't know what I would have done without him.

During my short hospital stay, I was bombarded with several therapists and child psychologists for weeks after the accident. They threw words at me like PTSD, depression and anxiety. They warned my uncle to watch out for any suicidal signs or unusual behaviours that might indicate I'm not coping. They tried waving fingers and lights across my vision in hopes of dissuading the memories, but nothing worked. The pills they prescribed made me numb and feeling nothing at all was worse. Not mourning the loss of my mother felt like a betrayal, so I stopped taking them. The problem with stopping the medication cold turkey is that the flashbacks are hitting me harder than I had imagined.

The clock on the nightstand mocks me, flashing its claim to three am. I'm suddenly regretting how hard I pushed the idea of going back to school. In a few short hours, I'll be starting my new life without my best friend to help guide me through. I continue to shift between the ghosts of my dreams and the nightmares of my reality. I finally wear myself out and fall asleep, if only for a little while.

I press the snooze button for the fourth and final time before I drag my exhausted body out of bed. I fuss with my hair longer than necessary and try to find the right balance of makeup. I've only attended private schools that require mandatory uniforms and I'm struggling to know what to wear. With the clock ticking away, I need to make a decision and stick to it. I adorn a black and white striped singlet top and some comfortable black jeans. Once I add my tan boots and match it with the leather jacket I'm happy enough with my efforts. Before leaving the safety of the second level and descending the stairs I pause, taking a deep breath to ready myself. I catch a glimpse of my reflection in the mirror, I fake a smile, but I can see it's forced. I'm finding it harder and harder to recognise myself anymore. I feel like I'm playing dress up, wearing a skin that's not my own.

The sensational aroma of bacon ascends the staircase shattering my negative thoughts. My stomach churns feeling light and it's not from the smell. Something inside me feels wrong. I suddenly feel weightless and before I have time to grab onto anything my legs buckle beneath me. Cumbersomely I tumble down the staircase, grazing my forehead on the wooden banister before landing squarely at the bottom of the stairs. I correct myself into a sitting position, taking stock of my injuries. I touch my finger to my temple, a thundering ache traces across my forehead making me wince. I look up to see Jerry towering above me with tongs in one hand and his 'greatest uncle' apron tied securely at his waist.

"What are you doing on the floor?" He asks.

"I tripped. I cut my head on the banister. Is it bad?" I ask.

Jerry gently tilts my head upwards to get a better look, I see the dread in his eyes. It's a look he's been wearing far too often these days. He assures me it's only a slight graze and no blood has been spilled. All too eagerly, I follow him into the kitchen and drop my body heavily into one of the chairs. Jerry shuffles through items in the freezer until he finds what he's looking for. He places the cold bag of peas on my forehead and the relief is almost instant.

"Maybe you should stay home another day. The school would understand," he offers.

"The longer I put it off the worse it will be; besides I need to focus on something other than these four walls," I smile reassuringly. "I'll be okay," I promise.

"Well if your minds set you had better get going. Are you sure you don't want me to drive you?" He asks.

"Thanks, but I'll be okay," I say.

He kisses me on the top of my head and offers me an apple for the road which I slip into my bag. Teasingly, I snatch a piece of bacon off his plate as I run out the back door. As I walk down the driveway I take in the sunshine and savour the saltiness of the crispy bacon strip as it touches my tongue. I don't know if it's the bacon or the sun, but I feel my mood begin to brighten.

- 5 -

SETH

I have never been a fan of aeroplanes, I'd prefer to travel by car or on foot, but when you're racing against a ticking clock taking to the sky is unavoidable. I'm relieved when Jason takes the first shift; he flies the plane smoothly and with minimal turbulence. I look out the window at the open skies before me; feeling relaxed enough to fall asleep. Unfortunately, it's a fleeting sense of security as I'm rocketed from my seat as the plane makes an angled decent. I leap out of my seat and push my way through the jolting shocks and frightened people. By the time I reach the front of the plane I can see Aedan sitting in the captain seat. My brother is accomplished in many things, but flying planes are at the bottom of his resume. If only my brother didn't view his capabilities through rose coloured glasses. My eyes search eagerly for Jason; peering through the small crowd of confused and shaken vampires in our company. Our eyes lock as he emerges from one of the bathrooms in the back.

As Jason passes I offer him a disgruntled look and he mutters a hushed apology under his breath. Jason should know better than to let Aedan take command of the flight, I still have flashbacks of the last trip we took together and if it wasn't for compulsion we would be locked in a third world gaol cell right now. I settle back into my seat once Aedan is securely buckled in beside me, and despite his actions, we manage to make it to Texas in one piece.

It's been a long time since I set foot in Texas, but the air still smells as I remember, hot and overcrowded with overweight tourists wearing stupid shirts while they sweat all over the place. I must be scrunching my nose because Aedan rolls his eyes in my direction.

"What?" I hiss.

"Nothing brother, I can just tell what you're thinking. Leave the poor humans alone they can't help it. Jason and the others are going on to set up at the hotel. You and I are heading straight to the school. Shall we grab something to eat beforehand?" He asks.

"I don't smell anyone worth dirtying my shirt for. Let's just get this done," I reply. I don't mean to be so short with him, but I can't help it. Since the plane took off I've had this overwhelming sense of urgency and the longer it's taking the more irritated I'm becoming.

The drive is uneventful and quieter than the usual trips I have taken with my brother. I could blame my mood on lack of sleep or the fact that I've hardly eaten, but I'm distracted by a girl I've never met. Images of her innocent face and trusting eyes attack my mind and other things. It's been a while since I had female contact. Maura's second in command Shaylin used to be the woman who would take care of my urges, but that ended when she became too attached. I was surprised to see her yesterday and even more surprised that she's riding alongside Jason in the car behind us. Maura insisted her right hand come along, like Aedan and I couldn't be trusted. If anyone's not trustworthy it's that cold bitch. I welcome my hatred for Maura, it's a pleasant distraction from the other unseemly thoughts I'm having. I sit quietly stewing in my loathing for Maura until I'm mentally drained and allow myself to catch up on some much-needed sleep.

I wake abruptly when Aedan brakes forcefully making us jolt forward. When I'm finished cursing at my brothers driving I wipe away the sleep from my eyes until they adjust to the lighting. The sun has come out while I've slept, and I find us parked across the street from a small high school.

The school grounds are basic at best, all squares and triangles. A structure built for functionality, not beauty. The classrooms are run down with aging desks and stacks of overly used books piled high in the back. I use the guise of being a new student to ask around for the girl, while Aedan waits in the car. The only problem is the children are more interested in myself rather than telling me what I want to know. I even resort to using compulsion on a few, but I only encounter one stupid person after another. Eventually, I stumble onto a group of girls who look about the same age as the one I'm after. I flash a flirtatious smile that makes the girls giggle like infants, at least one of the girls gives me something I can use. The new girl was absent from homeroom this morning. So much for a simple snatch and grab.

As I approach the black SUV I notice that my brother is missing from the driver's seat. The keys are in the ignition, but the car has been turned off and there's no sign of a struggle. My inquisition inside the school grounds did take longer than I had expected, but he still could have waited for me. I take over the driver's seat and settle in to wait for his return.

- 6 -
Adaline

I'm one street away from the school when I look down at my watch and I realise I've already missed the start of roll call. I consider taking up my uncles offer to stay home but going home would be like admitting defeat. I continue to march myself forward, but with each step, I feel my nerves pulling tighter and tighter in my chest. My march slows to a crawl. I fiddle with my shirt and the zipper on my bag, allowing more time to pass the longer I fidget. I shift the part in my hair to strategically cover the raised lump on my forehead. I look up at the heavens and ask them if I'm ready for this, but I receive no guidance. I reach an old wooden bus stop and throw my bag against the seat. Pacing back and forth, I know I'm working myself into a frenzy. I must decide, go home or go to school; I'm equally strong enough and weak enough for either option. I decide on neither. I make myself comfortable under the bus shelter and retrieve a book from my bag. Delving into the pages of another person's tragedy might make my woes seem a little less.

I become so lost in a world of imagination I almost dismiss the vicious clouds settling in around me. The sudden shift in temperature catches my attention more than the dulled hue of the sky. I can smell the rain before it hits the pavement. It's a clean familiar scent that has always found me comfort. When other children would run to their mother's beds at the first shriek of thunder, I would race the stairs to the attic or whatever window our current home had and cast open the shutters. I would curl up on the window sill and drink in the steady rain. My tense muscles would relax as bolts of lightning would strike down from the heavens and by the end of the storm, I always felt renewed.

This storm is exactly what I need right now, I lower my book and set my eyes to the sky. I watch in awe as a battle unfolds before me. An overshadowing cloud dances to its own tune as it doubles in size. A smaller cloud that's been left behind tries to evade the path of the colossal monster, but it's not quick enough. The little cloud abandons its futile attempt at escape and is swallowed by the beast.

Transfixed by the state of the heavens I barely notice the young man trying to escape the onslaught of rain. My breath catches nervously in my chest as his eyes fall on me. I shy away from his gaze as he edges closer and I turn my attention to the sky.

"Crazy weather you American's have, isn't it? At least at home, I expect the constant rain," he says.

"I suppose," I whisper over the top of my tattered book.

"Pleasure to meet you, Adaline," he say's reaching out a friendly hand. I ignore his polite gesture, I'm more concerned with how this stranger knows my name. I slip my book back into my bag and smile sweetly at him.

"I have to go, my uncles waiting for me," I lie.

I turn my back to him and enter the curtain of rain. Just when I think I'm making a smooth getaway, I stumble on the uneven sidewalk and tumble to the ground. Everything in my bag empties in front of me and a few items roll into the sodden street. Hastily I try to correct myself beneath the moisture of fading rain.

I hear the scraping of metal on tar; the man begins picking up my belongings. I look up to find us almost cheek to cheek. His bright blue eyes devour me, and his smile deepens as he hands me my muddy jar of lip gloss.

"I didn't mean to startle you before. I saw your name on your keychain," he says pointing to the chain on my bag.

I glance down at the purple and gold keychain my mother had brought me. She had ordered it especially online since my name is not easy to find in gift shops. She wanted to be sure I wouldn't confuse my bag with the other kids at school. The young man continues speaking and the words flow from his mouth effortlessly, but my thoughts are no longer focused on his smile or delicate words. I'm lost in the memory of my first day of high school and the proud look on my mother's teary face. I was so scared. It was another new town and another new school. I felt much like I do right now.

"Courage and kindness," I whisper to myself. I'm pretty sure my mother read it on a bumper sticker somewhere, but it's the motto she lived by. She said it to me that first day and every day until she died. She would have said it to me this morning if she was here with me. The young man looks confused and a nervous smile hides in the corner of his perfectly formed mouth. "I'm sorry for being rude. It's been a while since I've conversed with people, my manners are out of practice," I say nervously and outstretch my hand to him. "I'm Adaline, officially," I say.

"Aedan," he says taking my hand in his. He squeezes firmly, and a smirk breaks his lips and I smile back.

"I really need to get going, I'm already late," I say.

"Well then, until next time Miss Adaline," he says.

I watch the handsome figure disappear into the fading fog and my heart skips a little beat. As if on cue the clouds part revealing a bursting sun that's desperate to shine its light on me. Maybe this small town won't be so bad after all.

- 7 -

SETH

Thirty excruciating minutes pass before Aedan returns to the car. He climbs into the passenger seat dripping wet, the smell of rain still clings to his skin and fills the car with its freshness. Aedan turns the heater on and removes his soggy jacket discarding it to the back seat. He smiles distractedly as if the fact that he abandoned me here like an idiot has escaped his mind.

"What happened to you?" I ask. I'm tempted to snap his neck in sheer frustration. I watch his damp face and small smile transform into a broad mischievous grin. I can't stop myself and I punch him in the jaw.

"What the hell was that for?" He asks making an exaggerated rubbing gesture of his chin.

To be honest I don't know why I hit him or why I find his face so infuriating all of a sudden. I'm used to his overconfidence and often childlike charm. A subtle breeze drifts through the open window allowing me to recognise where my hostility is stemming from. It's not what my brother did, it's a smell lingering on his damp clothing. The smell of sunshine and fresh spring flowers hiding beneath the guise of rain. It's an unusual scent, but it's distinctly feminine.

"You left me sitting here to run off and get a snack," I say. The anger that's been building inside my chest explodes. I'm not angry with my brother, I'm angry with the world and poor Aedan is caught in the flames, literally. Small sparks of fire flicker on his shirt despite the moisture they keep. The flames start to burn bright and hot. He rips the shirt from his body and casts it out the window before it can cause any real damage. I feel the flames die in the dirt.

"Calm down Seth," he whispers as he cradles my face. "Why are you so worked up? Calm yourself. While I waited for you the earth called out and I followed. I found her just sitting there at a bus stop reading. It was the strangest sensation," He says. I breathe deeply and the fire inside me settles. Aedan pats my shoulder once more, I focus on the steady vibration of the earth that's radiating from within him. "Are you okay?" He asks.

"I'm sorry. I lost control for a minute, but I'm okay," I tell him. "And sorry about your shirt," I add.

"What's one piece of Prada between brothers? If you feel you can hold yourself together can you head back into school? Your enrolment is prearranged," Aedan says.

"Why can't you do it?" I plead.

"Firstly, I'm not wearing a shirt. Secondly, you've already met some of the students, we don't want to draw too much attention to ourselves and after meeting her I think we should approach this differently. We need to get her to trust us. She needs to see that working with us is in her own best interest," Aedan says.

"After setting you on fire I guess it's the least I can do. Do you have the paperwork?" I ask.

"Packed them yesterday, figured they might come in handy," he leans over the seat and pulls out a backpack. "I even have books and supplies. Have fun, I'll see you at three," he says.

"Yeah thanks," I reply.

It takes me a few seconds to regain my composure after he abruptly shoves me out of the car. I look down at his partially melted shirt and I'm glad I burnt it. I cast my eyes towards the metallic school gates and decide to face my demons and get this over with. At the very least, once I meet her I will be able to settle this irrational feeling that's taking root inside of me.

- 8 -
Adaline

My feet hit the pavement of the school parking lot. I straighten my back and lift my head proudly, trying to emulate the strength I wish I had. I stride to the office with purpose, ignoring my dishevelled appearance the rain has caused. The gates surrounding the school appear welcoming at first glance. They give the illusion of hope and bright futures, but I see them as the farce they are. As I walk through the gates I feel them closing in, imprisoning me on a path of structure and normalcy. My earlier panic starts flooding back. Just breathe, I tell myself.

A not so polite elderly woman with serious fashion issues signs me in and hands me my class schedule. I thank her sweetly and smile, she rolls her eyes and hurries back to her typing task. I sit outside the glass doors of the office and look at my schedule and the map provided. I'm happy to find I have just enough time to skulk around the grounds and find the science lab before the bell rings.

As I arrive, the classroom is overcrowded by chaotic students fighting over seating preferences. Many of them are still coming down from their lunchtime high. They laugh wildly and speak volumes with hand gestures. It's hard to believe these children and I are the same age. I feel older. I feel worn. I miss the innocence I once shared with them. I sift through all the chaos and I find an unmanned seat in the back row and claim it quickly.

A short chubby man, possibly in his late fifties with a predominantly large nose and a shiny-balled head enters the room. His eyes explore the crowd of youths as they continue flooding in. He rolls his eyes at the group before him and disgust is clearly written all over his face. Just when I think my presence has gone unnoticed his sour eyes fall on me. He smiles, making me feel sick in my stomach.

"If you could all shut your traps for one minute I could tell you that we have a new student hiding in the back," he says smugly. "Why don't you stand up and introduce yourself," he says.

I stand slowly, feeling the flush come to my cheeks. I smile uncomfortably and offer a small awkward wave to my new classmates.

"Hi I'm Adaline," I say.

I lower myself back and grip the seat firmly, careful not to miss my landing. I hear people whisper and snicker as their eyes dart toward me. My uncle warned me about small-town gossip. Between the crash and the local newspaper calling me 'miracle child,' the town has had much to talk about.

The teacher passes out some handouts and the items for our remedial task. He has us place seeds in damp cotton wool and set up charts to follow their growth. He swears it's to enhance our documentation skills and analysis abilities, but I have a suspicion this task requires little effort on his part. Unlike my classmates, I like the simplicity of the project and the continued need to maintain it. It will be a nice distraction from my life.

I look down at the tip of the sunflower seed peeking through the cotton wool, I close my eyes and envision the sunflower in bloom.

When I open my eyes, the seedling begins to split, bursting open as a small green stem sprouts from within. A sunflower no bigger than my thumbnail opens before my eyes. It's the most beautiful and fragile thing I have ever seen. I stroke its delicate petals and feel the life glowing within it.

I look at the desks beside me and no one else has flowers in front of them. A blonde bombshell is twisting her hair while she whispers to the boy on my right, another girl is engrossed in her phone that she has hidden creatively under her desk. I grab my flower and quickly conceal it in my bag before anyone notices. There's a ringing in my ears and I begin to panic. I sit frozen while my heart beats like a drum drowning out all other sounds in the room. I watch students start to collect their bags and begin leaving their desks. The herd movement spurs me into action and I follow suit. I'm last to exit the classroom, my head feels light and my vision begins to blur. The hallway seems to have darkened. I strain to focus as I reach towards the handrail for support, but the corridor begins spinning out of control and I lose my balance. In the blink of an eye, the world turns black.

- 9 -

SETH

Sign up took a little longer than usual because the office 'lost' my transfer papers, lucky for me my brother had given me a second copy just in case. I insist that I can find my way to science class and the portly receptionist is all too happy to abide. I wander between corridors using my senses to guide me. I follow the scent of chemicals. I turn into a bricked hallway and I know I've almost arrived. A piercing bell rings and the hall becomes flooded with children. Each of them shoving their way past one another, a stampede of animals being freed from the zoo. The corridor clears as I round the corner. The darkened hallway seems to brighten a little. I glance around confused, the sun hasn't shifted and the cheap lights hovering on the ceiling remain dull and lifeless. I'm overwhelmed by the smell of spring and a fiery light that awakens all my senses. I look for the reason behind these sensations, but all I see is a girl, surrounded by an ethereal spark. A smile forces itself to my lips making me feel like I belong with these stupid school boys.

The girl is alone as she walks towards me, she raises her head. Her eyes connecting with mine. My fangs quiver beneath my gum line. Everything around me stops, the air catches in my chest, and my blood ceases to flow beneath my skin. I brace myself waiting for the world to begin breathing again. I open my mouth and try to think of something witty to say, but instead, the girl collapses. My body reacts before my mind has time to catch up and next thing I know she's cradled safely in my arms.

All my earlier concerns now seem insignificant. The only question that matters is what am I supposed to do with the unconscious girl in my arms? I know my brother wanted to take a different approach, but he's not the one with a girl passed out in his arms. I could easily take her from the grounds and no one would be the wiser. Maybe they might think she ran away. I look down at her innocent face and move a stray hair that's caught in her lashes.

I wonder how she would feel waking up in a strange place with a strange man standing over her. Not to mention how she's going to feel when she finds out her life as she knows it is about to end.

Strangely enough, I feel bad for her. I'm sorry for the world she's about to be forced into. I silence my usual line of thinking and do what my brother would do if he was in this situation. I carry the girl to the nurse's office and decide to watch over her until she wakes.

- 10 -
Adaline

I moan loudly to myself, my heads pounding worse than ever. I open my eyes to see the room still has a blurry quality to it but at least it's stopped spinning. I allow my eyes time to adjust to the faint lighting and I realise I'm not in the school corridor anymore. I'm on a mattress. It's thin and cheap. There's a layer of harsh plastic between my aching body and the lumpy mattress beneath. I shuffle uncomfortably trying to release some of the pressure that's building in my head. I see pictures of children washing their hands on the walls and the distinct smell of antiseptic fills my nostrils. I must be in the nurse's office, the rooms too small and dark to be in a hospital ward.

"Anyone ever told you that you make a great first impression?" An unfamiliar voice asks. "I know I'm attractive, but you barely even looked at me before falling at my feet," he says.

"Don't get too excited it's the third time I've fallen today. Are we in the nurse's office?" I ask.

"We are. You fainted in the hallway. Lucky for you I was able to catch you before you kissed the pavement. Heroic of me I know," he says. Overconfidence radiating from his voice like heat from a flame.

"I'm sure you were more interested in skipping class then tending my wounds, feel free to leave," I tell him.

Before he gets a chance to respond he is silenced by the school nurse. A sweet plump little woman in her late sixties squeezes through the door. She gently places an ice pack on my forehead and gives my shoulder an affectionate squeeze before removing her hand.

"How does that feel?" she asks. Her hands are warm and caring and remind me of my mother's touch. A tear threatens to escape but I close my eyes tightly forcing it to retreat. "I spoke to your uncle, he insisted there was no need to call an ambulance. He said he's on his way to get you," she tells me, stroking my head once more before she waddles out of the room.

I feel the pull of penetrating eyes watching me; I turn myself to my side to catch a glimpse of the man behind the arrogant voice. As my eyes scan his features I follow the direction of his stare. It's clear he doesn't share the same fondness I have for the kindly nurse who's humming happily to herself outside. I smile listening to her song and the tap of her heels. I feel his unkind eyes leave the nurse and fall on me. I feel nervous under his steady gaze, so I keep my eyes trained on the door.

"Thanks for your help, but you can go," I tell him.

Cumbersomely I try moving into a sitting position on the stiff cot. The young man's intense stare never wavers, making the moment more awkward. Now I've righted myself I pull my eyes from the door and take in the sight of the man before me. I'm transfixed in the deep russet of his eyes, they're not as unkind as I had been imagining. There is a sincere quality hidden within the molten tawny ring encircling the iris. My eyes follow the line of his face. He has a slight stubble growing like moss on a rock, but it doesn't hide the strength in his jaw. He leans in closer and my breath catches in my throat. I'm almost certain he's going to kiss me.

"What's your name?" I ask.

A coarse cough at the door frightens me; causing me to fall back into the rickety cot. The moment between us is broken, but I can still feel the warmth of the moment in my cheeks. My uncle stands in the door frame like a warden on duty. I clear the breath that had been caught in my throat, my uncle's watchful eyes never waver from the man sitting across from me. The nurse arrives with a piece of paper in hand, she smiles childishly at my uncle and his broad smile leaves her a little blushed as she leaves.

"I suppose introductions are in order. I'm Jerald Thomas and who may I ask is the young man who's sitting awfully close to my niece?" He says pointedly.

That's it. This is where I shrivel up and die. On this cheap plastic cot, it seems a fitting end to the humiliation I have already endured today. I can feel my face turning red, soon my cheeks will match the rose hue of the nurses.

"Please excuse me, Sir, my name is Seth," he says with an outstretched hand. Watching Seth in action I can see he's practised at this. Using his arrogance and charm to woo fathers along with their daughters. I'm sure it has worked for him in the past, but I don't buy his crap for a second.

"Oh, you're new in town. I believe I had the pleasure of meeting you brother no less than an hour ago. He seems a nice young man,"

Jerry says.

"Yes, I'd be lost without him that's for sure," Seth replies.

"Perhaps you and your brother would like to join us for dinner tonight, our way of welcoming you both to town?" Jerry asks.

"I know my brother already had plans for this evening, but I'll join you if you don't mind. It beats eating alone," Seth says.

"Great, let's say seven," Jerry adds removing a business card from his coat pocket. "Call me on that and I'll give you the address. Adaline I'll go get your bag from the nurse," Jerry says with a wink.

"I'll see you tonight then," Seth says as he walks out of the room.

What the hell just happened? It was like watching a car crash in slow motion. I could see where it was leading, but I couldn't do anything to stop it. I can almost feel flames of embarrassment starting to sizzle on my skin. I'm humiliated. My uncle returns with my belongings in hand. I walk behind following him in autopilot until we reach the car. I settle into the buttery leather seats and revel in the heat embedded in them. In the rearview mirror, the school begins to vanish, and I watch the steady stream of houses that map the journey back to my uncle's house.

"How's your head? We can stop by the surgery and pick up some painkillers if you want," Jerry asks innocently.

"No, my heads fine, I'm more preoccupied with the archaic mating ritual you seem to have thrown me into. What's next, will you call him to drop off a cow for my dowry?" I say.

"Please you're worth at least three cows," He jokes. I smack his arm in protest. "I'm sorry Adaline, I didn't mean to embarrass you. His brother came to the clinic this morning. The boys have lost both of their parent's and are new to town. When I realised who Seth was I just thought... I'm sorry. If you want me to cancel we can. Just say the word," he offers.

"No, it's fine, don't cancel," I reply. If anyone knows a thing or two about losing a parent it's me. Maybe Seth and I have more in common than I thought.

- 11 -

SETH

I text Aedan to pick me us as I slip outside the school gates. Since Adaline's gone home, there's no reason to spend the rest of the day in this hormone fuelled wasteland. Back when I was a small boy, schooling was a luxury that was always out of reach. Education only bestowed to the wealthy and I most certainly was not. Kids these days don't know how well-off they have it, squandering the opportunities they have been handed. It's such a waste.

My wretched excuse of a father started me working in the fields long before I reached puberty. Even at the tender age of five, the excruciating manual labour was better than the beating my father would have given me for not pulling my weight. I remember every time my skin blistered or broke, I had to push myself forward. Not because I was worried what would happen if I didn't, but because I didn't want to give my father the satisfaction he felt every time he justified beating me.

Life was different back then, harder, crueller and people didn't give a shit if your dad was beating you. I was my father's property, he could do with me as he saw fit.

The only reason I think I survived all the years of torture was because of my mother's love. Sadly, even she couldn't survive my father. Her body finally expired in my fourteenth year, but her spirit died long before that. I remember coming home from the fields earlier than usual; the blisters on my hands had burst and I couldn't stop the bleeding. My father was worried my blood would affect the quality of the crops, so he allowed me to go inside and let my mother bind my hands. At first, I didn't notice anything out of the ordinary. It was only when she refused to move from her chair that I noticed something was wrong.

Her body sat limply in her wooden seat by the failing fireplace. She was frail and gauntly thin; the season hadn't been good to any of us really. Her eyes were cloaked in a grey haze and pale-yellow bruises decorated her neckline like a delicate chain. As terrifying as it was to see my sweet mother that way I had never felt such relief. Knowing she was finally at peace gave me solace.

When I was younger she had a spark in her eyes, as I grew, that light dimmed until it was snuffed out completely. My father had beaten it out of her, leaving nothing but a hollow shell. I kissed her still warm cheek and pulled the thread bear rug a little higher on her shoulders.

It was then that I decided living with nothing was better than staying under the torment of my father. I walked out of the shabby farmhouse that I called home. I walked past the bales of hay that sat by the dilapidated barn where my father would drunkenly fuck the whores he would waste our family money on. I walked past the sickly cows that hadn't given milk in weeks and I held my breath. I marched past the dirt covered man who shares the colour of my hair and the stiffness of my jawline. I didn't release my breath until he was nothing but a black dot in the distance. When I was able to breathe again I finally felt free and I kept walking.

I haven't allowed these memories to invade my mind for centuries and I do my best to shake them off. I wrap them in a muslin cloth and put them back inside the locked box that's hidden deep in the back of my mind.

My stomach makes an uncomfortable sound making me suddenly aware how hungry I am. As I wait impatiently for my brother, another disturbing image floods my mind. Not images of my mother, but the vision of a beautiful girl sleeping peacefully on a cheap fold out cot. I become lost in the image as she sleeps in my memory and the world falls away. The earth tremors beneath my feet, not an earthquake, more like a nudge. I look up to see Aedan waiting across the street waving. I was too deep in thought and I hadn't realised he had pulled up.

"I hit the horn like five times and you didn't even look up. I literally had to move the earth to get your attention. Is something wrong?" Aedan asks. His expression quickly changing from mocking to concern.

"No, nothing's wrong, just hungry let's get something to eat," I say.

We choose a small diner around the corner from our hotel and settle into a booth, I order the burger and fries I have been craving and Aedan orders a garden salad.

"A salad, seriously? Only you could suck the life out of immortality," I tease.

"I like a salad; besides I get enough protein elsewhere," he says.

"I met the girl, she fainted. We spoke briefly, her uncle invited me to dinner this evening which I'm sure is due to your involvement,"

I say flatly.

"I like to cover all angles," he jokes. "You felt it when you saw her didn't you. There's something about her, something you can't quite put your finger on. Anyways I think gaining her uncles favour will go a long way to making her trust us," he says.

"You have always told me trust is a two-way street and trust has never been my forte. It took me thirty years to trust you. Maybe it's better if you try and get close to her," I say.

"I have faith you won't mess it up. Trust me, you got this," He says confidently.

The waitress returns with our meals in hand and we finish our food in silence, each of us lost in our own thoughts.

- 12 -
Adaline

After a long sleep and a few Advil, my head feels better. At least until it starts swirling with anxiety. The tension grows each time I remove an item of clothing from my wardrobe. I scrutinise every piece until it fails my inspection and is forsaken to the floor. My wardrobe has only one final garment left; as my finger grazes the soft fabric it dawns on me how ridiculous my behaviour is. Seth annoyed me almost as much as he enchanted me. The arrogant tone of his voice and the look of disdain on his face as he looked at the sweet nurse. He's nothing like me and he's not the kind of person I would want to associate with.

I rub my fingers once more over the ivory summer dress that still adorns its tags, it has thin straps with a scoop neckline and it hitches under the bust before flowing in draped layers down to my knees. It's plain but beautiful, it's the last dress mum and I brought together before she died.

My plan was to wear it to the birthday party I'll no longer be having. I slip the silken dress over my head and past my shoulders. It falls perfectly around my body, heightening not hindering my curves. Mum always did have impeccable taste.

When I was younger I thought that gene had skipped me, I often looked awkward and the clothes I chose never fit quite right. When I hit my teenage years, my body changed and so did my sense of style. With mum's help, I rarely felt awkward again. Since her death,

I feel all my insecurities clawing their way back into my mind. I apply a little eyeshadow and mascara absentmindedly. I reach into my school bag for some lip gloss, but my fingers find something soft and moist instead. I gently lift the curious object out of my bag, it's the sunflower I had hidden away. Between teenage hormones and medical drama, I had forgotten about the little flower. There's a soft knock at my door that shatters my daydream and I place the flower on my desk to worry about later.

"Are you ready it's almost seven?" Jerry asks.

"All done," I say and do a little curtsy at my uncle. He returns my foolishness with a grand bow.

"You look stunning, maybe we should cancel dinner. I may have to beat the boys away with a stick," he says.

"Or a gun," I add

"Exactly, depends how close they get," he jokes.

My face burns with embarrassment at his flattery, but I love it. It's nice to feel happy even for just a moment. He gives me a quick kiss on the forehead and runs downstairs. One last look in the mirror and I'm happy with my appearance. I take a few deep breaths and apply a final layer of peach scented lip gloss before descending the staircase.

Standing in the open doorway is the handsome boy who watched over me while I slept. His intense gaze holds me in place. The feverish feelings we shared in the dim lit room that smelled coarsely of disinfectant come flooding back. My body shivers making me almost lose my balance, unlike this morning I'm able to steady myself on the banister and confidently make my decent.

"Please be careful, I know my presence is overwhelming, but you're going to have to learn to control yourself," he says.

"Well, it's definitely not your modest charm that's affecting me," I say

He smiles at my comment making my heart beat faster so it can force the excess blood to my blushing cheeks. I admit I swoon a little, but he's still an arrogant jerk, I remind myself. I turn my gaze from his breathtaking smile and focus on something else, anything else. I focus on his shoes. Their simple Chuck Taylor's in a muted tone with dark splashes from the water. His jeans have the same damp look about them as well as his shirt. As my eyes raise higher I can hardly ignore the fact that his hairs dripping water droplets onto the floorboards.

"Forecast said clear skies tonight, shows what they know. My car almost got hit by lightning, I'm surprised I made it here alive," he says.

I grab a towel from the hallway closet and hand it to him, my mother did raise me with manners after all. Jerry calls us into the dining room and offers Seth a seat. Jerry places himself deliberately between us and handles the majority of the conversation.

Halfway through dinner, it's clear I'm not even needed. It's like having dinner with your parent's and one of their friends. The adults talk happily and joke amongst themselves while the child sits quietly, speaking only when spoken to. I doubt Seth or Jerry would notice if I got up and left the table. As dinner starts ending I consider doing just that. Seth recalls another saintly anecdote about himself while my uncle eats it up. My uncles smitten, but I can sense a falseness in Seth's words and it unnerves me.

My uncle excuses himself and wanders off to the kitchen, both hands full of dirty dishes, leaving Seth and me alone. I'm happy staring at my half-empty glass of coke, but I feel Seth's eyes watching me. I feel his eyes tickle the edges of my bare skin as they move over my body. I shift uncomfortably and pull my hair over my shoulders to cover my exposed skin.

"Your uncle is actually a really nice guy," he says.

"You sound surprised," I reply.

"I kind of am surprised," he says.

"I think that's the first sincere thing you have said all night," I scoff.

"You look beautiful tonight," he says honestly. Thankfully my uncle returns saving me from having to respond.

"Do you want dessert Seth," Jerry asks.

"Seth has to get going and I'm ready for bed, it's been a long day," I say.

Jerry looks at me confused, but he doesn't comment on my poor manners. The look on Seth's face is nothing less than complete shock. The bulging vein on his forehead and the open droop of his mouth, tells me he might be a little-pissed off too. I would bet money he has never been turned down before. I almost feel bad for him, but his overconfidence worries me, and my gut is telling me he's a liar. Jerry must sense the discomfort between us because he makes himself scarce, leaving me to show Seth to the door.

"Thank you for coming, I'll see you at school," I say politely, but I know my words don't sound right.

"Did I do something? If I did I'm sorry," he says.

"I don't want you to get the wrong impression, but I sense you're a little too good at all this. Flirting, making girls swoon and bending parents to your will. Which is a great skill for hooking up with the kind of girls I'm sure you've had plenty of, but that's not me. It would be cruel of me to make you think otherwise," I say. I'm not usually so brazen with my words, but something about being in Seth's presence forces my mouth to work before my mind can stop it.

"To be honest your right, you're not the kind of girl I want," he says. His words sting a little. A downpour unleashes from the heavens drenching him in rain, I feel sorry for him.

I lock the door behind him and climb the never-ending stairs to my bedroom. I peel off my dress that suddenly feels dirty and dump it on my chair. I slip on a nightgown and position myself on the window seat so I can see the stars while I comb the curls out of my hair. I spend a few minutes arguing with myself for my irrational behaviour and before long my eyes are heavy with exhaustion. I climb into bed and find myself flooded with images of a handsome young man. The features of his face shimmer in and out of focus as I drift into a blissful sleep.

- 13 -

SETH

I turn my back on her and walk into a storm that threatens to drown me for the second time today. The invisible thread that has tethered us tugs at my chest. I can feel its pull as it follows her upstairs until she disappears behind closed doors. It's true what I said. She's not the kind of girl I would choose for myself, she's more than a want, she is a need. This girl should mean nothing more to me than my next meal or a plaything to pass the time, but I find myself craving her presence. I feel lighter in her company. These stirring feelings are something I have never dealt with before. Perhaps if I push the feelings down deep enough they will fade.

I text Aedan and tell him I'll be back at the hotel soon since I couldn't get her alone to talk. I can hear the frustration in his texts, but he understands. My brother has already positioned a few of our guards around Adaline's house to watch over her tonight.

I start the ignition and the passenger door swings open to reveal a small dark-skinned woman, with well-toned arms and faded scars. She effortlessly lifts herself into the front passenger seat.

"You must be losing your touch, you couldn't even get the child to leave her house," Shaylin teases as she strokes my upper thigh.

This is exactly what I need. Physical contact with no emotions. I don't even comment on her insult. I lift her small frame up and onto my lap and start kissing her ferociously, she kisses back just as forcefully biting a cut on my lower lip and I taste blood. It arouses us both, spurring us into action.

Our secret liaison finishes soon enough; I zip my jeans and run my fingers through my dishevelled hair. Shaylin is out of the vehicle and running back to her patrol before I've even pulled myself back together. A flash of white catches in the corner of my eye, I look up to the second story to see Adaline sitting by the window gazing out at the night sky. The flash of white that had caught my attention is the soft moonlight reflecting off the brush she's using to comb her lustrous auburn hair.

It's clear that she's unaware of my presence across the street so I take advantage of my invisibility and soak in the image of her. My eyes trace the outline of her creamy porcelain skin that's unblemished by the sun. My body warms in the delicate rose of her cheeks and her blush coloured lips. Each time she finishes another pointed stroke of her hair I find another layer of beauty to commit to memory. Slowly she rises from her seat, her eyes still searching the heavens looking for something out of reach. She starts to draw the curtains closed but pauses, leaving a small gap to let the moonlight in. I watch her silhouette fade behind the curtains; it appears I'm not permitted another look tonight.

- 14 -
Adaline

Sunlight creeps through the small opening between my curtains and the increasing warmth forces me to move from the comfortable cocoon I've made of my covers. I wriggle my toes, extend my arms and welcome the blissful high of a waking stretch. All I want to do is fade into the covers and sleep the weekend away, but today's importance has made that dream impossible. The last few weeks I have been avoiding the thought of today but pretending it didn't exist hasn't stopped the day from arriving.

I wriggle in my bed once more allowing my body the time it needs to start moving. My eyesight hasn't even adjusted to the morning light and my thoughts turn to Seth. Dinner was more than three nights ago and he's been absent from school ever since.

Perhaps I was too harsh on him, though I doubt he would have taken my words to heart. I kept watching for him in the hallways at school. I even tried to delude myself, discarding my stalker tendencies as calculated avoidance, but a twinge of disappointment that I felt every time he didn't show is harder to deny.

It seems silly to worry so much about a boy I'm not interested in when my heart should only be focused on mourning my mother. Since the accident I know I have made a lot of progress and some days I almost feel better, almost normal. Then the wave hits me and the reality of what's missing sinks back in. Sometimes it's something small and insignificant that makes me think of my mother. It can be something as tiny as the smell of her coffee brand or the sound of Jerry switching off his shower and dropping the shampoo bottle on his way out. These broken moments take all my strength just to keep myself from falling apart.

Jerry enters my room with a proud smile stitched on his face. He sees the tears that have taken root in the corner of my eyes and his smile weans. The first time Jerry found me crying in a huddled mess on the bathroom floor he didn't know what to do and gave me a stiff pat on the shoulder. I responded by spinning around and hugging him so tightly he couldn't breathe. I clung to him desperately that night and he's been my lifeline ever since. Before I can make an excuse for my puffy eyes and shrug off my tears he reaches for me. He draws me into his broad chest and secures his arms tightly around my shoulders. For the first time in a long time, I feel safe. My tears fade, and I smile, thankful for what I have left.

"Your hugging skills have improved immensely," I say. He stands and makes a dramatic bow.

"Thank you, thank you. I'm here all week," he says gesturing graciously for me to stand and join him on our imaginary stage. I giggle wildly as my heartache is forgotten. "I want to thank my beautiful niece, I could not have become the experienced hugger I am today without her ongoing support and guidance. Now I must whisk her away to open birthday presents," he says excitedly.

Jerry leaves laughing foolishly so I have time to get myself dressed. It's surprisingly warm this morning, the heats already seeping into the house. I dress simply in some denim shorts and a white singlet.

I pull my hair into a high ponytail to stop it sticking to the sweat that's pooling at the nape of my neck. Rounding the corner to the staircase I'm taken back by the sight below. Every inch of the lower level of the house is consumed by purple balloons. Different shapes and sizes all floating along the roof while spiral ribbons dangle and dance below like rain. As I reach the last stair the ribbons tickle my arms and fingertips as I push my way through the purple haze. I can't even count how many balloons there are floating above my head. Jerry must have been up all night doing this, no wonder he was so excited. I make my way to the dining room where Jerry waits with a giant grin from ear to ear.

"What do you think? It's too much, I know it is, but I couldn't resist. You haven't had a birthday here since you were little," he asks.

"There's no such thing as too much. Thank you," I say.

I lurch forward and hug him. The tears take hold again, but it's not tears of sadness, I'm overwhelmed with adoration. I've been dreading my eighteenth birthday. I assumed it would be unbearable without my mother, but it seems Jerry's made it possible to be a day filled with joy, not sadness.

Jerry force feeds me an overly decadent breakfast of pancakes, eggs and bacon until I can barely move. Once he's finished his coffee and I feel like I'm not going to be sick he ushers me into the lounge room. He has placed one of the dining chairs in front of the coffee table and has covered it with purple ribbons and bows. I sit down on my throne as three immaculately wrapped presents are laid out before me. One slightly larger than a shoe box wrapped in purple and gold expensive paper with a large bouquet of gold curled ribbon adorning the top. The second is a small gold gift bag sealed with a purple bow. The third is no bigger than the size of a standard envelope and is wrapped in the same purple and gold fashion. Handing me the largest first Jerry tells me proudly that this one is from him. I ease the paper open and inside is the latest Apple laptop in purple.

"I didn't think these were out yet, let alone in purple! I love it, thank you," I say.

"Your welcome. I thought it would help with senior year and all. The man assured me it has all the bells and whistles you kids like these days, face chat, eye book, it has it all. Now, this little bag Seth dropped off this morning," he says handing me the small gift bag.

"How did he know it was my birthday?" I ask.

"I saw him at the store a few days ago when I was getting birthday supplies, I may have mentioned it. He stopped by early this morning, I told him he could wait and join us for brunch, but he had plans. He left his number, so you can let him know if you like it," Jerry says eagerly.

I gently untie the bow and ease open the bag. I brace myself ready for a fake tin filled with snakes ready to jump out and frighten me. To my surprise, there are no tricks inside, just a jewellery box the size of my palm. I open the lid with a small creek. Inside is a large teardrop jade pendant encased in rose gold. The chain it hangs on is strong but there's a sense of elegance and frailty about it.

"Wow, that's beautiful, honey. You must have made a real impression on that boy," Jerry says peering over my shoulder.

"I must have," I murmur. I slip it back into its casing, I'll return it to him later. It's far too extravagant and I can't possibly accept it.

"This last one I wasn't sure how to handle. It's something I wanted to talk to you about first, but then I thought there's no good way to warn you and I didn't want you getting upset. Your mother's attorney sent this to me last week. He had strict instructions that it was for your eyes only," he holds the package delicately between his thumb and forefinger careful not to squeeze it too tightly. "I didn't read it," he says with a grim look on his face.

"What do you think it is?" I ask.

"I don't know. Do you want me to read it first?" He asks.

"No, I'll do it. I'll read it in my room if you don't mind," I say.

"Of course not, I'll go clean up," he replies.

Jerry gives me an encouraging smile before he heads into the kitchen. As I walk through the purple haze it begins to stifle me, by the time I reach the stairs I feel like I'm suffocating. I climb the stairs to the second level, and when I'm finally free of the purple haze I can breathe again. I close my bedroom door securely behind me and place the parcel on the window seat where the sun's rays highlight the gold in the paper.

I need four deep breaths before I'm able to sit next to it. Once I've built my courage I make short work of the wrapping paper. I'm disappointed when a pale-yellow envelope is all that's inside, foolishly I hoped my mother would fall out of the pages like in a magic act. The front simply reads 'Adaline' and I recognise the handwriting immediately. I slip my finger under the seal and ease the envelope open. I take extra care removing the buttery paper from within.

My darling Adaline,

Today we would have celebrated your eighteenth birthday and I'm sorry I'm not here with you. I raised you to be strong of heart as well as mind and you have grown into more than I could have imagined. As much as I wish I could take credit for how wonderful you are I know it's because you were born filled with goodness. I know you will grow up to be the exceptional woman I have always envisioned. I am proud of the person you are and love you more than anything in my life. You are the greatest gift I have ever received and I'm thankful for the time we have had together.

My greatest fear is that you will hate me when you know the truth about what I have done, but please understand that anything I have done has always been in your best interests. I had rehearsed what I was going to say to you so many times over the years. Sometimes I came so close to giving in and telling you the truth, but my fear would get the better of me. Now it's too late and I can't keep it from you any longer.

I loved your father very much but despite our love for one another, it was impossible for us to be together. It took years before my heart was open to the idea of love and who would have thought I would find it in a parking lot behind a rundown hospital in London.

I had been working my way through Europe as a nurse and eventually settled in London working in a forgotten hospital on the rough side of town. One night after finishing the late shift I came out to my car to find your father waiting for me. I hadn't seen him in years, but my heart still beat wildly at the sight of him. At first, it took me a moment to realise he had a baby bundled in his arms.

He told me that people had tried to hurt you and that the only way to keep you safe was if no one knew the attack on your life had failed. Your father loved you so much he was willing to give up a life with you to keep you safe. I admit I considered turning him away, but when I looked into your eyes I fell in love with you and that was that. The next day I quit my job, packed up my apartment and moved back to the states. I gave up everything and it was the best decision I ever made.

Now that I'm gone you're no longer protected and need to be cautious. You father worried not everyone believed his tale of your demise and they may still be looking for you. I wish there was more I could do for you. I know my sweet brother will care for you in my absence, but he is unaware how dangerous your past is and the role I played in it. Please tell him I'm sorry for lying to him and I love him dearly.

Once it's safe your father will come to take you to your true home. Your father will explain everything to you. The most important thing you need to know is that even though you are not of my blood you are still MINE. I watched you grow from a fragile child into a beautiful and strong young woman. I have loved you every second of every day since you came into my life. You are the true love of my life. Adaline my darling daughter, I hope in time you can forgive me. Love always your mother xxx

Her writing is as gentle as the tone of her voice, I can hear her reciting the words to me in my mind. In my wildest nightmares, I never would have imagined I didn't belong to my mother. My heart starts beating violently until it breaks into a thousand tiny pieces. A pounding ache sweeps over me, rippling through my body like the tremors after an earthquake. It's like I'm losing my mother all over again. The pressure rises from my stomach and passes through my chest until it reaches my face. The sensation finally escapes my body in the form of tears. I burrow my head into a cushion and I let it all wash over me. Soon enough I'll be carried away like Alice in an ocean of her tears.

- 15 -

SETH

I dropped off the amulet early this morning. I spent the last two and a half days tracking it down. Finding the jade stone wasn't hard but finding a witch who was capable and willing to charm it, proved to be more difficult than I had thought. I found an old hag in Dallas who was able to do what I required. The bitch charged me a lot but at least it's done. Now all Adaline needs to do is put it on. Aedan and I have been waiting in the SUV for more than two hours since I dropped off my 'gift' and it's nearing noon. The clock ticks over once more and there's still no sign of Adaline.

"It's been years since a girl has been immune to your charms. What gift did you think would sway the lass's opinion of you?" Aedan asks, his accent escaping a fraction more than usual.

"It's just a necklace, women love jewellery, as you are well aware. Who was that girl you stole some of the crown jewels for?" I ask.

"Oh, Tatiana in 1631. She was worth every penny, the thought of her still makes my loins ache. Poor girl, I think she died of syphilis in the end. Such a waste," Aedan says.

"The last thing I need to hear about is your loins… You know you could have turned her, Tatiana I mean," I say.

"An eternity is an awfully long time. I love too much too often to be chained to one woman," he says.

I missed this, just sitting with my brother and talking like we used to. I'm tempted to tell him the truth, to divulge all the sordid thoughts I've had about Adaline since the moment I laid my eyes on her. I could do it, unburden myself from my feelings and the constant worry that lingers in my chest. The words find their way to the tip of my tongue, they are eager to escape my lips, but once again I'm distracted by the beautiful girl sitting in the window.

Adaline sits under the warm sunlight, the glow making her skin shimmer like porcelain. Her hair is pulled back exposing her tantalizing neckline and the few stray freckles that sit on the tips of her shoulders.

She is dressed simply but it allows her natural beauty to shine through. My heightened vision can see the envelope she's holding and the steady shaking of her hands. I watch as she opens the envelope carefully. She removes a piece of folded paper. I watch her shoulders rise as she takes a deep inhale of breath. Tears start flowing down her cheeks and the crinkle in the corner of her eyes tells me she's fighting desperately to hold them back.

"What do you think it says? The poor child doesn't deserve any sadder news," Aedan says.

"No idea, what should we do?" I ask. Dealing with emotional women is a job better suited for my brother, but the thought of him comforting her the way I wish I was, it fills me with resentment.

"Nothing, we keep watch, it's not like you can call her and say, 'hey why are you crying' she would think you were stalking her," Aedan says.

"We are stalking her," I add.

"Not like a creepy stalker. This is for her protection," he replies.

I wish I knew what the letter said because whatever it contains it's rattled her. Aedan and I continue to sit and watch her cry. It takes all of my self-control not to jump out of the car and scale the house to comfort her. By the time my fingernails have torn through the leather seat her crying slows and she curls up on the window seat and drifts off to sleep. She lays there immobile for the rest of the day, if it wasn't for the steady rise and fall of her shoulders I would think she was dead. When Jason and Shaylin arrive to relieve our shift, the sun is beginning to set behind the tree line and Adaline's still asleep.

- 16 -
Adaline

When I wake, the fear and pain I had felt earlier are gone. I raise my head from the damp cushion and my eyes are pained. The world around me feels cold and deserted. I look out the window and notice it's rained while I've slept, and everything outside has been washed clean, I wish I could say the same for my wounds. I lay cramped on the window seat for a little while longer allowing my body the time it needs to remember how to move. The sun no longer shines through my window, the moon must have chased it away. The stiffness in my back aches as my body regains some feeling. Laying uncomfortably for so long has taken its toll and I feel a slight sting on my cheeks from the sun that's hovered over my motionless body all day.

I catch a glimpse of my reflection in the window, I look like a racoon. I laugh mechanically to myself, so much for waterproof mascara. The movement helps as I walk to my dressing table and rummage through my draws to find some wet wipes to clean my face. In spite of the hours of sleep, I feel exhausted and tender. I steal a look at the letter resting innocently by the window, it's funny that a piece of paper can do such damage. I turn my back ignoring the pages and the secrets they hold. I'm not ready to share their contents with my uncle just yet. Telling someone else will make it real, and I'm not ready for real. I remove my hair from its ponytail and brush it vigorously. I apply a fresh coat of make-up to disguise my emotion-stricken features and brave the walk downstairs.

Jerry ordered Chinese for dinner and Mrs. Phyllis who lives next door came by when I was having my meltdown and dropped off a decadent chocolate sponge cake for me. While eating a second slice of cake, Jerry casually asks me about the letter and I tell him we can talk about it tomorrow.

Selfishly I crave one more day where my world still spins the same and my uncle still looks at me like I'm his family. I settle into my blissful delusion and a voice in the back of my mind whispers, don't get too comfortable, because the shit's about to hit the fan. I turn up the television to drown it out.

After the movie ends and Jerry yawns, I give him a kiss on the cheek and thank him again. Despite my aching body I decide to go for a run before bed to burn off any energy that would dare keep my anxious mind awake tonight. I change into black leggings, a baggy t-shirt that has seen better days and search for my joggers. While lacing up my shoes Seth's jewellery box catches my eye. Jerry had placed it on my dresser and next to it is a small square piece of paper with Seth's mobile number written messily on it. I add the number to my phone and write a quick text.

**Hey Seth its Adaline thanks for the gift but I can't accept it. When will you be at school so I can return it? Ty

Before I even finish tying my second shoe I hear a chirpy bird-like song as my phone begins to vibrate across the dresser. I catch it before it falls and retrieve the message.

*Happy birthday Adaline and I'm afraid it's not refundable. Accept it as an apology for offending you the other night. If you want to get together so you can thank me personally we can arrange that.

Regards Seth

Regards? Who says that, is he applying for an interview? I shouldn't laugh, but I do. Seth is the only person at school who's shown even the slightest interest in befriending me. I'm not really in a position to be picky. I'm also finding it hard to deny the fluttering sensation my stomach makes at the thought of seeing him.

**How about tomorrow? We can have lunch or something as friends??

*I'll be at your house at eleven. Good night Adaline

**Night

I smile genuinely for the first time since reading mum's letter. I open the box once more and linger on the beauty of the trinket. I place it back on the dresser where it can remain until I return it to Seth tomorrow.

On my way downstairs as I walk back through the purple haze, I wonder if Jerry has thought about what to do with the balloons tomorrow. I call out to my uncle and let him know that I'll be back in an hour. I make sure to put the porch light on before I leave. As I walk down the drive and start stretching my muscles I notice Mrs. Phyllis still has her porch lights on. I jog up to the front door and knock. Mrs. Phyllis is a born and bred Texan who's easily in her eighties and since her husband died ten years ago she has become an extension of our family. I remember her husband William's funeral. It was the first funeral I had ever attended. Everyone was draped in black and their eyes were stained red. People smiled when I greeted them, but their smiles never met their eyes. At my mother's funeral, I recognised the traditions I saw as a child. A different church and different songs were sung, but people still adorned the same red-stained eyes and the sea of black that followed.

I knock once more and hear four heavy locks being twisted and cranked into submission. When she opens the door, I realise she has left the safety chain attached. I don't remember her being this paranoid when I was younger. Maybe since losing her husband, she's frightened of being alone, which I understand.

"Adaline is that you? Every day y'all are gettin' more and more beautiful. Just like your mam," she says, closing the door to remove the final chain before she pulls me into a bear hug.

"I just wanted to stop by and thank you for the cake. I'm sorry I wasn't up for visitors," I say.

"Sugar it doesn't even matter. Y'all want to come in for a cup of tea?" She asks.

"Actually, I wanted to go for a run before bed. Can I come by tomorrow afternoon for tea?" I ask.

"Certainly darlin' any time. I do wish y'all wouldn't go out running at night, especially alone, it's not safe. You know I've seen people roaming the streets at night and there have been more cars hanging around than usual. I called the police, but they just think I'm an old fool," she says glancing worriedly over my shoulder.

"You are definitely not a fool. I have to go, but I promise I'll be careful," I say and give her a kiss on her cheek.

I press my earbuds securely in place and switch on my running playlist. As I take off down the street I realise how long it's been since I actually ran. Aside from the fact that my playlists grossly outdated the burn in my legs is nowhere near as pleasant as I remember. I'm running thirty minutes before my body remembers how to do it properly. I push past the mental wall and thrust my body's tension back into the earth. My favourite song makes its way through the shuffle and I start singing aloud through struggled breaths. I pick up my pace to match the music's beat.

Once I circle the block for the third time I know I've reached my limit, my legs know it too. I can see the porch light of my uncle's house ahead and I slow down to a gentle jog. I stop at the edge of the street and start cooling down my overworked muscles. There's a flash of movement in the corner of my eye. I feel the hairs on the back of my neck stand up and goosebumps rise on my forearms. I scan both sides but find nothing to warrant my attention. Something's out there; something's watching me.

I forget the cooldown and sprint toward my house. Something's gaining on me, I think I can hear the pounding of quickened footsteps, but my heart is thumping so loudly I can't be sure of anything. I cross the flower border in the front garden and practically fall up the steps into Jerry's arms.

"What's wrong?" He asks.

"I thought there was something out there," I tell him. I turn to look out into the darkness, but there's nothing, just an empty street. "I think Mrs. Phyllis is making me paranoid," I joke. My breathing slows as I shake off my paranoia and head upstairs to get ready for bed. I make sure to lock the front door behind me, safety chain and all.

- 17 -

SETH

The need for sleep is clawing at the insides of my eyelids, like sand burrowing into creases you never knew you had. I concede to the darkness that calls to me and allow myself to become weightless with sleep. The sensation of falling pulls all my weight back into my body at a hurtling speed. I wake to find my brother shaking my shoulder. I start to scold him for my rude awakening, but there's no time. Jason just chased off a werewolf that has been stalking Adaline. We haven't had negative encounters with werewolves since the clan signed the peace treaty with the Seelie. One thing is certain, if werewolves are coming after Adaline the treaty isn't going to last much longer.

We arrive outside Adaline's home within minutes but the streets quiet. Most houses in the street have turned dark with their inhabitants securely tucked into bed for the night.

A few homes like Adaline's still have their porch lights burning brightly seducing mosquitos and insects with their warmth. Adaline's bedroom light flicks to life behind her heavy curtains. I can make out the shape of her moving back and forth across her room. I watch her shadow quietly from the shrubbery across the street while Aedan barks orders at the guards. Before I realise what my fingers are doing the phone is pressed firmly against my ear. It rings once, twice and on the third ring, she answers.

"Hello?" She asks.

"Hi, I know it's late and I'm sorry if I woke you," I say.

"No, it's okay I just hopped out of the shower. I mean I'm just getting ready for bed, getting ready to sleep," she says in a blur. Her nervous high-pitched tone makes me laugh. "So, did you want something?" She asks.

"Yes, I was thinking about the necklace," I say.

"You were thinking about a necklace at twelve o'clock on a Saturday night?" She asks.

"Honestly, I was thinking about you and the necklace. I got it for you because I know that your whole world has been torn apart. That's something I can relate to better than anyone. Sometimes it's important to have something solid that you can draw strength from. I had hoped that pendant could be that strength for you," I admit.

"How can I refuse it when you go and say things like that?" She replies.

"I guess you're going to have to keep it then or people might think you're a jerk," I say.

"Thank you," she says with a suppressed laugh.

"You're welcome," I whisper.

"Are we still on for tomorrow then? After all, I was only meeting you to give the necklace back," she asks.

"I'm still game if you are," I reply.

"I'll see you in the morning. Goodnight Seth," she says disconnecting the call.

I watch her window until the light goes out and the house turns still. The air around me feels lighter and the pressure in my chest starts to ease. Despite my protests, my brother insists I go back to the hotel and rest. I'll be no good to Adaline or myself without sleep. At least with Aedan watching her tonight, I know she will be safe.

- 18 -
Adaline

I hang up the phone and my fingertips tremble with a nervous anticipation. Seth seemed different on the phone. Like he was able to let his guard down and I could finally see him through all his bullshit. Seth is probably one of the few people who can understand what I've been going through, and what he said about needing something to draw strength from resonates with me.

Still wearing nothing but a towel, I cross my bedroom to my dresser and open the velvet green box. The necklace is stunning to look at, but now I see it for more than just its physical beauty. It's a talisman, a symbol of strength. I unclip the clasp and drape the chain over my bare shoulders. It takes me a moment to fasten the clasp because my fingers are still trembling, but once secure I release it and the pendant falls just below my collarbone. I discard my wet towel and slip into a night dress.

The letter from my mother still sits on the window seat and the moonlight plays on it mischievously. I ignore its taunting and I climb under the covers. I turn over snuggling down into the warmth and let my heavy lids close. I feel the cool jade stone against my skin and it centres me making me feel safe.

- 19 -
Deklan

The Talbot line has ruled the Seelie since the end of the dark ages and our lands have been at peace ever since. When Theo took the throne, he announced me as his right hand. Regardless of title, I would protect him with my life, just like I have since we were children. Forty years ago, when Theo's first wife was murdered I almost lost him to a broken heart. It was hard to watch my best friend in such sorrow. In his grief, Theo left the Vale, and for years he drank and fornicated his way through the mortal realm. I had almost given up hope that his spirit would return until he met a mortal woman named Sarah who changed everything.

When Theo was with Sarah I saw the light come back into his eyes, I dare say she was the true love of his life. Unfortunately, fae Kings don't marry mortals and when the kingdom started to unravel and the fae whispered words of war Theo was forced to return.

To solidify his rightful place as King and reconnect the clans he had to form a political alliance. That meant marriage. Leonora was chosen by the council and Theo agreed to the match. At first, Leonora seemed the perfect choice for Queen. She came from a noble family, she was scandal-free and her beauty rivalled any maiden in the Vale, but within the walls of the castle, it soon became clear that her heart was as ugly as she was beautiful.

Eight and a half months after the royal wedding Queen Leonora gave birth to a child, a daughter. A princess was a shock to the kingdom since the Talbot line has only produced male heirs. Theo was enthralled to have a daughter and would have doted on the child. Unfortunately, not everyone was pleased with the princess's birth. I watched Theo pace outside the princess's chambers at all hours. He lived in constant fear for her safety. After three days without sleep, he could barely stand, he finally agreed to rest while I kept watch over the little princess. That was the night of the attack.

A hobgoblin broke into her chambers and tried to kill the princess while she slept. Luckily, I was able to tear the intruder apart before the child came to harm. As the swine bled out on the nursery floor he whispered to me a secret. He told me the name of the person who hired him to commit such a treasonous act. The Queen.

The day of the child's birth I had my suspicions about Leonora's affections. She never held her daughter, never kissed her rose coloured cheeks and every night when Theo paced outside his daughter's room after tucking her into sleep the Queen was nowhere to be found. I knew without a doubt in my mind that it was her hand that had paid for the kill.

The only proof I had was lying dead on the nursery floor. There was nothing else linking her to the attempted murder, only the word of a dead man and the werewolf that killed him. I placed my trust in Theo and told him everything. Despite how insane and treasonous my accusation was, Theo believed me. It was then that we decided to fake the princess's death.

I escaped with her into the night and after a few days had passed Theo joined us in the mortal realm. There was only one person who Theo trusted with the safety of his child and that lead us back to Sarah.

In a dark alley in London, we left the princess cradled lovingly in Sarah's arms. The princess was to be raised as a mortal by a mortal woman whose only power was that she was kind. That was the last time we saw the little princess. Theo and I returned to the Vale to wait until the princess came of age and we could bring her home.

That was almost eighteen years ago. Now that she's standing before me I can hardly believe the creature of beauty and grace that she has grown into. She has the same auburn hair as the Queen and the same flawless cream coloured skin, but everything else she inherited from her father.

I'm in wolf form as I run behind her, she's quick considering her change has only just begun. She sings along to music I can faintly hear escaping her earbuds and her voice is as angelic as her face. My nose catches the scent of two night walkers nearby and I start to panic. I should have gotten here sooner. The second Sarah died the cloaking spell was broken and the child was left unprotected. I quicken my speed keeping a watchful eye on our surroundings. She slows to a brisk jog and I scan the empty yards and houses. I can't see them, but they must be close by, their stench is overwhelming.

I need to get her inside where she will be safe. Before I approach her, something changes and she picks up her pace, she looks around nervously. She knows she is being watched. Smart girl, trust your instincts. She doubles her pace again and I speed up to match. Seconds later she's on the front porch of a colonial style home and she's in the arms of a man who resembles Sarah so closely it can only be her brother. She's safe.

Thanks to the hemlock root, the bloodsuckers aren't able to track my scent. I watch them circle Adaline's house like vultures surrounding a decaying meal. The first thing I notice about the vampires is that they are too organised to be rogues. If they belong to one of the clans I may be able to use that to my advantage. The last thing any fae wants is to break the treaty. I position myself on the roof of a house one street over, the colossal home gives me a good vantage point. Soon more vampires arrive and start spreading out their search for me.

I leap across the houses getting closer to the watchful vampires who are still too stupid to pick up my presence. As the vamps go about their business I overhear two of them talking.

From their conversation, it's clear they are watching Adaline, but the underlings have no idea why. I don't even think they sense that she is fae. If only they knew their future Queen was in their sights.

A blonde man arrives and starts barking orders at his people. I recognise his profile immediately. Aedan Dracott the leader of the western vampire clan. I continue watching him from the shadows in silence. He scolds his people for their sloppy work and inability to track me, eventually, he leads them around the neighbourhood for a final reconnaissance. His blood brother Seth waits behind, staring up at Adaline's window. I've met Seth once before and I'll admit I'm not a fan, but the concerned look on his face has me wondering if I might have been wrong about him. After a few hours, it's evident that the vampires mean no harm to Adaline and by all accounts, they appear to be keeping her safe tonight.

I arrive back at the bed and breakfast shortly before dawn. I crawl into bed and allow myself an hour of sleep.

- 20 -
Adaline

I wake to feel genuinely refreshed for the first time in weeks. I slept the whole night without the complication of disturbed nightmares forcing their way through my psyche. I've slept so well in fact that I've missed my alarm and there's little to no time to get ready for my date with Seth. I untie my hair from its knotted bun, it's still damp from my shower last night, the curse of thick hair. I let it fall past my shoulders and give it a brisk comb, thankfully my hair seems to be behaving itself today and falls in soft curls around my shoulders.

I slip into some skin-tight dark blue jeans and I only have a little trouble closing the top button. I'll admit I've put on a few pounds since the accident and I've completely negated my running schedule. I put on a push-up bra that gives my breasts the right attention and a thin white camisole.

Once I adorn the pink sheer blouse my outfit is complete. My womanhood is evident, but not overtly flaunted. I think mum would have approved. The voice in my head returns taunting that she's not really my mother. I turn up my music to drown out the voice, I'm not dealing with that today.

I apply a light layer of make-up and check the finished result in the mirror. I smile, happy that I look like my old self if only for a day. The necklace hangs gracefully against my collarbone, still cool against my skin. I blush at the thought of the man who gave it to me. Downstairs in the kitchen, I find Jerry's note that says he's been called into work and won't be home until late tonight and he's left some money for pizza. I could easily ask Seth to stay in and watch a movie or play a board game, but I dismiss that thought immediately. It's our first date and I don't know if I can trust myself to be alone with him.

The knock at the door startles me from my daydream. I open my phone to see the time, it's only ten, and he's early. I check my reflection in the glass of the fridge and make a deliberately slow walk toward the front door, so I don't appear too eager.

The pendant around my neck begins to warm and with each step, the heat intensifies. As I turn the door handle and pull open the door the pendant burns against my skin, I look down at my chest to see if there's any burn marks or explanation for the heat. The last thing I remember is a beautiful dark-skinned woman in my doorway and her tightly clenched fist coming toward my face.

- 21 -

SETH

I've been awake for hours; an uneasy feeling woke me from a dead sleep and I haven't been able to shake the feeling since. My brother joked that it's my nerves acting up because of the 'date' with Adaline. I won't admit it out loud, but I think he's right. I've been alive for centuries, but dating has been a pastime I never really took part in. It seemed an arbitrary waste of time and effort. Now I wish I had practised the mundane task more frequently so the unease in my stomach might subside.

Aedan's half-awake laying on his bed, he's exhausted from the night's events. They were unable to track the wolfen beast, but it hadn't returned. The mutt knew how to hide his scent and tracks which worries me. It's clear he's more than a random dog and it's possible that he could be a hired gun. It's not uncommon for vampires or werewolves to be hired as killers. Our talents make us uniquely qualified for such monstrous tasks.

My concern is shifting between Adaline's safety and the reaction she's going to have when I tell her the truth. I've spent all morning planning what I will say to her. I'm worried she will hate me for my deceptions. Worried she will think I've lost my mind and try to have me committed. If she tries to run, it will force us to hold her against her will. Then I worry if that's something I could do to her? Could I cage her like an animal if it came to it?

I leave Aedan to sleep and make my way down the hotel stairs. As I climb into the SUV I feel a rush of air beside me. Aedan has thrown himself into the passenger seat, looking as dishevelled as I feel.

"She's gone, drive," he says through gritted teeth.

"What do you mean she's gone? Where's Jason?" I yell.

"Just drive!" He screams. I thrust the car forward leaving nothing but dust in my wake. "Jason called said he was knocked out. At first, he thought the wolf had returned but there was no sign of him. He didn't realise until they started searching," Aedan says slamming his fist on the dashboard.

"Realise what?" I ask.

"They found some of Adaline's blood at the front door and Shaylin's missing, along with one of the cars. That treasonous bitch has taken her," he says furiously.

"How much blood?" I ask as I grow sicker with worry.

"Jason said the blood loss was minimal," he says.

Aedan continues to make calls to Samuel and the security team while I sink deeper and deeper into a fragmented dark rage. For years I have issued out justice among our kind and often it was unnecessarily cruel. After what Shaylin has done she will feel the full unbridled force of my torture techniques. The fifteen-minute drive takes me less than half that.

We arrive at the house and the front door is open. Even standing at the end of the footpath I can smell the blood. A few small drops have dried into mahogany brown circles on the wooden boards. I can also smell Shaylin's scent lingering in the doorway.

The room is overflowing with the scent of Adaline. It's a sweet unusual aroma, it's heady but delicate at the same time. It tickles the taste buds on my tongue like when you eat something sickly sweet and your body shivers automatically in response. A wave of panic starts washing over me and I have to step outside into the fresh air so I can breathe. Aedan places a steady hand on my shoulder to reassure me. A phone rings deep in his pocket and he releases his hold to answer. I stop breathing, my body shifts into a death-like stillness, straining to hear the words on the other side of the call. Have they found her?

- 22 -
Deklan

The hour was nowhere near as much sleep as my body wanted and it protests to waking. I didn't even undress myself this morning; once my boots are slipped on I'm ready to face the day. I retrieve the ancient mobile from the nightstand and I am connected to a direct line to Theo.

"You found her?" He asks eagerly.

"Yes, but it appears I'm not the only one watching her," I tell him.

"Do you need men? I can send an extraction team," he replies.

"No. We can't take the risk, word would spread through the kingdom if a party went out. From what I have witnessed so far it doesn't appear they want to bring the child harm. What I need is for you to get me the contact information of Aedan Dracott the vampire clan leader," I say.

"You will have it in five minutes. Is there anything else you need?" He offers.

"No, and Theo, don't worry I'll keep her safe you have my word," I reassure him.

I discard the phone and make my way to the rental car. The stupid thing is keyless and turns on before I'm even settled. I drive down to the small shopping village in the centre of town. To say the stores are basic is an understatement, but at least they can provide me what I need. After finishing my fourth sandwich from the deli I find my way into Kmart, thankfully they have a large supply of disposable cell phones which is the main thing I require. I start heading back to the car and unwrap one of the cell phones. I activate the sim and input the mobile number I received from Theo. The phone doesn't even get a chance to ring before he answers.

"Aedan speaking," he says.

"Aedan, this is Deklan, right hand to King Theodore. You and I will be having a meeting," I inform him.

"Of course. Shall we set up a time next week?" He asks.

"No. We can meet at your hotel in ten minutes or I can meet you wherever you are now. Which will it be?" I ask.

"Hotel. Room twenty-six, I will be there shortly," he replies.

I hang up as I leave the parking lot and drive straight to the hotel. I am the first to arrive. I take the liberty of picking the lock and letting myself into their room. The mini bar is stocked so I help myself to a beer and sit at the tiny attempt of a dining table to wait. I am about to call Aedan a second time when he and his brother enter. Aedan looks just as I remember; smartly dressed in a simple long sleeve button down and dark jeans. His dark-haired brother wears a worn green t-shirt and faded jeans. They are polar opposites, at the last treaty signing I recall thinking that Seth would have been better suited to join the Unseelie. Regardless, he joined us alongside his brother.

"Deklan, a pleasure to see you again it's been a long time," Aedan says shaking my hand firmly.

"Hi," Seth says.

"Excuse my brother's manners we are dealing with an urgent situation. What can we do for the King?" Aedan asks.

"Well, you can start by telling me why you are watching Adaline Thomas," I say. I see both of their jaws tighten and they are hesitant to answer. "Maybe I should start. I think you know the girl is the child of prophecy. I believe you either want to kill her or you want to keep her safe. I do hope for both your sakes it's the latter," I tell them.

"What do you want with her? That's what I want to know," Seth says boldly as his posture shifts into a defensive pose. Aedan quickly positions himself between us before the increasing tension turns into physical violence.

"I want to keep her safe and I will destroy anyone or anything that gets in my way boy, believe me," I reply.

"It appears we want the same thing then, perhaps we can help each other?" Aedan says.

"I don't trust wolves," Seth grunts.

"Very well. Let me ask you this. Who is Adaline really?" I ask.

"The chosen one," Aedan replies uncomprehendingly, while Seth simply glares.

"She's much more than that. Almost eighteen years ago the Queen gave birth to a daughter. Only days after her birth the princess was murdered. The truth is there was an attempt made on the princess's life, but they failed. The King and I put the princess into hiding. To keep her safe, she was raised in the mortal realm. On my honour as the hand of the king this is the truth," I say.

"She's a princess," Aedan says.

"She is 'the' princess. Not only is she the child of prophecy, but she is the next leader of the Seelie Court by birthright," I tell them.

"I don't care who she is. What matters is that she's been taken," Seth says.

- 23 -
Adaline

There's throbbing deeply ingrained in my skull; each time it beats I fear my brain might explode from the building pressure. I open my eyes but it's too dark to see anything. My wrists are bound in front of me and there's little room to move. What happened? I was in the kitchen getting ready to leave and someone was at the door. A girl, not much older than me, she had dark skin and a strong figure. She hit me. I touch my fingers to my right cheek. It's tender and a warm liquid begins coating my fingertips. I'm bleeding.

The room starts to shake and sway, then a steady vibration sets in. It's not a room, I'm in the boot of a car. I check my pockets for my phone but it's gone, I must have dropped it. My vision starts adjusting to the darkness and I can see there's a small ray of light peering through one of the seats. I roll myself over and begin pulling at the thick backing.

It's harder than I thought. The rough fabric hurts my fingers as I struggle against it, but eventually, my stinging fingers are able to make enough of a gap to shed a little light on my prison. I look around the boot for a weapon or a button to release the door, but there isn't any. I feel myself starting to panic, my breathing quickens and my pulse begins to race. I need to calm down, I need to be smart. I make a mental checklist.

1. Keep calm.

2. Find a weapon.

3. Find my chance to run.

4. Survive.

Trying to keep calm is becoming increasingly challenging as time drags on. I try chewing through the tape that's binding my hands but the plastic coating proves difficult. A muffled phone rings behind me. I turn back around and press my ear to the small hole I have made in the back of the seat.

"Yes. She's in the boot," there's a pause. "I could just kill her now..." more silence, "Yes, I understand. I'll arrive in Dallas within the next two hours. I won't be late, I assure you," she says.

I hear the smashing sound of plastic being crushed between vengeful breaths. Whoever my captor is she isn't happy. Which is not good for my situation. I start screaming. A deafening ear-splitting cry that sounds foreign to my own ears. Then I remember the last time I heard this tone in my voice. I see flashes of the plane going down, the faces of the passengers as they cried out for help. The feel of my mother's hand holding mine tightly. I continue screaming, the car radio begins to rise until it matches the volume of my cries. I become so worked up I feel nausea bubbling in my stomach, I push it down with a final blood-curdling shriek. My vocal torture has reached its limit as the car comes to an abrupt halt. The sudden jolt makes me jerk forward, hitting my head against the back seat.

The engine cuts off, I hear the creak of a door opening. There are loud stomping sounds and the grinding of gravel. My attacker is approaching the boot, the door unlocks and the assault of light forces me to squint my eyes.

It takes me a moment to be able to focus on the figure standing in front of me. It's the dark-skinned woman I remember. In this light, she seems older than I first thought. Her skin has traces of scars on her neck and arms. Her face is unmarked except for the vile curl of her lips.

"Shall I gag you, little girl?" She says with disgust.

"No, I'll be quiet. I just need some air, I'm going to be sick. Please let me walk a minute," I plead. "If I choke on my own vomit what good am I to you?" I add.

"Two minutes and if you run I will shoot you. Understand?" She reveals a large silver handgun to support her threat.

I nod in compliance. As I sit myself upright in the boot I look beyond my captive and take in my surroundings. We have travelled down a dusty dirt road that's filthy and overgrown. To my right, there's long grass carpeting a field beside us and just past the grass is lush green woods.

I swing my legs awkwardly over the back of the car, my captive digs her nails into my shoulder forcing me forward. My feet touch the ground, as I stand the world starts spinning. The nausea that I had been suppressing hits me and before I can move I reach forward and vomit on the ground. I'm overjoyed when some of the vomit lands on the woman's lovely black boots.

"Stupid child," she screams and hits me across the face, making me cry out.

"Why do you want me? I don't even know who you are, you're making a mistake." The necklace I had forgotten I was wearing burns against my skin. I look down and just like before there's no sign of a wound or redness. It simply dangles beautifully in place.

"I know who you are. You are nothing, a worthless little girl who will be dead soon enough." She says spitting her words, like a snake spitting its poison. "You're so stupid you can't even see he was lying to you," she adds.

"Who lied to me?" I ask.

"Don't you see it? Seth was playing you like a fucking fiddle. He was never interested in you. He was trying to get you exactly where he wanted you. Once I deliver you to my mistress I will be rewarded with a seat of power in the new order. Seth will bow down to me, they all will," she yells.

"What did he do to you that was so bad?" I ask. Maybe if I can sympathise with her she might let me go.

"He ruined me. Unfortunately for him, I found friends who will help me get my revenge," she says.

There's a crazed look in her eyes that I have never seen in another person and it scares me. I feel the wave of panic return; this woman has lost her mind and she is going to kill me for something that is out of my control. I'm not going to die today. I feel a strength rise deep within me, a primal need for survival. I feel an anchor tether itself to my chest, I follow the invisible pull that connects me to the roots of a nearby tree. The roots begin to grow and stretch.

They reach forward towards the woman and start clawing at her limbs. She's shocked by the assault. As a second branch comes toward her she regains her composure and shoots at the branches. I'm momentarily frozen in place, hypnotised by the swaying of the limbs of the tree. The forth gunshot releases me from my mental prison. Run, my head screams.

I turn on my heels and run across the open field, the undergrowth stirs and shifts out of my way creating a clear path for me to tread. As I reach the edge of the woods I hear my attacker hissing in the distance, but it doesn't slow me down. I follow the path the forest creates for me until it leads me to a cave on the far side of the mountain. As I enter the darkness of the cave, branches grow at the entrance sealing me inside. There's minimal light and I can hear the woman's gunfire and her screaming rage.

I use one of the bulging rocks to cut myself free from my restraints. The adrenalin coursing through my veins begins to fade and I sit weakly against the cave wall. I feel myself starting to sway and the corners of my vision start to blur, at least this time when I pass out I'm already sitting on the ground.

- 24 -

SETH

Adaline's been missing for five hours and against my better judgement, my brother and I have formed an alliance with the wolf. I'm willing to sink to unspeakable levels to get Adaline back. Aedan's driving and the wolf is sitting in the front passenger seat so he can track Shaylin's scent. While they make themselves useful I'm in the backseat kicking myself for not being there to protect her in the first place. I'm also thinking of all the ways I can bleed out Shaylin before she succumbs to death for her betrayal.

I've been so consumed with the emotions of losing Adaline I haven't stopped to think why. What could Shaylin have to gain from abducting Adaline? Maura? I saw how determined Maura was to kill Adaline and I have seen firsthand what that heartless bitch is capable of. Aedan was able to contact Samuel who is on his way to Russia to investigate Maura's stronghold.

All the rage I have towards Maura and Shaylin is making my blood boil and the thought of Adaline being injured pushes me to my limits. I feel my skin teetering on the edge of combustion.

"What's that smell?" Deklan yells casting a judgemental look in my direction. I look down where my hands are gripping the leather seats, the leather has begun decaying beneath my touch. The heat in my palms turns to flames. I leap from the car before my brother has a chance to come to a complete stop. "We don't have time for this, I cannot follow her scent with him burning things in the back seat.

Get your brother under control or he stays here. It's your fault she's been taken in the first place," the wolf screams.

My eyes widen and the flames burn brighter. It swirls into a hot blue inferno that I send hurtling directly at the wolf. He jumps out of the way, missing my assault. I start to build another fireball in my hands when Aedan grabs me by my shoulders and tries to wrestle me to the ground.

"Seth, we need to find Adaline. Fighting each other only hurts her," Aedan yells.

"He's right. It's my fault. She could be dead in a ditch somewhere and I'm to blame. I should have been there watching her, I should have…" I choke. Aedan still has me locked in his iron grip, he ignores my breakdown and keeps me focused on my breathing. I match my breath to his and the flames start to subside and so does the panic in my chest. When he's certain I have composed myself, he releases me.

"Deklan do you still have the scent?" Aedan asks.

"I do. Do you have your brother under control?" Deklan snaps.

"He's fine, get in the car," Aedan orders.

My brother ushers me into the car. He climbs back into the driver's seat and starts the engine. I can't understand why he doesn't appear as shocked by my emotional outburst as I was. Now I feel weak and broken, and it's not a feeling I'm comfortable with. The tension in the car increases the closer we get to Dallas. Jason and his team found the SUV abandoned roughly two hours from the city and we have been tracking her scent ever since. Vampire senses are heightened more than any humans, but nothing compares to the nose of a wolf. They can track things even vampires can't find.

"Turn here," Deklan orders.

"Why would they come here, this road is taking us to the middle of nowhere? Dallas would be the better escape route?" Aedan queries.

"Slow down, I can smell Adaline's scent, it's weak. It's strange her scent is confusing. It's like it's there but I can't get a lock on it. The vampires scent is strong though," Deklan says with his body half hanging out the car window, like a pet dog on holiday.

I curse myself for giving her the charm. It was meant to keep others from locating her not to stop us from protecting her. I keep my guilt to myself and bottle it away with the other emotions I have building in my chest.

"Here, take that road. I can smell her blood, its fresh. We are closing in," Deklan says.

"Adaline's blood or Shaylin's?" I ask. The thought of Adaline being hurt makes my stomach churn uncontrollably.

"Both. Adaline's is faint, the vampire's blood is dominant," Deklan replies.

We round the corner of a dirt road, I can see an abandoned sedan ahead. The boot door is wide open but the car looks to have been dumped years ago. Tree roots and undergrowth have grown around it trapping it in place. Some of the branches encasing the car have been shattered and broken, showing signs of a struggle.

"Adaline did this. I can sense it through the earth. She was afraid and the earth protected her. This is good news," Aedan says.

"Let's split up, you two follow the tracks as best you can and I will head towards the mountain to get a better line of sight. Watch out for Shaylin the bitch is capable of anything," I order.

Aedan and the wolf move forward into the forest in perfect unison. Adaline's natural instincts would have made her travel downhill and Shaylin would have gone to higher ground to get a better vantage point. I just hope the pendant is making Adaline as difficult to track for Shaylin as it has been for us.

- 25 -
Adaline

A chattering sound wakes me, I'm stunned by the darkness. As I arch my back against the rough wall behind me I remember where I am. I also recognise my teeth are responsible for the chattering that woke me. My fingertips are numb and tingle as I stretch them out. The rocks and dirt grind beneath me, clinging to any exposed skin it can find. I dust off the grime as I walk around the cavern and recount the turn of events that lead me here, alone in a cave consumed by darkness. I hug myself tightly praying for warmth. A small flicker of light steals my attention, I press back against the cave wall afraid that the woman has found my secret location. As my eyes shift into focus I see that a small grouping of branches in the corner of the cave has begun to burn.

I huddle by the fire and drink in its warmth. I should be concerned by the spontaneous combustion, but after the things I've seen, it pales in comparison. My stomach grumbles making sure I haven't forgotten its hunger. There's a rustling in the overgrowth at the entrance to the cave. I pick up one of the burning branches and approach the sound with caution. I can't see through the thickness of the overgrowth, but I do see that the branches aren't bare. They are covered with lush blueberries. I fill my shirt with the juicy berries and sit back by the fire. Once I've had my fill and my hands are stained violet from the berries juices I decide to sleep and save my energy. I will start moving at first light, and perhaps by then, my uncle will have the police looking for me. I just hope the lunatic woman has decided to give up the chase by then. As I lay down by the fire I feel the urge to cry and after everything that's happened, I think I deserve the right to have my own little pity party. So, on the floor of a deserted cave in the middle of nowhere I make my bed and cry myself to sleep.

- 26 -

SETH

My sharp eyes see through the darkness like the sun is still shining brightly in the sky. I look out along the tree line, but there's no sign of movement. I punch my fist into a tree fracturing the sapling with my rage. I just hope the others are having better luck than I am. I start the steady descent to catch up with them when my attention wavers. My fire element responds to nearby flames. The element detects it before any of my other senses are aware of the presence of the fire. It's no secret I have never been happy about my connection to the fire element, but right now I couldn't wish to be connected to anything else. I feel the draw of the fire calling out through the night, beckoning me into its alluring warmth.

The fire leads me through the trees and up a steep hill, in my haste, I trip on a root or two. When I finally reach the top there's nothing but a large grouping of blueberry bushes and no visible sign of fire, but my element tells me otherwise.

I start pulling the branches back violently, cutting lacerations into my palms as I go. I hear footsteps behind me. I turn ready to attack but instead of a villain, I see my brother with a confused look on his face.

"What are you doing?" Aedan asks.

"She's inside," the wolf answers for me. "Adaline, you can come out now, we're here to take you home," Deklan calls as he pushes me aside, I hiss at him in return. Aedan smacks my shoulder to curb my brashness. "Adaline, we promise it's safe," Deklan coos.

"How do I know you're not here to hurt me? That woman wasn't working alone," Adaline replies.

"Adaline, it's me, Seth, that necklace I gave you for your birthday is it warm or hot to touch?" I ask.

"No, it's cold," she says.

"It becomes warm when you're in danger, I'm sure you felt that at least once today. I promise you it is safe," I say.

"The woman said you lied to me, Seth. Was she telling the truth?" Adaline asks.

I freeze. I don't know how to reply. She will hate me once she knows the truth.

"We were trying to keep you safe. If you come out we can take you home and explain," Aedan says.

We wait in silence for what feels like an eternity before the branches begin to grow in opposing directions, opening like a curtain being drawn. In their absence, a girl sits on the ground. Her face streaked with blood and dirt. Her shirt has been torn and her jeans are covered in filth. I rush to her side and she flinches.

"It's okay Adaline, I'm going to carry you back to the car," I say gently. She seems too shocked to protest, so I bend down to lift her into my arms. As my hands reach the small of her back she punches me in the jaw. Her impact has more strength behind it than I would have guessed and it catches me off guard.

"Don't touch me," she orders and turns her attention towards my brother. "Is Aedan even your real name?" She asks firmly.

"It is," he replies.

"I assume our meeting was also a part of this game you two have been playing," she says.

"Technically I haven't lied to you, however, you're correct that our meeting was intentional," Aedan replies.

"Very well, you will take me home," Adaline says to Aedan. She turns her glare to the wolf and looks him up and down. "I don't know who you are, but you can take Seth home, I refuse to travel with him," she says confidently.

"My name is Deklan my lady and I will escort this fool if that is your wish," Deklan says bowing formally, before moving out of her path.

Adaline still looks nervous despite her display of confidence and she doesn't smile at Deklan's formality. She pushes past Deklan and starts trenching into the woods. Aedan is close at her heels and even though it's killing me to watch her walk away, at least I know she's safe and I can finally breathe again.

"She knows how to put a man in his place. I think I'm going to like having her as my Queen," the wolf laughs.

"Shut up dog. Let's get back to the road," I spit.

- 27 -
Adaline

I walk ahead of Aedan until I'm sure I can't feel Seth's gaze behind me. Once I'm out of sight I realise I have no idea where I'm actually going. I fall back and let Aedan take the lead.

"Are you okay, physically I mean?" He asks.

"I might need some stitches. Does my uncle know?" I ask.

"When we were at your house I found your phone. Our men removed any signs of a struggle and I sent him a message from your phone saying you were going out with some school friends. It's a little after seven now so we have time to get you home. I'm not sure what you want to tell him about your face," he says smiling sweetly.

We enter the clearing, but everything looks different at night. I can still make out the car I had travelled in and the grotesque way the trees have consumed the field.

We reach a large dark SUV and Aedan hurries to open the door for me. Once I'm securely locked inside he runs around and climbs into the driver's seat. As we pull away I see Seth's stricken face in the rear-view mirror. The sight of him causes a little pang of longing in my chest, but I turn away and ignore it.

"How far are we from home?" I ask

"About an hour and a half if I disregard the speed limits," he replies.

"Where are you staying tonight?" I ask.

"Hotel off Main Street," he says.

I take the cell phone that's sitting in his console and dial my uncle's number. The phone only rings once before he answers. I use every ounce of strength I have left to withhold my tears. I lie and tell him that one of the girls from school has asked me to sleep over tonight. He's so excited at the prospect of me making friends he approves automatically. I tell him I love him and promise I'll see him in the morning before he leaves for work.

"Now we have time for you to tell me the truth, because there's some serious shit happening and I feel like I'm losing my mind," I say.

Aedan delves into a story filled with prophecy and magic. He throws around tales of vampires and werewolves. The most insane story is the one about my birthright. He swears up and down that I'm the next in line to rule a fairy kingdom and once my powers arrive in full they expect me to go to another realm with them to reign. As he speaks I can hear the desire in his voice. He sees my heritage as some amazing gift I should be thankful for, but I'm not so sure I agree.

"You know what's funny is that when Seth and I first decided to come find you we had no idea who you really were. We thought you were just a gifted human. We never had any idea that you were fae, let alone the Talbot heir," he says. "I know you're unhappy with Seth but my brother really cares for you Adaline," my cheeks warm at his words. "Seth and I have been together for over two hundred years and I have never seen him act the way he has in the last few days. I don't know what it is about you that's incited this change, but I'm grateful he's finally letting his guard down," Aedan says lovingly.

"Stop. Please just stop, I don't want to hear any more about him or his lies. Can you please just take me to your hotel so I can shower and sleep?" I plead.

"Of cause princess," he replies.

I try to sift through all the information Aedan's thrown at me. I try sorting it into neat piles in my mind. Magic, monsters, murder. I eventually make my way back to the letter my mother left me and the flower sitting on my desk at home. Between my mother's words and the things I have seen, I find it hard to believe that what Aedan's said isn't the truth. The logical alternative is that I have suffered brain injuries in the plane crash and all of this is an ongoing hallucination. Then again the logical has not always been my first choice. Trusting my gut, on the other hand, has always proved to be the right decision and my gut tells me to trust Aedan.

- 28 -
Deklan

I admit I had concerns about the princess being raised as a human. I worried she wouldn't be strong enough for our world. I'm pleased to find she's stronger than I thought and watching her punch that vampire in the face was the best thing I have seen in years. It wasn't a ladylike response, but I think her father would approve none the less. Seth's quiet as we walk back to the road, he hasn't even made any more dog remarks.

"Thank you for helping find Adaline. I would not have been able to live with myself if she had come to harm. I will make sure the king is aware of your support in this matter. He will reward you and your brother handsomely," I say.

"Don't bother," Seth snaps back.

"If you insist… You know when Adaline was born I watched over her night and day alongside her father. She had this mess of auburn hair on her tiny head and she would smile when she slept. When my own son was born he didn't smile for months. She's not like other people, she has a warmth in her and I can't help but feel a love for her like she's my own. Giving her up to keep her safe was hard for me, but for her father, it was almost unbearable," I say. Seth sighs deeply and I hope he understands I'm not saying this to be cruel, I'm saying it to save him some heartache. "It's easy to love her Seth, but loving someone, truly loving someone, sometimes means letting them go," I say.

I place a gentle hand on his shoulder, his body tenses in response. I can feel the hope drain out of him. Seth knows as well as I do that the princess must marry in accordance with her station and it's a widely known fact that vampires are infertile. The princess could never marry someone who could not give her an heir.

Seth smacks away my hand and storms off towards the abandoned sedan. The headlights of the SUV graze us as Aedan drives past. I look at Seth and wonder if his infatuation for Adaline is a fleeting feeling or something more substantial. I never saw Seth as the loving type, but perhaps he has finally found something worthy of love. Poor kid, I feel bad for him.

- 29 -
SETH

Why is the bastard telling me this? Does he just like rubbing salt into my wounds? It's bad enough to know fate has decided my future with Adaline but to hear him drag on about it. It makes me want to punch him repeatedly in the face until it resembles a bloodied and deformed crushed tomato.

Jason arrives not long after Aedan's departure. I jump in the back seat trying to distance myself from the wolf and the situation his presence reminds me of. The gentle rocking of the car lulls me into a half sleep only slightly conscious of my surroundings, while the other half tries to drag me into the sleeping world.

"Aedan informed me that you're here to assist us with the human girl," Jason says. "Do you know why we are putting so much effort into a human?" Jason asks.

"Perhaps you should question your boss about his methods," Deklan replies in a gruff voice.

"Well, actually my boss is sleeping in the back. Usually, Aedan handles the majority of the leadership but I answer to Seth, though he has never been interested in his position," Jason says.

"If Seth has no desire to rule then why aren't you Aedan's second in command?" Deklan asks.

A question I have often wondered myself. Jason is basically Aedan's second, but he has made it clear on a few occasions that he follows me and not my brother. Why follow a man who doesn't lead? Why follow me at all?

"Seth has potential to be a great leader. He hides it well, but he has a good heart and he's the most loyal person I know. Sixty-one years ago, I broke into the stronghold. I was dirt poor and starving at the time, I thought I could find something worth stealing to get me through the winter. Safe to say I saw things I shouldn't have and the previous leader sentenced me to death. At this time Aedan and Seth were enforcers," Jason says.

"Aedan spared you?" Deklan asks.

"You would think so, but no Seth did. Aedan was ready to do his duty but Seth offered me a choice. Immortality or a swift death. I chose to be a vampire and he has been protecting me ever since," Jason's says.

"Why did he spare you?" Deklan asks.

"I don't know. I probably never will, he's not a sharer," he replies.

I hear Jason's seat squeak as he shifts his weight and settles into the drive. I know why I let him live. It was a moment of weakness. When I saw him huddled in the corner of the mildew covered dungeon I recognised something in his eyes. It is the same hopeless look my mother had the morning before she died. Like my father had beaten down my mother, Jason had been beaten down by the world. I made a choice to save him. Until now I haven't repeated that decision, caring for people makes you weak. Between Aedan and Jason, I already have too much to care about.

I must have finally drifted off because suddenly I wake to the sound of Jason's cell phone ringing. He answers through his earpiece and I can tell it's my brother on the other end by the way his body tenses.

"Yes, not a problem send it though. Yes sir, we should be back within the hour. Goodbye," Jason says.

"What did he want Jason?" I ask sleepily.

"He needs me to pick up some clothes on our way back," he replies.

"Why? We packed heaps of stuff. Did he run out of blazers?" I laugh, half asleep.

"Not for him, for the girl. Her clothes are ruined and she needs something to wear in the morning," he says turning off the highway.

"In the morning?" I ask.

"She's staying at the hotel tonight. You can bunk with me if they get too loud for you to handle," he jokes.

"That won't be necessary. There's no way she's spending the night alone with a bunch of vampires. I'll be joining you," Deklan declares.

"Great we can braid each other's hair," I reply.

My stomach panics and does a somersault at the thought of Adaline spending the night alone with my brother. At least with Deklan and myself present I know I needn't worry.

- 30 -
Adaline

We arrive at the hotel and Aedan escorts me up the flight of stairs to a row of doors. We make our way up to room twenty-six where he opens the door with a gold coloured credit card kind of key. It's swankier than any hotels I have ever stayed in and I'm surprised this town has one this lavish to offer. The room is dazzlingly bright with ivory textured walls and cream coloured curtains with gold accents. There are two single beds on the left with a door between them and two doubles on the right. On the far back wall, there's a large window and a small kitchenette, complete with a dining table and chairs.

"Who else will be sleeping here tonight?" I ask. My speech is low and raspy, the day has worn down my voice to inaudible levels.

"Myself and Seth, although I don't suppose Deklan will stray too far," he replies.

"I don't know how I feel about that," I tell him as he rummages through suitcases on the floor.

"Here you can put these on after you shower. The others will pick up some clothes for you to wear tomorrow. They belong to Seth. I hope you don't mind, but my clothes are all buttons and zippers. Not exactly comfortable to sleep in," he rambles.

"It's fine. Do you have a towel?" I ask.

I'm too tired to fight about whose clothes I'm going to wear, so I grab the bundle of clothing and Aedan hands me a velvety soft cream coloured towel that matches the room's décor. He also provides me with a toothbrush still in its plastic casing and gestures towards the bathroom. I lock the door securely behind me and turn the hot water on. It's slow to warm, but once the steam begins to rise I gingerly take my clothes off my aching body. I drop the rags into the empty bathtub. I find the shampoo and toothpaste on the counter and some bars of soap with the hotel's logo stamped on it. I never thought I would have to consider whether or not vampires brushed their teeth, judging by the two brushes on the sink it's a safe bet they do.

The hot water stings my feet and legs, I flinch as it comes into contact with the cut on my cheek. Slowly I ease the rest of my face under until I can bear the painful sensation. I lower myself to the floor of the shower and watch the dirt and blood trickle off my body. The rust coloured water runs down the drain, washing away the day's events. I start breathing heavily, at first I think it's the steam opening up my airways but it's because I've started crying. Like the traces of dirt, my tears become lost in the steady stream of water. I sit under its warmth until my skin feels too hot and I need to stand to change the temperature. I shampoo my hair twice and brush my teeth thoroughly. The hotel soap smells good against my skin. I lather myself until I'm raw, trying desperately to wash away my reality. Unfortunately, I can't hide in the shower forever.

I turn off the water and dry myself until the soft towel feels rough against my skin. The bathrooms filled with a steamy haze and I feel like I'm walking through a cloud. There's a comb in the top draw and I make short work of the knots in my hair and squeeze out as much excess water as I can.

The clothes Aedan gave me are far too big, the shirt hangs three inches above my knees and the boxer shorts look like swimming trunks. Aedan was right about one thing, these clothes will definitely be comfortable to sleep in. I try to ignore the fact that Seth's manly aroma still clings to his belongings, but beggars can't be choosers so I take a deep breath and emerge from the bathroom.

Aedan's sitting on one of the beds by the door deliberately looking away from the bathroom. He doesn't turn immediately, so I clear my throat.

"All done?" He asks trying to keep his eyes focused on mine and nothing else.

"As done as I can be," I reply. I move over to the double bed pressed up against the back wall. I pull back the sheets and climb in. I pull the covers up close and sink into their smoothness. Aedan suppresses a small laugh. "What?" I ask crankily.

"Nothing," he says through pursed lips.

"This is Seth's bed, isn't it?" I sigh.

"Afraid so," he says.

"What do you think would bother him more, me in his bed or me in yours?" I ask.

"I don't know, he has never been the jealous type," he says.

"Which one's yours?" I ask. Aedan gestures to the double bed next to Seth's, I stride over and pull back the covers.

"You're going to be a handful, aren't you?" He smirks and I can't help but smile in response.

I move a pillow against the headboard and position myself comfortably. I lean back into the pillow and rest my aching muscles. I open my eyes to find Aedan sitting on the bed facing me. He opens a small first aid kit and starts pulling pieces out and laying them on the bed. He holds up a piece of gauze and raises an eyebrow asking my consent. I nod. He presses the wet gauze against my cheek, it stings but it's nothing compared to the caress of the shower.

His eyes sparkle with a kindness, a quality I recognise from my mother. He begins to dry my wound and pinches the cut together while artfully placing the butterfly stitches to pull it shut. The hotel door opens abruptly. Seth's presence in the doorway consumes the frame making the entrance look small. He recovers his shocked expression but I can tell my proximity to Aedan has rattled him. Good, I think to myself. Deklan enters behind him carrying a small shopping bag.

"Princess," Seth addresses me coldly, "Aedan can we have a word outside?" He asks. I feel guilty and hope I haven't gotten Aedan in too much trouble with his brother.

"Sure thing," Aedan replies. He turns to me offering a reassuring smile and a wink before he follows his brother outside.

"Thank you for everything," I murmur.

"You're welcome princess," Aedan says sweetly, closing the door behind him.

With the vampires outside I'm left alone with the werewolf. Deklan actually looks like a wolf as I come to think of it. He has large loyal eyes and a rough looking beard. There are signs of an abundance of chest hair peeking through the top button of his shirt. He has a scruffy quality about him which I find comforting.

"You know my father?" I ask.

"I do," Deklan replies.

"Is his name really Theo? When I was younger I asked about him often. Mum only ever gave me his name and nothing else," I tell him.

"Yes, he's Theo. Your father is a wonderful man. He and I have been best friends since we were kids. He loves you a great deal and he loved your mother too," Deklan says encouragingly.

"Ha, which mother," I say.

"Can I be honest?" He asks cautiously. I nod in response. "Sarah was your mother. She loved you unconditionally and raised you as her own, it's more than others get," he says.

I lay down and snuggle into the feathered covers. I close my eyes and ponder all the things I have discovered about myself today and not just myself, but about the world. I almost think I'm going to struggle to find sleep, luckily my weakened body wins the battle against my racing mind.

- 31 -

SETH

I didn't prepare myself to see Adaline scantily dressed cozied up to my brother in his bed. His hand was against her cheek and she was looking attentively into his eyes. Indignation burns inside me and my fingers begin to sizzle. I hold my breath attempting to steady myself while I wait for Aedan. I hear her thank him and I want to spit on her words. Aedan closes the door softly and joins me at the end of the porch.

"Should we talk about what happened today?" Aedan asks.

"Perhaps we should talk about what you were just doing," I say. I can still smell the remnants of the extinguished fire in my palms. My hands may not be burning, but my insides are a different story.

"It was nothing, I was tending to her wound. Do you honestly think I would make a move on a girl you are infatuated with? I'm your brother Seth, I wouldn't do that to you," he says.

"Well she was in your bed, I find it hard to believe that's just a coincidence," I say. I know I'm overreacting and my words have more venom than I would like.

"My bed wasn't her first choice. Let's get some rest it's been an emotional day," he says.

When I enter the room, her head has sunk low into the cushions,

I make my way into the bathroom and close the door. The room smells of her. Her blood lingers in the air, I consider leaving, but then I would need to face her. I decide to shower and shave, taking great care to wash every inch methodically to pass the time. The best thing I can do for any of us now is my job. I will keep her safe and deliver her to her father. Once that's done I can move on with my life.

Eventually, I withdraw from the bathroom and glance in her direction, her head is hidden beneath the heavy blankets and I can hear even steady breaths escaping her cocoon, she's sleeping. Wearing only a towel I creep up to her bedside to open my suitcase and search for my shirt and underwear.

Not finding what I'm looking for I steal another glance at Adaline and notice she is wearing my shirt. This time the fires in my heart, not my hands. I find something else to put on and slide into my bed. When my head hits the pillow, I'm taken back by its unusual scent. It smells of soap and sunshine with a hint of spring flowers. Adaline was in my bed, now I know what Aedan had meant. She had chosen my bed first and moved to spite me. I smile secretly to myself and settle into the crisp linen sheets.

Wakefulness comes easily as I inhale the fresh scent that morning light brings. When I open my eyes, I'm surprised that there is no light to be found. It's dark and raindrops dance along the tiled roof. The oversized bed across the room cradles Adaline lovingly in its blankets making her look younger than her years. I quickly notice that Adaline's the source of warmth in the room, even when sleeping she's a radiating light. She begins murmuring in her sleep and tossing from side to side. She's having a nightmare. I ease myself out of bed, careful not to wake anyone. I walk over to her side and crouch low beside the bed. She rolls over again making us face to face.

Her features are tense and she bites down on her lower lip. I reach out a hand to stroke a stray hair off her face. She flinches and her eyes open wide with surprise. Usually, her eyes have a violet quality to them, but in this light, they are a rich emerald, like the depths of the ocean. She studies me for a moment and before she has a chance to scold me I recoil my hand.

"Forgive me, you were having a nightmare," I whisper.

"My mother used to rub my head like that when I was little," she replies in a hushed tone.

"Mine too, I guess it's something mothers do," I reply.

I shift from my crouched position and lean back against the wall, resting my arm on the side of the bed. We sit in perfect silence listening to each other breathe, I could stay like this forever.

"I actually thought you liked me, you know before, but it was all just a lie," she says sadly.

"You're a princess, you have certain obligations and I'm not worthy. Just ask wolfman he will be happy to tell you," I admit.

"Aedan seems to think very highly of you," she says.

"Aedan's a kind-hearted fool," I say, but I find myself smiling in the dim light.

"If you promise not to lie to me again do you think we can be friends? Due to current circumstances, I find myself at a disadvantage when it comes to friends," she asks. I can hear her smile and I laugh low in my throat. Her innocence is refreshing.

"Yes, I think I can manage that," I reply. I make a move to stand, but her hand encloses mine forcing me to lower myself back to the floor.

"Can you just stay until I fall asleep?" She pleads holding my hand intimately.

"Yes princess," I reply.

"And I'm sorry for punching you today, although you did deserve it," she yawns and lowers her head into the pillows, her breathing evens out and I know she's drifting off. "Thanks for finding me," she whispers. I rest my head on the bed and close my eyes relaxing in her presence. Grounded by her touch, I follow her into sleep.

- 32 -
Deklan

My body can sense that dawn is approaching and it protests to waking. During the last few days, sleep has been an afterthought. Adaline is sleeping safely one bed away, I lift my head to reassure my mind and then I will indulge myself and go back to sleep. Regrettably, I see a foreign object resting beside her head. I sit upright and leap from the bed, I arrive at her bedside in two strides. She is asleep in the bed while Seth sits on the floor next to her. His head is leaning on the bed resting alongside her pillow. I can see they are holding each other's hands securely.

"Deklan," Aedan whispers and nods his head for me to follow him outside.

"This won't do Aedan, she has a higher calling than slumming it with a vampire," I yell.

"Don't forget who you're talking to. As for Seth, he knows there is no future for them. That doesn't mean his feelings can disappear overnight. Seth will protect her with his life and the way I see it the princess needs as much protection as she can get right now," he says.

"What if he breaks her heart?" I ask.

"What if she breaks his? People survive broken hearts. You have a son, right?" He asks. I nod my response. "If you told your son he couldn't see a girl because it wasn't meant to be what would he do?"

Aedan asks.

"He would dig in his heels and just want her more. Your right, I'm not happy about it but you're right," I admit.

I realise my fear runs deeper than protecting her physically. I want to protect her emotionally too like any father wants to protect his child. Since she has been gone I have been responsible for all communication with Sarah, I saw the photos of Adaline growing and I read the letters Sarah wrote containing everything detail of Adaline's life. In a way, she's my daughter too.

Aedan and I sneak back into the hotel, careful not to wake Adaline. Aedan pours two cups of coffee and offers me one. As I approach the kitchenette to collect my much-needed caffeine hit, I kick Seth's outstretched leg. What can I say, I couldn't help myself but take the opportunity. He wakes instantly looking ready for a fight. Then his eyes fall on the hand gripping his. He gently releases her hold and joins us for coffee. Aedan gives me a knowing eye and I shrug.

"Deklan when can she return to court?" Aedan asks.

"The problem is that she can't claim her throne until she turns eighteen. On her eighteenth birthday, she will receive her powers in full and then she will be eligible for the crown. Until then she is too vulnerable to have at court. Only the two of you know that she is the princess, but that doesn't mean others aren't looking for the child of prophecy. When Sarah died the cloaking spell began to fade, which I assume is how the two of you found her," I say.

"But Adaline just had her eighteenth birthday," Seth comments, between yawns.

"Not really, we had to falsify records when we put her into hiding, she's not eighteen until December thirty first," I explain.

"Why can't we just take her to court now? They have more magic and guards than we can offer her," Seth queries.

"The castle isn't safe. Not for her. We can't prove who tried to kill her, which means she's still in great danger," I explain.

"Who was it?" Aedan asks

"I told you I don't have any proof," I reply.

"Regardless of proof, you know who it was," Seth says.

"The King and I believe it was the Queen," I confess. It's the first time I have said it aloud since the night of Adaline's attack.

"Why would the Queen want to kill her own child, that's madness?" Seth's asks.

"The Queen is vicious and cruel. She got her position by default and she's not the kind of woman who would give up her crown or her youth to anyone, not even her daughter. With Adaline dead, the Queen can continue to rule and stay young and beautiful. After Adaline's eighteenth birthday the King will renounce his claim on the throne handing it over to Adaline. Since the Queen is not royal by blood there's nothing she can do to stop it," I tell them.

"So, what are we going to do now?" Aedan asks.

"I plan on staying here and finishing school. We better get home so I can explain things to my uncle," Adaline orders.

Her intrusion on our bedside meeting makes me jump and spill my coffee over my chest. Her voice is strong and defiant. I turn to see her sitting on the side of the bed. Even dressed in a baggy shirt with mussed hair she looks like a leader. Her face is held high and her shoulders are arched back. She's wearing a stubborn expression I recognise from her father. If she's half his daughter there will be no changing her mind once it's made up. She stands gracefully collecting the bag of clothes from the table and walks into the bathroom with purpose.

- 33 -
Adaline

I guess that's why Deklan didn't want me hung up on my birth mother. She tried to kill me as a baby and my father shipped me away to save me. What kind of mother would kill her own child? I know Sarah would never have harmed me in any way, she was always my pillar of strength. I wonder how Jerry will take all this. Maybe he will have me committed to a psychiatric ward, which may not be the worst thing that could happen.

I'll show him the letter first, once he wraps his head around that I'll tell him the rest. I wonder if I can show him my powers, although I'm not really sure how to make them work on command. Maybe Deklan can turn into a wolf, it's something I would defiantly like to see. I brush my teeth absentmindedly and consider the possibilities of my new life.

As I open the plastic bag and remove the clothes they had picked up for me. I wonder who was responsible for picking them out.

My guess would be Deklan, he seems as conservative as the clothing I have in front of me. A floor length heavy dark skirt and a long sleeve button up navy blouse, the kind with a collar and buttons to my chin. I abandon the skirt and collect my jeans from the tub, they aren't as far gone as I thought. I sponge away the visible dirt and dry them with the hotel hair dryer. The underwear they brought are white sensible cotton tops, unfortunately, they didn't buy a bra so I will just wear my dirty one. I slip into the underwear and pull on my jeans. I put on the new blouse and leave the two top buttons undone. I fold over the sleeves until they rest securely at my elbows. I tie the excess fabric at the bottom of the shirt into a knot just over my belly button exposing a small amount of midriff. It's not a raunchy outfit by today's standards, but I don't look like I've rolled out of an Amish community either.

I look in the mirror and aside from the cut on my cheek and some bruising around my eye I don't look too dishevelled. Strangely enough, I feel more like myself than I have since before the accident. There is a knock at the bathroom door and I open it hoping to see Seth, but it's Deklan.

"Didn't the skirt fit?" He asks.

"I'm sure it would have, but after everything that's happened I want to feel like myself," I say. He gives a small smile and nods. Then he looks at my exposed stomach and he rolls his eyes before walking off.

"I knew you were going to be a handful," Aedan laughs as he passes me on his way to the bathroom.

It's a little after six when the four of us load into the SUV. I had told Jerry I would be home by seven thirty to get ready for school so he hasn't called to check in yet, but I think I can safely assume I won't be going to school today. The car ride is silent, everyone focused on the road ahead, while I have a thousand questions running through my mind.

"Do you need to wait for the full moon to change?" I blurt out.

My question catches everyone off guard and there's a moment of silence. "I just mean in movies werewolves need the full moon to change and I guess you two don't burst into flames from sunlight so what's the deal?" I ask inquisitively.

"Bitten wolves will change on the first full moon after they are bitten. Then they can change with every full moon after that. If they are strong enough they can change whenever they choose. Born wolves like myself are stronger than the bitten. Our first change is on our eighteenth birthday and we can change at will, regardless of the phase of the moon," Deklan replies.

"Do you think I can watch you change, into a wolf I mean?" I ask. Seth laughs and I shoot him a furious glare.

"I don't know if that's appropriate princess," Deklan mutters. Aedan begins laughing alongside Seth.

"What's so funny?" I ask. Seth looks at me and clears his throat.

"When werewolves change it can be messy so they usually do it naked," he says.

"Well I have seen a penis before so I guess it wouldn't completely ruin me," I say. All the laughter dies down and the air feels uncomfortable. "I've had like ten sexual education classes at school since I was twelve and I have Netflix you pervert's," I chaste.

"What can you guys do then? You drink blood and don't age I figured that much, oh and Aedan told me about his earth elemental gift and your gift for fire. Can you turn into bats?" I start rambling.

All three start laughing and sadly they are laughing at me, not with me. "Look there's no need to be mean I only found out about all this less than twenty-four hours ago and I think I'm handling it pretty well considering. It's not like someone dropped off a magical encyclopedia for me to study you know," I say. I try to ignore their laughter, but end up sulking like a child for the rest of the drive.

We arrive at the house to find Jerry's car in the driveway. As we enter the house, I direct the men to the dining room to sit and wait. I climb the stairs reluctantly and linger at Jerry's door. Timidly I knock. He opens the door whilst fumbling with the buttons on his shirt. He smiles broadly at me until his eyes fall on my cheek.

"What happened?" He asks

"I had an accident, you know how clumsy I am. I'm fine I promise. I actually need to talk to you about something important. Can you come to my room with me?" I ask.

"Lead the way," he says.

Jerry sits on my chair at the dressing table and I collect the letter from the window seat. I sit across from him at the end of my bed and brace myself.

"Jerry, I just want you to know that whatever happens, I love you and whatever you decide to do I understand," I say apprehensively. I hand him the letter and wait as he reads.

"At least she told us the truth," he says.

"What do you mean, aren't you angry?" I ask confused.

"I always figured there was something. You didn't look like her, but you and she behaved the same, so I told myself that you just looked like your father. I also never believed that she would have hidden a pregnancy from me. After our parents died we always had each other's back. I loved her no matter what and she knew that. You know this changes nothing. You're still my niece and I love you just as much as I always have," he says.

I propel myself into his arms like I've been released from a catapult and squeeze him until he has trouble breathing. I want to freeze this moment in time, this perfect moment where he loves me.

"There's more, there are some people downstairs you need to talk to," I tell him.

- 34 -
Adaline

I usher my uncle into the dining room and I imagine how introducing him to a werewolf and two vampires is going to play out. I envision them soaring around a table in shredded clothes with blood dripping from their teeth, but what I see is three men sitting at a table drinking tea and coffee. I'm disappointed, it would be easier to convince my uncle if they showed their true colours. If I didn't know any better, they could pass for an adult study group. The truth is that anyone of these men could turn into a monster and despite what they are, I feel comfortable with who they are. Jerry enters behind me, it's clear he recognises Seth and Aedan but glances around the table curiously before taking his seat.

"I see you helped yourselves to coffee. Does anyone want something to eat?" I ask. No one answers so I take the seat next to my uncle.

"Jerry, you know Seth and Aedan and this is Deklan. Deklan works for my father," I say cautiously.

"Are you his attorney? I can assure you my sister would never have broken any laws, she wasn't that kind of person and you can't take Adaline away, I'm her legal guardian and I have the paperwork to prove it," Jerry babbles.

"No sir, I was actually present when he asked Sarah to take Adaline as her own. She was a good woman your sister and I'm sorry for your loss," Deklan says sincerely. "See the thing is, Adaline is rather special," Deklan says.

"I know better than anyone how special she is, I have been a part of her life since the day my sister brought her home. Even after every time they moved, I was in constant contact with them," Jerry snaps.

"You're lucky you had the option. Her father wasn't that lucky," Deklan remarks.

"So, he wants to be a part of her life now is that it?" Jerry asks.

No one responds. Seth and Aedan look awkwardly at one another and Deklan looks to me for guidance. Cowards the lot of them.

"My fathers a King and I am his successor, at least I will be after my eighteenth birthday. Turns out they lied about my birthday as well," I blurt out.

"King of what country?" Jerry asks.

"Well, that's more complicated. My father is King of the Seelie Court. He rules in a realm called The Vale. He's a fairy just like I am," I tell him. His jaw tightens and the colour in his eyes darkens.

"What are you people telling her, do you even know what she has been through, she's vulnerable and you're messing with her mind? Everyone out," Jerry yells but no one moves. "Out!" He screams. I can feel the air around him vibrate with rage and it makes me feel a little angry myself.

"No Jerry, listen its real. Everything we ever read about in fairy tales is real. Deklan is a werewolf, Aedan and Seth are vampires and I'm a fairy," I explain.

"Actually, you're fae, not a fairy. Fae is a term for the whole species and fairies are a subset of the species. Just like vampires and werewolves are also a subset, but we are all fae," Seth interrupts.

"Thanks for the clarification," I say sarcastically. "Jerry, I have never lied to you. Trust me that this is real. I've seen it with my own eyes… Deklan do your wolf thing," I request.

"What right now, I don't know if that's a good idea," Deklan replies.

"Just do it, my uncles, ready to have me committed!" I command.

Deklan stands to remove his shirt, he takes off his shoes and trousers, and he leaves on his underwear. My uncle stands, but I pull him back down to his seat and hold onto his hand tightly. At first, nothing happens and Jerry looks more frustrated with every passing second. Then Deklan's skin starts to quiver and move like ripples on a lake. The skin on his hands begins to tear and split apart. The tearing spreads up his arms and over his chest. Faint traces of blood follow the cracked wounds in his skin. Dark black fur starts to sprout from the raw open spaces between his cracked flesh. His torso elongates forcing him to hunch over in a distorted painful looking position. The black fur spreads over his body the same way moss grows over rocks by the river. His mouth stretches to expose monstrous fangs. His body begins shaking rapidly and I can't see straight.

When my eyes finally fixate on the space where Deklan once stood, a mammoth black wolf stands in his place. The tall proud creature lowers his head and front paws into a formal bow. I'm overwhelmed by his beauty, I rise from my seat and stroll over to stroke his silken fur and tell him what a beautiful creature he is. I look at Jerry whose expression has gone completely blank. I wave a hand across his face and he doesn't react. I gently squeeze his shoulder, still nothing. I think we broke him.

"Well?" I ask Seth.

"Don't know, we haven't told humans before. At least none that lived long enough to share their feelings on the matter," Seth replies.

"Jerry it's okay, he's just a big puppy," I tell him.

Deklan growls, clearly offended by my choice of words and Seth laughs. I glare at him and he shuts up. Aedan rounds the table to place a hand on Jerry's shoulder and guides his face away from Deklan.

"Jerry look at me. This is very difficult to come to terms with, but we can help you. Right now, we need to focus on Adaline's safety. Someone wants to hurt her," Aedan says.

Jerry's still in a state of shock, but with a little magic from Aedan, he seems to relax. Aedan begins explaining the world of monsters that I belong too. Jerry seems to be taking it well, but I still see his eyes glance towards his gun cabinet every so often. Deklan the wolf collects his discarded clothes in his mouth and wonders off. Deklan the man returns a few minutes later wearing only his pants and a partly buttoned shirt.

I sit quietly and listen while Jerry takes everything in. The sharing shifts between Aedan and Deklan, while Seth appears more interested in the state of his hands than the state of my uncle. Deklan leaves out the fact that it was my birth mother that tried to kill me which I'm grateful for, hearing it once was bad enough. Then the topic shifts from my past to my future, it's the only time Seth starts putting his opinion forward.

Deklan is adamant about taking me somewhere remote to hide for the next few months until after my birthday, before returning me to court. Seth wants to take me back to their castle in Ireland where I can be under guard twenty-four seven. Seth and Deklan continue fighting back and forth while Aedan tries to mediate. Jerry interjects every so often with questions of schooling and a normal life, things I'm concerned with myself.

These men are chess players and I'm their pawn. They are willing to move me around as they desire with no thought to what I want. Do I even know what I want? Do I want to be solely responsible for the future of the Vale? Deklan has spoken of his home at great length. He describes a land full of beauty and wonder. A place where the practice of magic is open and people don't need to hide who they are. The world he speaks of so fondly sounds like a place I really want to visit, but to live there and rule over it, I'm not so sure. It would be like ruling a foreign country and not understanding the language. Making decisions for a world I haven't been raised in, for people I know nothing of seems unreasonable.

My mother raised me human, I grew up with humans. Humanity has a brutality that has always confused and concerned me. I admit it, I'm scared. I'm scared this new world will be crueller than the mortal world I live in and I won't be strong enough to make a difference that matters. It should be my choice, if I'm really the princess the decision should rest with me alone. If I decide not to take the crown what are they going to do? Super glue a tiara to my head and force me onto the throne?

"Stop." My voice is quiet but firm. "I'm not sure I want this. Everything is happening so fast. What happens if I choose not to be queen?" I ask.

"If you refuse the throne your father and mother will continue to rule, though I fear that something may happen to your father if he continues to overrule certain decisions," Deklan replies.

"I have until my eighteenth birthday to decide if I want to rule correct?" I ask firmly.

"That's right princess," Deklan says.

"Well until my birthday I want to stay here. I want to finish school, I want to stay with my uncle and I will use the time to decide if I want to go through with this," I tell them.

"It's not safe here," Seth remarks.

"On that matter, I agree," says Deklan.

"One of your own people tried to kill me, Seth, I don't think I would be any safer at your home than mine and as for spending the next few months in isolation, I won't do it… I understand that I will need people to protect me, so you can work out some security or whatever, but my decision is final and I'm staying here," I say and exit the room.

- 35 -

SETH

Adaline's grand exit was regal if nothing else, she was resolute and elegant. I can hear her ascending the staircase and the click of her door handle as it closes behind her. I smile inside. I find it hard to look past her fragile exterior. Between her youth and innocence, I keep expecting her to break. In the last twenty-four hours, she has been through more turmoil and tragedy than most people endure in a lifetime and she has managed to keep her composure and self-confidence; she's more resilient than I could have imagined.

Looking around the table it's clear not everyone shares my delight at Adaline's independence. Deklan's nostrils are flaring and the air around him has become sickly stale. Aedan sits patiently waiting for the hostility in the room to dwindle, but my fire element can feel the anger resonating with my present company and it's not going to die down anytime soon.

"Well, I guess the princess has spoken. Shall we discuss security?" I ask to break the silence.

"This isn't a game boy. We cannot protect her here, not adequately. We both know how you would feel if she was killed, this needs to be dealt with," Deklan's words sting. It was a cheap shot at my moment of weakness.

"I have money. We can hire personal security, some ex-military or something, whatever it costs," Jerry offers.

"That's a generous offer Jerry, but humans won't be strong enough to withstand an attack from the fae," Aedan says.

"She needs to be taken to a safe house. Isolation is better than death. It's the only way to protect her," Deklan declares.

"As far as we know aside from Maura and Shaylin, it's possible that no one else knows she's here. The smart course of action would be to move Adaline immediately, which is what Maura would expect us to do, what she wouldn't expect is us keeping Adaline here," Aedan says.

I'm almost tempted to agree with Deklan. I would rather take her into isolation than let Maura get her hands on her. But I could hear it in Adaline's voice, she needs her uncle and this mortal life, it gives her strength and that's something she needs right now. Forcing her into hiding would destroy her and what good is a queen if she's damaged? It was a small window when her cloaking spell was down, Aedan's right to think that her existence may have gone unnoticed. Our men are closing in on Shaylin and once she is apprehended she will be killed, which will stop the spread of information. Adaline can be safe and stay here's where she's happy.

"I have two spare rooms. Seth and Aedan can stay in one, Deklan you're welcome to the other. I assume having three uniquely qualified persons like yourselves under the same roof will make it easier to protect her," Jerry adds.

I eye Deklan wearily, it's obvious he's not on board but short of kidnapping her, he doesn't have any other options either. It's decided, the princess stays. I take it upon myself to inform our princess of the arrangements and hope that she will be happy with the outcome.

Finding her bedroom is something of a game, I follow her scent weaving through the house, tracking a lingering trail of flowers until I reach a pale blue door. I knock sheepishly on the wooden frame, feeling more nervous than I should. As she opens the door her scent flows into the hall, bringing me back to the moment in the nurse's office when we sat inches apart. I remember how intimate our time together had felt, now it seems like a century has passed.

She shifts her eyes from mine and looks down at her feet. I can tell she feels uncomfortable under my gaze but her beauty leaves me breathless, I reach out a finger and gently lift her chin until she meets my eyes and smiles. She stands aside so I can follow her into her room. I turn to close the bedroom door, but think better of it and leave it open. She crosses to the window seat and curls up in the corner making her look childlike. She's bathed in the late afternoon sun making her skin appear luminous. How on earth could I have mistaken her otherworldly beauty as human?

"I'm sorry," she says softly as she stares into her imaginary world among the clouds.

"For what?" I ask.

"For being difficult. I know you're all trying to protect me and I'm grateful, but I feel like I'm losing myself. Everyone's telling me who I am, what I'm going to do and I just need some time to see what I want for myself. I guess it's quite selfish in the grand scheme of things," she says.

I've known many royals in my time. Some fae, some human, they all shared a quality. Arrogance and entitlement. Some greater than others but Adaline is different. At times, she's so strong and self-assured I can practically taste the blue in her blood and then there are moments like now. She sits apologising to a lying monster like myself when she has done nothing wrong. Royals don't apologise, even if they are wrong. Selfish is not a word I would associate with this beautiful creature before me.

"I don't think you're being selfish. I can't imagine how you must be feeling right now. I have some good news though, the others have agreed to keep you here, under close guard of cause, and at the end of the year, it's your choice what you want to do," I assure her.

"Thanks," she says absentmindedly. I think I expected her to be a little more relieved, instead, she seems lost.

"Aedan, Deklan and I will be staying here, your uncle has offered to host us so we can be close," I add.

"That's going to be a bit awkward don't you think?" She asks.

"Why would it be awkward? We're going to be friends, aren't we?" I say encouragingly.

She draws her hair loosely over her shoulder exposing her neck, making my throat quiver with thirst, and I know exactly how she feels. She turns to face me and offers a soft smile in response.

"Friends," she says.

- 36 -
Adaline

I try to find the words to pinpoint the feeling invading my chest, but anything I can think of falls short. All the chaos from the last few days begins to overwhelm me. Now more than ever I wish my mother was here, she would tell me what to do. The world has shifted and everything is being pulled out of my control.

I watch Seth and the others walk down the driveway and quickly pile into the SUV. I hear the house phone ring and soon after Jerry follows suit, leaving me alone. The house is empty, the sound of silence has never been so sweet. I'm surprised they've left me unattended, it won't be long before someone rushes back to skulk around the house and watch my every move. This is the last moment of freedom I'm going to get. I've made up my mind before Jerry's car has left the end of the street. There's one thing I need to do before all my choices have been taken from me.

I collect my savings from my dresser drawer and stuff the crumpled notes into a small purse. I pull out my phone and look up the destination I've got in mind. Fate must be on my side, there's a bus leaving in less than ten minutes that will take me exactly where I need to go. I don't bother changing my clothes, I throw on some shoes and make a run to the bus stop. I run faster than necessary, I'm not afraid of missing the bus, but worried that someone might be watching me. I keep a lookout over my shoulder, but no movement catches my attention and the charm around my neck remains cool against my skin. The bus pulls around the corner in time for me to flag it down. A kindly older gentleman welcomes me on board and he assures me I will arrive at my destination in just under half an hour. I just hope no one notices I'm gone before then.

The bus is quiet with few passengers at this time in the afternoon and I revel in the normality of it all. An elderly woman with her trolley sits behind the driver laughing pleasantly at his cheerful banter. A tired mother answers the millionth question her child has asked about the inner workings of the bus and two teens laugh deeply while they switch seats back and forth like it's a game.

The boys brag about skipping school earlier today, when they reach the back seat they finally settle into boyish whispers. These little moments never meant much to me before, now I can't imagine anything more significant.

The bus pulls up outside a strip of small boutiques, anything from formal gowns to beauty spa's and at the end of the strip, I find the only store that holds any value. The street is deserted as many businesses have closed for the day. As I approach the poorly lit storefront I worry they may have shut early. I push open the darkly painted glass door and to my surprise, it moves easily under my touch. I enter warily, there's a soft bell ringing somewhere out the back. I look down to see I activated a sensor on the floor disguised as a small ceramic pit bull in a leather vest with flashing red eyes. A heavily bearded man in his late fifties wearing a black singlet and dark heavy pants appears behind the counter. He looks me up and down questioningly and for a second I think I have made a mistake. Before I lose my nerve, I square my shoulders and approach the counter.

"Are you able to help me with this?" I ask as I hand him a folded piece of paper that has seen better days.

"Are you eighteen?" He asks gruffly.

"Honestly, no, but if you don't help me I'll just find someone else who will. It's very important that I get this done today," I say.

I attempt to make my features stern and challenging, but I can't hold it for long before I feel pathetic. Surprisingly he agrees to help me in half an hour. I take a seat in one of the large leather chairs and flip through one of the books on display. The time passes slowly, even slower since I turned my phone off. I dare not switch it back on until I'm finished.

"Come into the back girl," he hollers. I swallow my fears and march towards his booming voice. "Take a seat there, do you want it this size?" He gestures to my picture.

"Yes please, I want it just here on my left wrist... Will it hurt?" I ask nervously.

"It might, depends on you. Why is it so important that you get this done?" He asks while rubbing an alcohol wipe on my wrist.

"My mum and I were going to get them done on my eighteenth birthday. I drew it two years ago. She said if I still liked it when I was eighteen we would both get one," I say through a choked breath.

He stamps a faint marking of the picture on my wrist and has me confirm its position. I watch him prepare the needles and squeeze black liquid into tiny pots. The mixed smells remind me of when mum would come home from work smelling of hospital disinfectant. It's comforting like she's here with me.

"Did she change her mind?" He asks casually.

"No, she died not long ago," I say quietly.

"I'm sorry to hear that darling, I'm going to start and if it's too painful, tell me and we can stop," His voice warms and I feel his mood shift.

The vibration of the needle shifting from fast to slow as he eases his pressure on the pedal makes me stiffen. I prepare myself for pain, but when the needle connects with my skin the sensation is surreal.

It hurts in parts, but mostly it's a steady vibrating pressure gliding over my wrist. I close my eyes and relax into the chair. It doesn't take as long as I thought. He squirts more disinfectant smelling liquid over my wrist and wipes away any excess ink with some paper towel. Once clean, he steps back so I can look closely at his work. This time the tears don't just teeter on the cusp of my eyelids they spill over and fall down my cheeks. The man hands me a tissue and offers me a small smile. He seems a brutish man, but after feeling his gentle touch and watching the features of his face, I see only a kind heart beneath the bravado. He smooths a Vaseline-like cream over the tattoo and wraps my wrist in cling film. He gives me a rundown of the aftercare instructions as I follow him to the cash register and open my purse to retrieve his payment.

"Save it honey. We can call it my good deed for the week," he says. His smile fades returning to his stern resting face. "Hurry along girl

I'm closing up," he says.

"Thank you," I reply.

I make it back to the bus stop with minutes to spare and by now it's probably time I face the music. I turn my phone back on and it starts blowing up before it's fully loaded. Sixteen missed calls and as many messages from Seth and a few from numbers I don't recognise. I hold my breath and call Seth. He must have been hovering over his phone because it doesn't even have time to ring.

"Where are you?" He yells.

"I'm sorry, I just had to do something," I cower, feeling instantly guilty.

"You couldn't have waited until we got back for fuck sake Adaline," He screeches. I jerk away from the phone before his shrill voice bursts my eardrums.

"It's fine, I'm okay, the bus has just pulled up. I'll be home soon," I say.

I turn my phone off before he gets a chance to respond. I know there's going to be hell to pay when I get home, but when I look down at my wrist I also know I did the right thing.

Mum had given me the freedom to create the tattoo I wanted when I first asked at sixteen. It's nothing fancy, a small circle with a cross through its centre. Each point of the cross has an arrowhead, like a compass with no directions. One of the arrows is longer than the rest, it underlines the word freedom written in the perfect cursive script.

Mum would have liked it and as crazy as it sounds it makes me feel stronger. Not that a tattoo can change everything that's happening, but having it reminds me that I have a choice, no matter what anyone else has to say about it.

- 37 -

SETH

Adaline hangs up the phone before divulging her location. I'm on the brink of madness as she hangs up on me. I squeeze the cell phone in my hand tightly and it crumbles like sand between my fingers. The only thing I can do now is to wait. I stare at my reflection in the hallway mirror, I still look younger than the years I've seen but now while my face is red with rage I look withered. I inhale deeply trying to calm myself. The redness eases from my face and my pale complexion returns. There's tension in the corners of my eyes, a clear sign of the turmoil that's bubbling beneath the surface. No matter how hard I try I can't shake the expression from my face.

My fingertips tingle and I raise my fist and pass it through the mirror before the fire has time to spread. I pace back and forth. First from the front door to the dining room until the sight of the broken mirror makes my anger flare. Fuming at my own foolishness I retreat to the front veranda and sit on the porch swing, slowly rocking back and forth while I wait. In the corner of my eye, I notice I have an audience. An old woman next door is not so stealthily peering through her heavy lace curtains. I turn to face her and pointedly stare, she freezes, and I lift my hand and wave. She shoots me a hostile look and pulls down the blinds.

My body turns to stone as the minute's pass. I hear the bus drawing near before I can see it. I stand and see it turn onto the street. I propel my body from the swing. I clench my fists, drawing a little blood as my fingernails sink in, but it's better than turning to flames.

I release my nails from the open skin on my palms and the wounds heal almost instantly. Calmly I walk down the footpath to wait by the fence.

The bus pulls to a halt two houses down and an elderly man gets off, followed by three young children. My heart beats in anticipation until finally, she emerges. She's wearing the same clothes she had on this afternoon. Her hair has been pulled into a high ponytail and I can see something foreign is wrapped around her wrist. A bandage perhaps? As she gets closer I forget about her appearance and hurry to meet her.

"What the hell were you thinking? You could have been killed. Get inside now!" I scream. I had planned on being calm and forgiving of her behaviour, but as I look at her my intentions are forgotten and my fear takes control. My anxiety makes my words louder and more forceful than I wanted, I feel guilty for their harsh tone.

"No," She says firmly.

"Get inside now Adaline!" I yell.

"Stop it. You are not my boyfriend or my father and you're sure as hell not in charge of me. Stop telling me what to do!" She screams.

Her anger matches my own, the fire inside me sparks at the thrill of competition. Consumed by rage I wrap my arms around her legs and lift her over my shoulders. As I begin carrying her towards the house she starts hitting my back and yelling like she's being kidnapped. Once I reach the front porch I place her down. As I begin to step away from her she swings and punches me squarely in the jaw. She turns abruptly, slamming the front door in my face.

I hear the crunch of the broken mirror under her feet and the stomping of her shoes as she ascends the staircase. The slamming of her bedroom door is the last thing I hear and then the house falls silent. I slam my palm against the door frame and exhale deeply. I decide it's best to wait out on the porch until Aedan arrives or the old woman next door calls the police, whichever happens first. By the time Aedan and Deklan reach the house the warm evening air has vanished and a storm has overtaken the night's sky.

"What did you do to her?" Deklan asks.

"What makes you think I did something? She was the one acting like a spoilt brat," I say.

"The sudden weather change tells me she's very upset," He says as he glances out toward the lightning that's dancing in the distance. "I may not know much of teenage girls, but one thing my wife taught me was that regardless of whose fault it is, you're to blame. So, go and apologise to her before she brings a tsunami down on all of us," Deklan advises.

"I have to give the wolf some credit Seth, he knows women. Go apologise to her, even if it wasn't your fault. At least she's home and she's safe," Aedan says following Deklan inside.

Lightning strikes a tree a few streets overemphasising their point with vivid colour. I had better heed their advice and make amends before I become the lightning's ideal target.

- 38 -
Adaline

How dare he think he can just order me around like that? Who does he think he is? He's a self-centred jerk who wants everything his own way. I've never been an angry kind of person, usually, I'm calm and level-headed but right now I feel like I could explode. Something about Seth just makes my blood boil. He was overreacting, nothing bad happened to me, I made it home safe and sound without anyone's help. Seth's nothing but a drama queen.

I pace back and forth in my room, obsessing over how stupid and irrational Seth's behaviour has been. The stupid smart-ass smirk he constantly wears, his sparkling eyes that were full of judgement and the way he carried me into the house like I was a child throwing a tantrum. I just want to scream. I settle for throwing my stuffed animals onto the floor, cursing each one as I do. There's a knock at my door. I swear to god if it's him...

"Who is it?" I say venomously.

"It's Aedan, I just wanted to let you know that Deklan and I are here, we're just setting up down the hall if you need anything," he says politely.

"You can tell me how to kill vampires. Will a stake to the heart do it?" I ask.

He laughs in response. I feel a sudden sense of calm wash over me, like an intangible hug filled with warmth. I can feel my anger starting to die down and I know it's because of Aedan's influence of his earth element. I start collecting my toy animals that suffered my wrath and place them back on the loveseat at the end of my bed. There's another knock at my door, I walk over and open it expecting to see Aedan. Instead, it's Seth.

"I'm sorry, can I come in?" He asks. His usual smirk has vanished and he looks grim.

"I suppose if I say no you'll just throw me over your shoulder and force your way in any way," I reply. I stand aside so he can enter my room. I walk over to the window seat and sit down purposefully, I gesture to the love seat for him to sit. "Well? Are you going to yell at me some more?" I ask. The hostility in my voice sounds foreign to me and I don't think I like it.

"I don't want to yell at you. I'm sorry about before. I was just so worried that something had happened to you. I didn't mean to be such a..."

"Dick," I say, finishing his sentence. "Look I get it, but you can't just order me around all the time. I need some space to breathe, I need some freedom," I say looking down at my wrist.

"I understand and I am sorry," he says with a small smile.

I look into his soulful eyes and I believe him. We sit in silence as the air between us grows warm. The storm outside has died down to a drizzle and the clouds are parting to reveal a brightly lit moon. I remove the plastic wrap from my wrist and hold it out for him to see. He crosses the room towards me and places my hand in his and inspects the tattoo. I feel an electric jolt when his thumb strokes the back of my hand, I pull back in shock.

"Mum and I were going to get matching ones on my birthday and I just thought, I don't know what I thought but I needed to do it," I admit openly.

"I wonder how your people will view a tattooed princess," he laughs. "It's lovely though, but when your uncle asks about it, make sure you tell him I had no part in it. I'll see you at dinner, your uncle said he would be home shortly and the wolf's cooking," he rolls his eyes at the thought and closes the door behind him as he leaves.

I look back to my window to find the sky has completely cleared and the stars are shining brightly in the darkness. Just like the weather, my anger towards Seth seems to have fizzled out.

- 39 -
Deklan

I unpack my bag of clothing and put my things in the empty drawers. My personals are few. I have four bags of weapons and a small bag filled with potions, but only one with personal items. The only thing of true value is the photograph of my son and wife. It's not in a frame and it's worn around the edges. My son is only a babe in the photo, his green eyes sparkle like a forest at dusk and his sun-kissed hair shines like gold. In the photograph, my wife is as stunning as the day I met her. Her silken fair hair flows down her shoulders, curling around her hips. She's wearing a long blue gown and my sons in a crisp white shirt and black bow tie.

The photo was taken a few days after Adaline was born. Chloe had forced us to try on fancy attire for the upcoming ball and insisted I took a photo, to remember a time when my son wasn't covered in dirt or food.

The Ball was supposed to be an opportunity for the royal family to present the princess to the leaders of the clans, but it never went ahead. Tears start to build behind my eyes, but they are suppressed by a knock at the door.

"Deklan, its Adaline may I come in?" She calls out through the closed door. I stand to open it for her. "Are you mad at me? For going out today," she asks while nervously pulling at her hair.

"No princess I'm not mad. It was a careless action though and you need to be smarter than that. It's your safety I'm concerned with," I say gently.

Raising my son alone these past years I found myself being harder on him than I wanted. I wasn't hard because I didn't love him, I was hard because I love him more than anything in this world. Treating Adaline the way I treated my son won't get me anywhere. If I could go back in time I would have raised my son differently. Now he's grown up and training for a war I know is far too close for comfort and there's nothing I can do for him.

"I am sorry and it won't happen again. I promise," she says and picks up the photo from the dressing table. "She's beautiful and the boy is lovely. Are they your family?" She asks. I turn to my bag of weapons and begin unpacking. I feel her lingering eyes burning through the back of my skull so I turn to answer her.

"Yes. My wife Chloe and my son Patrick. He's off training for the royal guard," I say casually.

"Does your wife mind you being gone for so long?" She asks innocently.

"She's dead princess," I whisper.

"Deklan I'm so sorry, I didn't know," she leans forward and hugs me. I'm startled by her forwardness and it takes a moment to regain my self-control. I reach my arm around her tiny shoulders and hug her back. It's been so long since someone has hugged me. I can't remember the last time I've held someone in my embrace. I think my son was ten or so the last time he hugged me and I realise now how much I've missed it and how much I miss him.

"Thank you, princess. I think I best go start dinner," I tell her.

"Deklan, can you do something for me?" She asks.

"Anything princess," I oblige.

"Call me Adaline, the princess stuff is a bit much," she says smiling warmly and I feel some of the sadness leave the room.

"I'll try. Dinner will be ready in two hours, don't be late," I order.

"Yes sir," she says as she raises her hand to her forehead giving a military address. She giggles as she wanders off towards her bedroom, the sound of her laughter brings a welcome joy to the quiet halls.

Before going downstairs to the kitchen, I place a quick call to Theo. He answers immediately like always. I inform him of the current circumstances, he's uneasy, to say the least, but he trusts my judgement and agrees to my methods. I leave out the fact that I'm concerned about Seth and Adaline getting too close and I assure him that the boys can be trusted. I have arranged a postal box under a false name for him to send funds and letters if required. Once again, our conversation is short lived, I bid him farewell and promise to contact him next week with updates.

- 40 -
Adaline

After making the rounds and apologising to Aedan and Deklan I feel a tiny bit less guilty for my actions. There's just under two hours until dinner, enough time to have a quick power nap, shower and change. As I lay my head on my pillow I have no trouble getting to sleep, the events of the day have wiped me completely.

My alarm chimes incessantly and I wake feeling more refreshed than I thought possible. Maybe it's the knowledge that my uncle's unconditional love for me still remains or the thrill of magic I feel quivering under my skin. Regardless of the reasons, it's gratifying to feel renewed.

I grab a long lightweight floral dress and fresh underwear from my closet, with all these men roaming around the house I can't exactly walk to and from the bathroom in a towel like usual. I step into the shower and welcome the sense of security the warm water brings. I feel it start healing the core of my body.

The cut on my cheek still hurts, but only a fraction less than my wrist. I flinch when the heat trickles over my tattoo, but the stinging soon fades. It's easy to forget the pain as I feel my body beginning to repair itself; both mentally and physically. Eventually, I have to leave the comfort of the water. I take more care than usual as I fix my hair and I even apply a little makeup. Just enough to distract from the wound on my face.

As I open the bathroom door, I'm bombarded by a half-naked and very handsome man. As I take in Seth's uncovered chest I feel my jaw not only drop, but my tongue may as well be licking the bathroom tiles. I'm transfixed on his immaculate form and my eyes eagerly trace the defined lines of his abdomen. My eyes dart to the faint trail of fine brown hair that disappears into his low-cut jeans. I reach out a hand towards his bare chest. Seth makes a small noise low in his throat. I recoil my hand like I've accidentally touched a hot stove. Mortified beyond belief at my actions I push past him and run back to my room, locking the door behind me. I don't know how I'm going to handle these kinds of distractions.

- 41 -

SETH

How can I expect to keep some semblance of morals when she looks at me like that? The lustful way she regarded my bare chest was nothing compared to how indecently obsessed I am with every inch of her. As her hand reached out to touch me a moan of anticipation escaped my lips and frightened her off.

The hallway falls flat in her absence and free of her distraction, I realise how close I was to giving into my sordid desires. I was seconds away from sweeping her into my arms and kissing her. If I'm being totally honest with myself I wouldn't have just kissed her. I would have pushed her back onto the bathroom counter, hiked up her dress and ran my fingers over every inch of her body until I consumed her entire being. I'm just lucky she pulled away when she did. If her hand had touched my skin I wouldn't have been able to stop myself. It looks like I'm going to have to get used to cold showers.

I wait out my impure thoughts under the ice-cold water until I worry the showers going to run dry. Once I'm comfortably dressed I head downstairs where everyone else is waiting patiently for my arrival. As I open the dining room doors all eyes fall on me, except for Adaline's. She seems extremely interested in the empty plate in front of her. I take the empty seat next to my brother and Deklan invites us to dig in. Jerry lifts the lids on the covered dishes laid out before us and to my surprise this meal is meat-free. No animals in sight, only an abundance of green. What kind of werewolf cooks a meal without any meat? I can identify a salad with pumpkin, cheese and some kind of nuts. Sadly, I discover the stuffed bell peppers are of cause filled with vegetables and there's an abundance of weird green coloured pancakes.

"No offence wolf but what the hell is this, did you think you were feeding a family of rabbits tonight?" I ask.

"It's suggested to only have red meat three times a week. Besides you get all the protein and iron you need from these," Deklan says proudly. He places a green pancake on my plate. I sniff it first before taking a small bite. To my surprise it's actually not too bad, it's not a steak but it's edible.

"What is it?" I ask cautiously.

"Zucchini and mushroom fritter," Deklan says with a wide grin.

"Thank you for cooking Deklan," Jerry adds politely.

Everyone starts into their food and we begin to discuss what the next few months will entail for Adaline. I try hard to focus on the topic at hand, but every so often my eyes find their way to Adaline and a subtle cough from my brother reminds me that my eyes should not be lingering. Once dinner is concluded, Aedan volunteers both of us to clean the dishes while everyone else gets to escape to their rooms. Aedan hums happily to himself as he passes me another wet dish, which I dry off and stack into a neat pile.

"This is weird, isn't it?" Aedan says absentmindedly.

"What?" I ask.

"You know a house, having dinner like a family, washing dishes. I could almost get used to this," he says.

"Maybe one day you will find the girl of your dreams, adopt a bunch of kids and play house. You could be the Brangelina couple of Seelie Court," I joke.

"At least I don't have school tomorrow. You should go to bed," he mocks.

"You're a dick," I tell him.

He responds by splashing me with water and I hit him with the tea towel before throwing it over his head. As I lay in bed I find myself speculating about what a normal life would be like. A life filled with children and a wife to share my bed. It's a life I never considered for myself, it's a life that has never been an option for me and until now I have always been content with that. As I lay in bed fanciful possibilities dance along the edges of my consciousness until I fall asleep.

- 42 -
Adaline

Despite all the formalities and discussions regarding my safety at last night's dinner, I enjoyed the familiarity of it. Recent events have made mealtimes a chore and my uncle and I haven't had much to discuss. But last night having everyone come together, swapping stories and banter, it somehow made the dinner table feel a little less bare. As I wandered off to bed I found the stirring feelings in my stomach making it impossible to find rest. Images of Seth's naked chest kept delving into my weakened mind and it took all my willpower not to sneak into his room and crawl into his bed. As a result of my disreputable dreams I've had very little sleep and the grey bags under my eyes are all the evidence anyone needs.

I force myself out of bed and glance out the window to check the weather. I can see the sun hiding behind the trees, but I can still feel the warmth sneaking through. I dress in some denim shorts and a lightweight top. My pendant still hangs firmly around my neck and every once in a while, it catches in the light reminding me of its presence. When I come downstairs Seth is sitting at the breakfast bar sipping coffee from an overly large mug, at least I hope its coffee. I notice his shoulders stiffen as I enter. He politely offers me the pot of coffee, but I decline and make myself some tea.

"Where is everyone?" I ask.

"Wolf left hours ago, something about installing cameras at the school and putting up some protection wards. Your uncle and Aedan are at the surgery," he replies casually.

"Can I ask you something?" I ask. Seth nods in response. "What do you and Aedan do for blood? Should I expect some classmates to go missing anytime soon?" I ask, suddenly aware of my own exposed neck.

"That's a big question this early in the morning," he says. I take a seat at the kitchen table and wait patiently for him to answer.

"We only need to feed a few times a week, but we need to maintain our strength so we will be feeding daily. Don't look at me like that, we aren't killing anyone. Aedan's picking up some blood bags this afternoon from the hospital. Are you ready to leave?" He asks in a hurried breath.

Seth waits by the front door while I collect my things for school. I take my time finding my misplaced items and tying my shoes. Seth's expression hardens, clearly annoyed by my dawdling. I give captain cranky a sarcastic salute and gather the last of my belongings while dragging my feet toward the front door. It's hard to deny the unfriendly tone Seth's behaviour has taken this morning, perhaps the romantic notions I felt stirring between us are only one-sided.

- 43 -

SETH

When I woke this morning at daybreak the only thoughts racing through my mind were of Adaline. Which should be a blessing, but I know it's a curse. The problem is every time she enters my mind I feel my concentration begin to waver and I'm no good to Adaline if I'm not one hundred percent focused on her safety. So, this morning before she came downstairs I decided that my feelings had to be different, that I had to be different. I will keep things strictly professional between us and I'll remove every passionate thought of her from my mind.

The school isn't far from Adaline's house so we decide to walk. I keep vigilant for signs we are being followed but nothing warrants my attention. Which allows my mind time to wander. I count six times that I have scolded myself for impure thoughts by the time we arrive at the school gates.

Adaline is surprisingly quiet and seems lost in thought. We agree to meet up for lunch after her music class and she rolls her eyes when I ask her to text me regularly to let me know she's okay. I scan our surroundings once more for anything out of the ordinary before I let her go to homeroom. I give her a nod to take her leave and watch her walk away.

As she walks away I notice how snug the pair of shorts are that she's wearing and I realise I'm not the only guy who has taken notice. Bloody teenage hormones. A well-built young man starts to follow her too closely which cause my adrenalin levels to rise into the thousands. Before I have a moment to rationalise the situation, I catch up to the young man and grasp the strap of his bag between my fingers.

"What the fuck do you think you're doing?" He snaps at me.

"I just wanted to introduce myself, I'm Seth. I also just wanted to let you know that Adaline's out of your league so don't bother wasting your time," I say.

"Is she your girlfriend or something, because with an ass like that I would be happy to take her off your hands?" He says jokingly to his friends.

I would like to say I'm the bigger man and decide to walk away, but I don't. I punch him and his stupid smirk squarely in the jaw. He drops his bag to the ground clearly shaken by my attack. He collects himself and postures for a fight. I effortlessly deflect his pitiful attempts to strike my face and when I hit him the second time a teacher arrives to break up our brawl. I also notice Adaline peering around the corner with a disapproving look stamped on her face, which hurt more than any punishment the principals going to lash out.

The meeting in the principal's office was just as I expected. We both had to apologise for our behaviour and were given three afternoon detentions. The principal warned us if it happens again it's a week's suspension. Our parents were called, so Aedan will have some words for me when I get home from detention.

Once allowed to return to class I send Deklan a quick message to have him meet Adaline after school since I'll be otherwise detained. I make it through my first two periods without any further provocation from hormonal teenagers and my last class before lunch is a study period, so I ditch it and wander towards the music rooms to wait for Adaline.

I reach the double pine doors of the music room and through the small pane glass window, I see a worn baby grand piano at the forefront of the classroom and a girl delicately stroking its keys. Adaline. She's playing a slow song I haven't heard before; each note flows into the next effortlessly. I didn't think there was a more divine sound until she starts to sing.

- 44 -

Adaline

I spent most of the morning angry with Seth's behaviour and by the time music class rolls around I'm tempted to skip and go home. Music has always been one of my favourite classes and it's one I have never left angry, so I decide to stay. The teacher is enthusiastic at the sight of a new student and he is even more enthused when I tell him the expanse of my musical knowledge. So much so he asks me to perform in front of the whole class. He assures me there was no judgement just art. In light of recent events stage fright should be one of my least concerns. I know exactly what song to sing. I know the lyrics by heart and I'm confident with the keystrokes. 'If I die young' by The Band Perry. It was the first song I played start to finish without any mistakes. I remember playing it for my mother in the small music studio down the street from our house in Montana. I remember the way the sounds echoed off the walls making the notes linger, I recall the subtle sobbing sounds of my mother crying in the corner as I played.

I sit down at the ancient piano and despite its shabby appearance, the notes ring clear. I feel the words flow from me as easily as breathing, my fingers seducing each key flawlessly and before I know it, the moments over. I lift my eyes from the keys and find myself in unfamiliar territory, for a moment I was back in the music school with my mother watching me practice. The music teacher grins tightly and I worry the force of his smile will squeeze his teeth free from his mouth. The students are a mix of awes and dropped jaws. They begin applauding loudly and holla. I rise from the piano seat and smile uncomfortably at the admiration as I walk back to my seat. During my performance, I hadn't even noticed the young man Seth had been fighting is in my class and he's sitting directly behind me. I slide into my seat gracefully and settle into the worksheets that are handed out. A light tap on my shoulder makes me jump in surprise.

"Hey, your voice is amazing, you could be on American Idol or something," the boy whispers.

"Thanks," I reply.

"I was wondering if you wanted to hang out sometime, that's if your boyfriend doesn't mind?" He asks.

"Seth's not my boyfriend, just a friend. I guess we could hang out sometime, I don't really know anyone here yet," I say.

"I'm Chris by the way, look here's my number give me a call sometime," he says as he reaches out for my arm and writes his number across the back of my hand.

The bell rings too quickly and I feel a little disoriented. As I collect my things three girls approach me, all in short skirts with low cut tops. Two of the girls are identical twins, one is a fraction shorter and has a freckle on her chin. Both girls have short brunette bobs, well made up faces and figures I would die for. The third girl is in a league all her own. She has long platinum blonde hair styled into an extravagant side ponytail. To say she is flawless would be an understatement, the twins are beautiful, but this girl is a goddess. Tall and slender with perfect high cheekbones and sparkling blue eyes. I admit even I flutter slightly. I hope she never sets her sights on Seth, I'd have no chance. The goddess introduces herself as Hailey and the twins are Becca and Bree, Bree has the freckle I note to myself.

Hailey tell's me how impressive my singing was and asked if I wanted to hang out with them after school sometime. We exchange numbers and agree to go shopping and have dinner on Friday night. Hailey gives me a quick embrace while the twins blow air kisses and follow their queen's exit. Two dates in one class, I admit I'm pretty impressed with myself.

The cafeteria reminds me of my old school. There's a clear distinction between the school's hierarchy system. The beautiful people sit by the large windows bathed in glistening sunlight while pimpled skin and sad ensembles sit near trash cans hidden behind piles of books. Between the two defined groups are a few scattered tables with a mix of people, the common folk. The people who aren't pretty enough for the cool kids or lame enough for the geeks. I spot Seth seated among them and to my surprise I see a pretty blonde practically hanging from his arm. I quickly notice it's not Hayley and I breathe a sigh of relief. This girl isn't the goddess, but she's still pretty none the less.

She's talking to him passionately and touching his shoulder. My senses hone and I hear her moronic giggle above all the other sounds floating across the cafeteria. I'm tempted to throw my water bottle at her, but it's hardly ladylike. Seth turns in my direction locking his eyes with mine. I smile inside as he signals a pained expression, clearly, he's not as smitten as the blonde seems to be. I plaster a confident smile on my face and stride over to join them.

- 45 -

SETH

When I watched Adaline sing my heart stopped. My breath held tight in my chest until she finished. The song she sang was pure and sad, but she was a siren. All eyes fell on her, it was impossible not to be drawn into her ethereal light. When she finished I had to tear myself away when a teacher scolded me for lingering in the halls.

As I wait for Adaline in the lunch room an annoying blonde positions herself practically on my lap. She continues to probe me with stupid questions, desperately trying to know everything about me. I give her the standard cover lines and politely smile while she pathetically flips her hair. The only appealing thing about her is the pulse beating in her neck that makes an appearance every time she flicks her stupid hair. I'm about to tell her I'm gay just so she will leave, but then the air changes.

It's suddenly warmer and the scent of flowers is carried in on a breeze. I turn to see Adaline across the room and she looks mad. I instantly think it's because of my boxing antics, I hope she won't yell at me for my behaviour in a public place. I brace myself for her disappointment until I notice her anger isn't pointed at me, her eyes are focused on the moron beside me. She's jealous. Satisfaction burns inside me and I give her an annoyed look. As if I could be interested in the meat stick next to me. She smiles unwaveringly toward us.

"Seth, I see you made a new friend. Hi, I'm Adaline, it's nice to meet you," Adaline says, all sugar and spice. She holds out her hand to the girl who introduces herself as Emily. Emily understands the underlying subtext in Adaline's voice and leaves us alone. I can't help but be pleased that she's so twisted up with jealousy. A feeling I'm becoming far too intimate with myself. "You going to tell me why you hit that guy. Is he a fairy monster I should watch out for?" She says smartly as she sits down.

"Not fae, but dangerous none the less," I say with disdain. I notice the ink marks on her hand, it's a number."Who's number is that?" I ask and her expression tells me exactly who it belongs to. "It's that dickhead's isn't it? Are you seriously going to go out with that prick?" The same rage I felt earlier starts to bubble under my skin.

"You're the one being a dick, why did you attack him in the first place. His eye has already started to bruise," she says. Her anger calms and her voice lowers. "He was nice, he just asked me to hang out, that's all," she says softly.

"Oh please he's only interested in your ass, he's not interested in who you are. Don't be so fucking blind Adaline," as soon as I say it she slaps me, hard.

I watch her walk away and what's more painful is I have to watch that snivelling piece of crap Chris follow after her like a dog. All eyes in the cafeteria have fallen on me. I gather my composure, empty my full tray of food into the trash and leave for my next class.

The rest of the day is uneventful. I receive no messages from Adaline or Deklan. I do get a text from Aedan telling me to stop acting like a moron. When the final bell rings I hurry out to the front of the school and search for Adaline. Her bright auburn hair catches in the sunlight and I see her getting into the car with Deklan. He offers me a friendly wave while Adaline doesn't even glance in my direction.

Chris is already waiting at the office when I arrive. We are each given black rubbish bags and pointed spikes to collect the trash from the school grounds. As I pick up empty bottles and plastic wrappings I contemplate how easily I could slide the metal spike through Chris's neck. I can imagine the blood dripping slowly around the edges of the spike until I pull it straight through the other side. That's when the blood would cascade over every inch of his body, what a glorious sight it would be. I smile at the thought and it helps me pass the time. By the time we both finish our labour, both of Chris's eyes have blackened and his pretty face resembles a swollen raccoon. I can't kill the prick, but at least I can be happy with my handy work.

- 46 -
Deklan

Adaline retires to her room to do homework while I finish installing the household security cameras and sensors. When Seth returns at five thirty I'm finished and I'm watching the video playback on the television in the family room. Seth drops his bag by the front door and strolls to the sofa. He sits silently watching me work, it's obvious he doesn't want to go upstairs and risk facing Adaline.

"What did you do wrong this time?" I ask. I knew Adaline was upset when I picked her up and even though Seth's message had said he had detention for fighting with another boy, I knew there was something more to it.

"I told Adaline the truth. This loser was checking her out and made a snide comment, I gave him a chance to move on but he didn't. He even asked her out after I kicked his ass and she said yes. She's behaving like a child," Seth says.

The frustration straining in his voice almost makes me feel sorry for him, but I can see Adaline's not the only one acting like a child.

"She's a beautiful young girl Seth. You're going to have to get used to males noticing her. Look at yourself, you have only known her for a few weeks and your head over heals," I say. His eyes turn dark.

"I'm not in love with her. I just want her safe," he says. I believe his words less then he does. I know how he feels about her, even if he's trying not to show it. It's a constant worry in the back of my mind.

"If you tell her to back off she will only want to rebel more. My advice is to stand aside and wait until she needs your protection and then you can step in, but not before," I tell him. I take his silence as an agreement.

Seth helps me finish setting up the rest of the motion sensors inside the house and we watch Aedan and Jerry pull into the driveway on the television. The cameras follow them as they walk across the grass and onto the footpath. There's an extreme close up of Jerry's nose as he opens the front door.

When they enter we exchange the usual pleasantries, Aedan and Seth go upstairs and I'm left alone with Jerry. I go over the security system and give him the lock codes which I will change weekly. He seems overwhelmed by it all. I guess if I was in his situation I would be too. He's lost a lot and to have all this madness thrown at him, he's handling it better than expected. I hope he will be able to cope when Adaline moves to court. My personal phone starts ringing and I excuse myself. Only Theodore has the disposables number, him calling me is out of character. Something must be wrong.

"Deklan, I don't have long, but I want to let you know that rumours are spreading through the kingdom. They don't know the child is my daughter, but people are talking about her arrival. A few witches claim knowledge of her location. The Queen has offered a handsome bounty to the fae who can bring her to court. Hunters are leaving through the portals by the truckload. I'll update you if I hear anything more. Keep her safe," he says in a blur, hanging up the phone before I can reply.

This complicates things. It's one thing when all we had to worry about was the one or two vampires that know about Adaline; having a bounty on her head means all fae, good and bad will be coming after her now. I know what I must do before the plan is even fully formed. I also know the princess isn't going to like it.

- 47 -
Adaline

The last few weeks have been uncharacteristically normal, no one has died, no one has made any attempts on my life and I'm even up to date on all my school work. Everyone seems to have settled into a routine, Aedan goes to work with Jerry every morning and I walk to school in continued silence with Seth. Deklan has been pretty elusive, he's been in an out of the house at strange hours and constantly making secret phone calls. He assures me it's just arranging security and organising a safe trip to court after my birthday. He has been so highly strung since moving into our house, I don't press the issue and leave him with his secrets.

I've spent my lunches with Hailey and the twins partly because embracing a normal life seems paramount at the moment and partly to spite Seth. Chris hangs in the same circle, so I've been getting to know him better as well.

Seth is always lurking in the distance and keeps to himself but his eyes are never far from me, even when he's nowhere in sight I feel his lingering gaze. We seem to have an unspoken agreement to keep some distance between us, perhaps it's for the best. Whenever we are alone, he's quiet and tense, and all I feel is a frostiness towards me. I'm sorry he's angry with me, but I'm not his puppet on a string and I won't be bullied by anyone, least of all him. Truthfully, I hate how far away he is and even with my new friends I still feel alone.

It's Friday night, I'm with Hailey and the twins at the mall for dinner and another round of shopping. The schools having a winter formal in a few weeks so I need to buy a dress and the goddess can definitely help me with that. Deklan and Aedan are at the mall too as a safety net, but they have promised to keep their distance. Seth's staying home with Jerry so I don't have to worry about him or his continual bad mood. The girls want sushi, I agree even though I'm not really a fan. I settle on some teriyaki chicken, at least it's cooked. Hailey talks about all the boyfriends she has had.

From what I can gather it seems like half the school has had a crack at her in one way or another and the twins aren't far behind. When the topic turns to me the twins can't contain their laughter at the fact that I'm still a virgin. Hailey just pats my hand and says it's darling that I'm so innocent. Her smile is sickly sweet and her tone is condescending, I never thought of my inexperience as a negative until this very moment. Why do beautiful girls always make the rest of us feel like crap?

By the time we reach the formal wear shop I'm second guessing everything about myself. Hailey made a few sly comments about my hair and makeup, minor improvements she called them. I try to shake off my unease and forget the 'friendly' judgmental looks from the Barbie trio. I try desperately not to be overly sensitive and attempt to enjoy the feminine experience.

The dress store is the most expensive one the mall has to offer and the girls feel right at home. Mum and I never shopped high end like this, we always bought things from Kmart or small boutiques and never in my life would I spend eight hundred dollars on a sundress. Becca and Bree emerge from the change rooms wearing the same dress, one in pink and one in blue.

The dresses they have chosen have a strap on one side with very low cut sweetheart necklines. With the right bra and the cut of the dress, their breasts easily look double their normal size. Both dresses are tightly fitted and so short I'm worried if they bend the wrong way I will know them as intimately as their many ex's. Hailey jumps and squeals with excitement at the slutty outfits. The twins join her in unison. Their eyes fall on me making me feel uncomfortable, do they expect me to jump around and carry on like a puppy on speed? I plaster the largest grin I can fake and tell them how fabulous they look, once they are satisfied with my approval their attention turns to the search for Hailey's outfit.

Two hours pass and Hailey has tried on more dresses than I can count and everything looked flawless on her perfect figure. Just when I'm prepared to make an escape she finally decides on a long red strapless gown with a split that reaches her underwear line. I do hope she plans on wearing underwear to the formal, although I wouldn't be surprised if she went commando.

At this point, I'm mentally drained and dying to leave. I lie and tell the girls I already have a dress at home and send Aedan an SOS text to meet me at the dress shop. The girls ring up their purchases and hurry off to buy makeup and accessories. They each give me a quick hug and air kisses with overtly loud sound effects as they leave.

I'm so relieved when Aedan arrives to take me home I could almost cry tears of joy. Aedan's dressed as impeccably as ever and I'm glad the girls have already left or he would be batting them off with a stick.

"Where's Deklan?" I ask.

"He had to go pick up some things, I thought you would be longer so we have an hour until he returns with the car. I can call Seth to come get us if you want?" He offers. I would rather wait. I guess while we wait I can try on some dresses. At least with Aedan here I won't feel like the ugly duckling standing alongside three breathtaking swans.

"Would you mind helping me pick a dress for the winter formal while we wait?" I ask him. At least with his keen fashion sense, he might be able to offer some perspective for someone fashionably challenged like me.

"Of cause Adaline, what did you have in mind?" He asks while I scan the racks.

"Honestly, I don't know, mum always had the best fashion sense. This would be right up her alley. I think a long dress would be nice. The other girls looked a little cheap in their short dresses and I want to avoid that," I say truthfully.

"I think we can manage that," he says and starts confidently pushing dresses aside. He dismisses dresses like a professional. I worry when even Aedan seems to be having difficulty finding something for me to wear and I'm about to give up hope. Aedan however, refuses to admit defeat and wanders off to the counter. I wait patiently while he has a short conversation with a pretty redhead. She smiles and giggles and they glance over at me. I smile and wave nervously. She disappears into the back and Aedan make his way back over to my side.

"She has the perfect dress for you, it's one of a kind. It's expensive so she doesn't have it out on display, but I assured her money was no object," he smiles brilliantly and I feel myself turn red under his gaze.

The redhead returns with a large white dress bag spilling over her tiny arms. She ushers me into the change room and removes the dress from its casing. It's stunning. I couldn't dream of wearing anything so beautiful, it seems too perfect to belong to me. She helps me into the long gown and expertly closes the buttons on the back. When I emerge from the change room I'm equally nervous and excited to see myself. The first thing I notice is Aedan's jaw almost hitting the floor and any nervous energy I have dissipates. The gowns top layer is a soft delicate champagne coloured lace. It has a high scoop neckline and cap sleeves. Under the lace is a pale silken fabric that clings to my body in all the right places, showing off my curvy figure. The lace drapes perfectly on top of the silk and the small train glides angelically across the floor when I move. My favourite part is the keyhole back, it's a little bit sexy but definitely not slutty. In this gown, I feel beautiful and all the comments Hailey and her clones had made earlier are a forgotten memory. I feel like the princess everyone keeps telling me I am.

Aedan escorts the redhead to the counter and pulls out a credit card and pays for the dress. When I change back into my normal clothes I feel a little shabby. The girl places the dress back in the bag and hands it to Aedan to carry for me. I thank her graciously and follow Aedan to the parking lot out back to wait for Deklan.

"How much was the dress? I can give you the money for it," I offer.

"Don't worry about it. You looked so lovely it would have been a crime not to buy it for you," he says with a wink. I turn away as I start to blush.

I'm ready to file away the day and start getting ready for bed. Just as I'm slipping under my covers I receive a message from Chris asking if I wanted to see a movie with him tomorrow night. I think about Seth for a minute and chaste myself for being so stupid. I send Chris my address so he can pick me up and I glance one more time at my beautiful dress that's hanging on the back of my bedroom door. It hasn't been too bad a day after all.

- 48 -
Adaline

I spent the morning lazily reading magazines and painting my fingernails and toes to match. I studied for an hour and finished all my homework, which seems silly since I doubt college is in my near future. Before I know it dinner time rolls around and I'm getting ready for Chris to pick me up. Aedan knows what movie we were seeing and the time, so he and Deklan can watch from a distance. I'm getting used to having my shadows around and often I'm more thankful for them than not. I wear a nice pink and purple dress and strappy sandals, the weather has been surprisingly warm, and a light cardigan is all I'll need. I braid three small sections of my hair and pin them up securely, the rest of my hair hangs loosely in its natural waves. The cut on my cheek has healed except for a small scar that is impossible to see when I've finished my makeup, and in a few weeks, the scar should fade completely.

The doorbell rings and I hurry downstairs before anyone else has a chance to answer it. Unfortunately, my house is filled with people with superhuman reflexes and Seth's standing at the open door glaring at Chris. The stance between the two boys is fierce, but my attention is drawn to the flicker of light in Seth's hand. Oh, my god, he's starting a fire in my living room. He's going to melt Chris's face like he's a candle. I push Seth aside and tell Chris I will be out in a minute and make sure to secure the door between us. I forget the flames in Seth's fingers and I enclose his hand in mine. Even though his fingers still have bright flames dancing on them my hand remains unharmed. I stare down at my unblemished fingers in disbelief. There are no burn marks or blisters to be seen, they aren't even red.

"How's that possible?" I whisper.

"When you have an affinity for an element it can't hurt you. Your connection to fire keeps you safe." The flames in his hand vanish as I release it from my grasp. "Don't go out with this guy Adaline, trust me he's bad news." His voice sounds defeated and I'm tempted to send Chris on his way.

"Give me a reason to stay," I tell him. He considers my words, I can see the thought turning over in his mind, but he doesn't respond. "I'll be okay, besides Aedan and Deklan will be following us," I smile convincingly but he still seems unsure.

As if on cue Aedan and Deklan appear on the staircase and announce they are ready to go. I leave all three of them inside while I go out to meet Chris. He's waiting by his green pickup truck smoking a cigarette which he extinguishes on the ground as I approach.

"What's that asshole doing at your house?" He says coldly.

"He and his brother are living with us. There was a problem with their house so my uncle invited them to stay," I say, it's not entirely a lie, but it's not the whole truth.

"Let's get a move on or we are going to miss the movie." Chris graciously opens the passenger door and I can climb into the raised truck. He's polite but I can sense his mood is less than content.

- 49 -

SETH

"You knew about this?" I scream at Aedan. He should have told me the second he knew Adaline was going out with that jerk.

"She only told me this morning and I didn't want to worry you," Aedan says as he slides into his leather jacket. Deklan follows close at his heels.

"Deklan you need a night in. I'll go with my brother, you can relax and watch the house," I propose. Deklan eyes Aedan for a moment who simply shrugs his shoulders. I push past Aedan and walk into the cool night air. The jerk's stupid pickup has already left by the time Aedan follows me outside, but we know where they are going and catch up quickly. I watch them pull into the parking lot outside the cinema and park a few spaces away.

"Are you going to be able to hold it together in here Seth? The last thing we need is you burning down the cinema," Aedan asks, but I'm already halfway out the car ignoring his concerns.

I follow them to the cinema doors when Aedan appears at my side. We linger at the entrance and I watch Adaline through the glass doors. Chris tries to take her hand in his, I'm about to smash the glass along with his face, but she withdraws her hand from his embrace and tucks her hair behind her ears. Clearly, she's not as interested in holding hands as he is. Once they disappear into the dark theatre, we hurry to purchase our tickets and Aedan buys some popcorn. I spot

Adaline's head down near the front, Aedan and I position ourselves a few rows behind. The movie is a crappy rom-com and if I wasn't engrossed with every move Adaline makes I would claw my own eyes out and use them as earplugs just so I wouldn't have to see or hear this dribble.

Aedan laughs every now and then between stuffing his face with popcorn, for a guy who eats healthy all the time he's really enjoying the butter-soaked heart attack in a box. I can't even comprehend how he finds this trash so amusing, he laughs again and I knock the popcorn out of his hand.

Chris's movement catches my eye, he's moving his head closer to Adaline and I'm almost certain he's going to try and kiss her. Adaline whispers something in his ear, but I can't hear what she's said over the speakers. Whatever she said it makes him keep his distance.

No sooner have I settled back into my seat I see Adaline standing abruptly and pushing other patron's out of the way as she escapes the confinements of the aisle. All the while Chris makes unsettling groans I haven't heard before. Aedan and I are hurdling the rows, Aedan is closer to Chris so I chase after Adaline. She reaches the exit doors before I get to her. She's making her way out past the concession stand when I grab hold of her wrist and she spins around to hit me, but I catch her fist in mine. Her face is streaked with tears and mascara. The security guard approaches us and asks Adaline if she's okay. She assures him she's fine and I let go of her wrists.

"Can you just get me out of here please?" She whimpers. I half carry her to the car and help her in. As I climb into the driver's seat I feel my phone vibrating. It's Aedan. I tell him I'm taking Adaline home and he offers to grab a cab once he sees Chris out.

I start the engine and before I pull the car out onto the street I remove my hoodie and drape it over Adaline's shivering frame. "Can we not go home straight away; can we go somewhere else?" She asks.

"Where do you want to go?" I ask.

"There's a lookout about fifteen minutes from here, we can go there," she offers. I follow her directions and we arrive at a lookout at the peak of a cliff. In the darkness, all the lights of the town twinkle as brightly as the stars that shine above. Adaline gets out of the car and sits on a large flat rock that's covered in spray paint and haphazard tags. I stand behind her and listen to her breathe.

"If I tell you what happened are you going to kill him?" She asks me quietly. I think I'm going to kill him no matter what happened unless Aedan has already beaten me to it. I know that's not what she wants to hear though so I stay silent rather than lie to her. "He tried to kiss me and I told him I wasn't interested like that. He seemed okay though, I thought he understood. Then he put his hand up my dress and made some crack about me putting out for scum like you. That's when I punched him in the balls." She says with a strained laugh. A laugh I can tell she's forcing for my benefit.

"I'm going to destroy the bastard," I whisper to myself. I'm contemplating the ways in which I'm going to torture him when she reaches out for my hand. She grabs it and pulls me to sit beside her.

"You won't do that because if you did it would make things worse for me," she says and rests her head against my shoulder. Suddenly all the rage I was feeling seems like a distant memory. "His face was pretty priceless when I hit him. His eyes bulged out of his head like a fish." This time her laugh was genuine. "You were right about him. I guess I overlooked my instincts so I could pretend to be a normal girl," she sighs deeply.

"Not even normal girls would want that guy. He's a tool and doesn't deserve someone as wonderful as you," I tell her. She tilts her head so she's looking up at me and her eyes are sparkling brighter than the stars and city lights combined.

"He's not really what I want," she says and she presses her lips to mine.

At first, I'm in shock, she's kissing me and I'm frozen like it's the first time someone's kissed me. My body reacts before my mind catches up and I kiss her back. Her lips on mine transform the atmosphere around us. The air warms, I can feel the heat of the electricity burning in it. I run my fingers through her hair and draw her nearer to me. Her body is pressed against mine, like a puzzle that's found its missing piece. My hand finds the curve of her back while the other caresses her thigh and reaches the hem of her dress. Her fingers trace the waistband of my jeans and her nails tickle my stomach. My phone vibrates loudly in my pocket and she pulls away. I have to catch my breath before I answer it.

Deklan's on the other end. He has already picked up Aedan from the cinema and they are both at home waiting for us. I tell him we will be back soon and hang up. The fiery energy still clings to the air, forcing us to breathe heavier than necessary. My heads clouded with confusion, but one thing that's crystal clear is that I have never felt anything like that before. The intensity, the passion, the fire that was burning between us was palpable.

"We should get home before they come looking for us," she says.

I nod and follow her to the car. I'm too lost in thought to say anything on the drive home and when we arrive at the house I wait patiently for her to say something. Instead, she gives me a small smile and goes inside. So much for keeping things professional.

- 50 -
Adaline

How could I sleep after the night I just experienced? The ordeal of being sexually harassed by that asshole and then the most amazing kiss I have ever experienced. I didn't know what to say on the drive home, I was so nervous and the attraction I felt for Seth still tingled in my veins. He never said anything either, maybe it wasn't as incredible for him as it was for me. Seth does have at least a hundred years more experience than I do, maybe I'm a bad kisser and he didn't have the heart to tell me. When I walked up the stairs to the house I felt like I was floating on air, I was on top of the world when I had my shower and I felt euphoric when I settled into bed. But here, laying in the darkness I find myself second guessing everything that happened. I feel insecure and frankly a tad pathetic. Why didn't he just say something, anything? I would have settled for him giving me a sincere thank you and sending me on my way.

I can't take tossing and turning in my bed any longer, so I decide to go downstairs and get something to eat instead, I can never sleep on an empty stomach. A cup of tea and some toast will help me settle. The kettle boils and I pour absentmindedly, spilling hot water all over the kitchen counter. I almost drop the kettle when I turn around and see Aedan standing in the doorway.

"Forgive me, I didn't mean to startle you. How are you feeling after tonight?" He asks as he collects a tea towel and starts mopping up my mess.

"I'm okay I guess. It could have been worse. Seth was right about him, he really was a jerk," I admit.

"The last thing Seth needs is to be told he's right all the time. He will probably hunt him down at school on Monday and tear his throat out," Aedan says casually and I'm not entirely certain he's kidding.

"He won't do that. How was he when we got back? Did he seem angry or upset?" I ask. It's after two in the morning and I'm probing Aedan for info on his brother, I can officially add desperate to my list of shortcomings.

"Actually, he seemed very happy, but then again that probably had something to do with what the two of you got up to," he replies. I feel my jaw unhinge as it hits the floor.

"He told you?" I ask. The toast springs from the toaster and I jump in shock.

"He didn't say anything, but I guessed. Do me a favour though, don't let Deklan find out because I'll have to deal with it. The last thing we need is fighting inside the house," Aedan says. He continues fussing around me packing away the jam and butter and scooping the crumbs off the counter while I eat my toast. Once Aedan's certain I'm settled he makes his way back to bed. It appears Aedan's the only person not judging my choices and I'm grateful for it. I hope Seth realises how lucky he is to have a brother like that, even if he seems a little OCD.

- 51 -

SETH

I can feel Aedan's knowing gaze on me as he opens the bedroom door. I can still smell her skin on mine and the sweet seductive taste of her mouth lingers on my lips. There's no way Aedan can't smell what I'm smelling. I ready myself for a lecture from my responsible brother.

"Adaline's back in bed. She just wanted something to eat," Aedan says.

He never asked me what happened when I got home and now laying here in the silence I find myself wanting to share. I try to stop myself but I can't. I start divulging every thought and feeling I felt with Adaline tonight and every other night since we met. More surprising than my willingness to share is his reaction to my disclosure. He simply smiles and reminds me to be careful.

Aedan has never thought less of me for my lacking judgement or the multitude of idiotic choices I have made in the past. Even now as I commit a crime against the crown he loves me still. He has always been a better brother than I deserved.

My once soft mattress on my bed now resembles the stony path outside our castle, a bed of jagged broken rubble and grit. My troubled mind plays tricks on my body, feeling abrasive bulges and discomfort where there is none. I toss and turn trying to shift the imaginative rocks I rest upon. I replay the moment over in my mind.

The clear night sky, the lights twinkling below us a world away. The dreamy way her eyes made me feel like I was falling and the moment when she held me captive in her embrace. I was trapped. All the reasons we can't be together escaped my mind, leaving me utterly vulnerable. It was a moment of complete selfishness, a moment when duty and family were never further from my mind. It was a stolen second for myself. If the wolf hadn't called when he did and put an end to my treasonous actions, I don't know what would have happened. Would I have been strong enough to stop myself? Would I have wanted to?

She clouds my thoughts and makes it impossible for me to find reason or logic when I'm with her. Now that she's gone my mind is hauntingly clear and all I can see is a tragedy. Treason for consorting with the princess, the possible banishment of myself and my brother from the fae community. I can only imagine what other punishment the king would cast upon me. A more heartbreaking thought crosses my mind, what if she realises the truth about me? I have done unspeakable things and it's more probable than not that I'll do many more. What happens when she sees me for the monster I am and realises that I'm not good enough for her.

The sun rises and irritates my aching eyes. I wasn't able to sleep for more than a few minutes before my mind would provoke horrific images. Unspeakable acts of torture aimed at Adaline by unseen forces. Each time the dream became too real I would wake with smoking hands. By the time I stopped my hands turning to flames I was too restless to sleep and again the cycle would begin. Emotions, how the hell do normal people deal with these kinds of feelings every day?

At least it's Sunday and I don't need to hurry to take Adaline to school so I have time to hide away from reality.

Aedan's neatly made bed is empty beside me, I vaguely remember him getting up a little before first light. His phone had buzzed on the nightstand, waking me. It was clearly unimportant or he wouldn't have let me fall back to sleep. I lay on the bed for another hour until I can't tolerate the mattress any longer. My nerves are so tightly wound I need to move before they snap.

I forgo showering but brush my teeth and hair. As I walk downstairs I hear disgruntled chatter coming from the kitchen. Aedan and Deklan are in a heated debate. At first, it's unclear what they are fighting about until I hear a name. Shaylin.

"Have they located her?" I ask.

"Yes, Jason and his team found her hiding with some rogue vamps in a dive bar in Dallas. They have her prisoner and are on route. They will return within the hour," Aedan says looking slightly grim.

"So, what's the problem?" I ask confused. Killing her should be an open and shut case, I can't imagine what they need to discuss.

"Deklan wants her killed on sight. However, we aren't any closer to providing any evidence against Maura. If we want her removed from her position and imprisoned, we need to prove her betrayal to the crown. The best way to do that is to keep Shaylin alive," Aedan says diplomatically.

"She tried to kill Adaline and she damn near succeeded. She needs to die for what she has done. I'm sorry brother, but I agree with the wolf on this one," I say. The idea of having Shaylin breathe another breath after what she tried to do to Adaline fills me with rage. I imagine sinking my teeth into her treasonous throat and tearing out her flesh, the thought fills me with pleasure.

"See even your pigheaded brother understands this situation for what it is. We cannot risk Adaline's life, she's too important," Deklan says echoing my thoughts. I never thought I would see the day the wolf and I were on the same page.

"Aedan's right," a small voice calls from behind me. I turn to see Adaline looking like an angel in a long white nightgown. The light from the kitchen window makes her skin glow with warmth. It still amazes me how she can sneak up on us like that. "We need to think long-term. Shaylin is just the pawn. We need to find who's sending out the orders and that means keeping her alive. Besides I honestly don't know how I feel about people killing in my name," she says.

"Are you serious, that bitch tried to kill you, Adaline? She was going to slit your throat or worse deliver you to someone who would force you to be their weapon. Is that what you want?" I ask her. My anger bubbles, how can she have such a disregard for her own safety?

"I want to see her," she declares like she's saying she wants to see a movie after curfew, not visiting the person who tried to kill her.

Deklan and I are equally outraged and make our thoughts clear. Granted I use more aggressive words than he does. Adaline turns to Aedan and pleads for him to let her see Shaylin. At least my brother still has some common sense and tells her he doesn't think it's a good idea.

"I'm not a fragile doll!" she screams as she storms out of the room.

Jason calls to inform us that Shaylin is securely bound at the hotel and they are awaiting our instructions.

She will have to wait a little while longer while Deklan and I talk Aedan into doing the right thing.

- 52 -
Adaline

I overheard the phone call from their friend Jason, I know where Shaylin is and it's clear they aren't going to permit me to see her, it's now or never. I change as quickly as I can and sneak out the front door while they are still busy fighting in the kitchen. Luckily the keys for their SUV are hanging on the key rack by the door and since the cars parked across the street they may not even notice when I start it up. Getting a ticket for driving unlicensed seems a trivial concern, I barely second guess my rebellious actions and turn the ignition over.

The car starts seamlessly, I put the gear into drive and make sure I fasten my seat belt. It would be a sad end to my story if I died from ignoring road safety regulations.

I cautiously pull out into the street; the acceleration is more powerful than my old schools Honda and the car heave's forward when I press too firmly. Mum insisted I didn't need a full license with all the public transport around us, but I know enough from my driver's education classes to get me to the hotel in one piece. Fingers crossed I don't get pulled over.

I make it to the hotel in good time despite my nerves and my phone sits silently on the passenger seat. They mustn't have noticed I've left yet and I'm seriously starting to question their security system. I remember that Jason has a room on the lower level of the hotel but I don't know which number. I climb the stairs to the room Seth and

Aedan had occupied and knock. There are hurried noises inside, the shuffling of footsteps and the moving of chairs. A pale young man with red hair opens the door, I instantly recognise his similarities to Seth and Aedan.

This man is a vampire and he's one of their men. I tell him that Aedan sent me to get something from Jason but I forgot the room number. I must be believable enough because he escorts me to the room directly below theirs.

He knocks loudly and Jason appears in the door frame. I thank the red-haired boy and tell Jason we need to speak in private. Jason is taller than I had imagined and he towers over me. He has big brown eyes and a youthful face, he and Seth could almost be related.

"You know who I am?" I ask.

"Yes, you're the girl everyone's fussing about. Why are you here?" He asks glancing over my shoulder as if looking for someone else to appear. It's obvious he knows I shouldn't be without one of my bodyguards. I doubt I will have long before he calls one of them to tattle on me.

"I'm here to speak to Shaylin. Aedan sent me alone because Seth didn't want me to come. Aedan will be along shortly," I say, trying painfully to sink sincerity into my words. I've never been a good liar and I'm not getting any better.

"I don't believe you. From what I have been told you shouldn't be left alone period, let alone with the woman who tried to kill you," he says.

"Aedan and Seth are fighting about whether to kill her or not and since it's my life that was threatened I want to know why. Please, let me talk to her for a minute," I plead. He weighs his options carefully, I'm almost certain he's going to restrain me while he sends word to the others.

"I'm going to call Aedan. It will take him ten minutes to get here so you have until then. She is secure, but don't get too close," he says. I follow him to a connecting door which leads to an adjoining room and he pulls out his cell phone. He holds up his hand ushering me inside.

I step over the threshold and scan the scantily lit room; my eyes are drawn to the dark woman bound to one of the hotel chairs. She looks thinner than I remember. Her face is gaunt, and her limbs hang weakly. I sit on the end of one of the beds facing her. She lifts her head slowly, it's a clear moment when recognition dawns on her. Her eyes lock with mine and her head snaps into a formal position. She looks at me with the same disdain I remember from the woods.

"What do you want little bitch, did you want to spit on me before I die?" She asks. Her words are harsh but weak. A growl from a lion that's lost its fight, more show than scare.

"I'd never do that... I wanted to see you... Seth wants you dead and Aedan wants to keep you alive until they get the information they need. Then they would kill you, but what makes my life worth more than yours. Did you really want to kill me because another person told you to or was it because of Seth?" I ask. She sits silently. "They will be here soon, we don't have much time," I urge.

"Partly because of him and partly for my mistress. She wants you dead. She says you're a threat to our kind. If I killed you she would help make me a leader of my own clan and I wouldn't have to take orders from anyone ever again," she says. Maybe she's telling me this to scare me or maybe it's just that she knows she's lost, either way, I know it's the truth.

"I understand not wanting to take orders from others. If I set you free what would you do?" I ask. I know what she tried to do to me and her reasons don't excuse her actions, but often people's poor choices are simply reactions to their own troubles.

"I won't be given a pass on this, stop trying to torment me further," she hisses. I ignore her outrage and wait for her answer. "If I was to go free I wouldn't be welcome back home because of my failure. Maura would not permit it, she despises failure. I suppose I would become one of the rogues, just as bad as dead," she says sadly.

I can feel her heartache bouncing around the room like it has a life of its own. I approach her slowly and place my hand on hers. She's taken back by my gentle touch. I feel the energy inside her, I feel her lungs breathing, her body struggles as it heals her injuries from within. Her pulse beats weakly under her cold skin and her eyes become hazy and unfocused. I watch as they roll around aimlessly until they fall on me. For a second we are connected, her heartache and pain is my own. I see the darkness that has taken root within her, it consumes everything it touches. When the darkness is almost too much to endure I pull back, but before I let go I see a small flicker of light. A tiny candle burning in the darkness.

"What are you?" She asks amazedly.

"I'm just a girl and perhaps it's time we both stop being pawns in the games of others," I tell her and offer a warm smile. I untie the ropes that have bound her to the chair. Some of her skin has fused to the cords and tears off when I pull them away. She grunts her teeth together and holds her breath while I remove the rest of her bindings. "They will be here soon. If you hurry out the window you will have a chance, I'll do what I can here to spare you," I say.

"Why?" She asks, looking at me like I'm playing a cruel trick.

"I think you still have something good in you to offer, and my mother taught me that hope isn't something you give up on. At least now, whatever you decide it will be because it's entirely your own decision." I give her a gentle forgiving hug, and she stiffens under my embrace unsure how to respond. I release her and the small flame I felt inside her is burning a little brighter and I pray that it's enough.

She jumps through the window like a cat off a ledge. Once she has crossed the empty lot she vanishes into the dense woods that surround the back of the hotel.

I know she won't be responsible for any harm that's coming my way. I will live to see another day and so will she. I feel the compassion within me grow and I know I made the right choice. Hatred destroys the spirit and I'm not ready to give up on mine just yet.

The screeching of raised voices outside wakes me from the surreal dream I'm caught in. Seth practically breaks down the hotel door and I'm thrown startlingly back into reality. Aedan's eyes fall upon me and I feel like a disobedient child who has been caught red-handed and the ferocious look on Seth's face tells me I'm in for way more than a round of grounding. Maybe I won't live that much longer after all.

- 53 -

SETH

Any warm feelings I had for Adaline turn to pure rage when Jason calls. She just doesn't seem to understand that her fucking life is in danger. Instead of letting us handle it she runs directly into the eye of the storm, or in her case the 'Adaline Slaughter House'. Not only does she disobey us, but she steals the fucking car and we have to run all the way to the hotel.

Deklan is the first to arrive but Aedan and I are close on his tail. Deklan hurdles the stairs to our old room, Aedan and I address the lower level to find Jason in his. He directs us to the adjoining room next door. I waste no time with locks and bust the door open with my shoulder. Adaline stands between an open window and a vacant chair containing nothing more than a pile of flesh streaked ropes.

"Are you hurt?" I ask as I rush to her side and squeeze her shoulders tightly in my hands. She looks a little dazed. "Are you okay?" I yell.

"Yes, I'm fine," she says simply.

"What the hell were you thinking, she could have killed you? And you, what the fuck were you thinking letting her in here," I say turning my rage towards Jason, who's standing guiltily in the door frame. "She could have been killed and obviously you didn't restrain the bitch properly because she fucking got loose," I rant. Jason flinches at my anger.

"Seth, don't be mad at Jason, he did secure her. I untied her ropes," she says casually like she let a kitten outside to use the bathroom.

"What the hell is wrong with you? Did she use compulsion?" I ask. Maybe Shaylin had enough strength to force Adaline to untie her and let her go.

"There's nothing wrong with me, you're the one who wanted to waltz in here and kill someone. Shaylin and I talked, and I decided to let her go," she says.

I realise Adaline may not even know that Shaylin used compulsion on her. I focus my will on Adaline, compelling her to obey my commands, I don't usually bother with compulsion on people, but it doesn't mean I don't have the strength or skill to do it.

"You will tell me the truth. Did she control you?" Adaline looks at me a little confused. Then she looks to Aedan for guidance. "Adaline tell me the truth," I command.

"What are you doing? I told you the damn truth, I let her go because it was the right thing to do. Stop looking at me like that, you're creeping me out," she says as she withdraws from my grasp.

Aedan walks over curiously and takes my place in front of Adaline. I know what he's going to try before he does it. His gaze intensifies on Adaline and he tells her to touch her finger to her nose. She doesn't comply. He tells her to bark like a dog and she bursts into a fit of laughter.

"Are you trying to mind control me?" She says through snickering breaths.

"Clearly, she is immune to our talents," Aedan says. "Come, Adaline, we can discuss your actions at home," he escorts her out to the car and I turn my attention towards Jason.

He is well aware how dangerous I can be, but he has never been the target of my rage before. My anger at Adaline, my rage at Shaylin and all of my disappointment at Jason are unleashed. I give him a verbal lashing that appears to hurt him more than if I had physically hit him. He apologises and swears to never fail me again. I tell him that he is on strict twenty four hour surveillance of Adaline. If she tries to shake her security again he will be solely responsible for detaining her.

I join the others in the car to catch the end of Deklan's lecture. I hear him say the word all parents across the world say to their children when they want to cut them deeply, disappointed. I swear I can hear Adaline's heartbreak in response. I see tears start to well up in the corners of her eyes. My heart tightens in my chest and I tell him it's enough. I'm just as angry with her as he is, but I can't stand to see her upset.

"Why did you do it, Adaline? You know all the reasons we are trying to keep you safe. She tried to kill you, why would you let her go? I just can't understand it," Aedan asks calmly.

"I'm not like you. I can't just say that someone deserves to die," she says. I scoff at her words. She ignores me and continues. "I know what she did and if I thought she would have done it again maybe I wouldn't have let her go, but when I touched her I knew," she says with that dreamy look in her eye. She's no longer crying and looks more dignified than I have ever seen her.

"Knew what?" Deklan asks.

"That she was in pain. The reason she had tried to kill me was that she was trying to save herself. She was hurt and lost, and this Maura exploited that. Her heart was broken, and she tried to build herself up, so it wouldn't happen again. She won't come after me. Can't you just let her go, please?" She begs. Her question is addressed to everyone in the car, but it feels directly pointed at me.

I knew Shaylin had been unhappy when we had consorted. She wanted me to be in love with her, but I wasn't. My heart has never been something I have been able to give to another. When she began to spiral out of control I found a position opening in Maura's clan, I thought that offering it to her was the best thing. A fresh start for her. She might find someone who could give her what she wanted. I guess I was wrong. Perhaps I'm a little to blame for some of Shaylin's actions. Adaline closes the car door firmly and enters the house unescorted. We sit idly for a few minutes each pondering Adaline's request.

"She really is powerful. It's a short list of fae that can withstand our gaze. She didn't even appear to be trying to fight it and as for the things she said about Shaylin, have you ever heard of such a thing Deklan?" Aedan asks.

"There are fae that can read peoples inner thoughts and sense emotion but I think what she described is different. It's like she can see into the essence of a being, she can see their soul. It will be a useful gift when she takes the crown," Deklan says. He keeps talking about when she will be queen but I find myself wondering if she will go through with it. To be a ruler you need to make the hard choices, sometimes that means killing others.

"Her compassion may very well be the end of her. A soft heart makes for weak rulers," I say out loud.

"I disagree, brother, soft is not the word I would use. Her heart is kind and I believe it will be her salvation," Aedan declares.

- 54 -
Deklan

Adaline's powers are growing quickly, when she reaches her birthday in a few short months I fear it may be too much for her to control. If she had been raised at court she would have had years of training to prepare. I remember the first time I changed. The power was so intense I could have died from the pain I endured. My father had conditioned me from birth. He had pushed me physically. Strength training, endurance training and weightlifting. Anything to make me stronger, I can't imagine how I would have survived if he hadn't prepared me. I don't think a few gym sessions will help prepare Adaline for what's coming her way, my powers were a physical trait, but hers are mental and require precise preparation.

Theodore's package arrived today but with all the excitement and Adaline running off every time I turn around I haven't had time to open it.

Now that she is safely tucked away in her room I can see what he was able to get done in the short time I gave him. Inside is twenty thousand in cash, a potion vial and a thick stack of documents. As I flip through the pages I see he was able to provide everything I asked for. When the time comes I will have what I need to keep Adaline safe. Tomorrow I will have Aedan and Seth assist Adaline with power training, hopefully, since they share elements they will be able to give her some direction and support. Regrettably, I know I'm going to need someone else to help prepare her, I just wish I didn't have to make the call.

After a night of broken sleep, I'm thankful Adaline has school today. I don't think any fae would attack her in such a public place and risk exposure, it's when she's home that I worry most. I spend the day checking the security systems and coordinating watch detail with Jason. As far as vamps go he's a pretty good guy. He talks too much for my liking, but from what I can see, I believe him to be trustworthy and competent at his job. He offers to collect Adaline and Seth from school so I can catch up on some much-needed sleep. Two hours isn't enough, however, it's plenty for the afternoon activities I have planned.

The backyard has high fences and ample open space which will provide us with a perfect training ground. I told the vamps and Adaline to be here at four sharp. Aedan and Adaline arrive promptly on time, Seth wanders in at quarter past. Adaline is dressed in tight pink and black workout gear and running shoes. Aedan remains in his usual button-down shirt and fitted pants, although today he has his sleeves rolled up making him look rather casual. Seth is in his usual minimal effort ensemble, t-shirt and jeans.

"Adaline has missed years of training, so over the coming months, both of you will be helping her with her elements. Aedan, this week we will focus on the earth element and Seth next week will be fire. Then we will move onto offence and defence," I explain.

Aedan is a natural teacher, he guides Adaline with encouragement and sound instruction. Aedan uses his abilities to grow a tree from nothing. It starts as a simple blade of grass, it begins taking form and sprouting roots. The branches expand to cover us and bright coloured leaves explode to life. At first, it takes her an hour to be able to grow a seedling, but once she has a hold of it, she grows a tree that rivals Aedan's.

At the end of the first day, Adaline's so tired she goes straight to bed without dinner and I'm worried I pushed her too hard. Aedan explains the fatigue is normal when starting out and I shouldn't worry. I hope he is right because this is nothing compared to the training Florence will dish out when she arrives. When I called her last evening, she didn't hang up as I thought she might, she did, however, call me a prick and tell me the ways she plans on removing my genitals. Once I offered her a very handsome payment and the instructions from her King she agreed to assist us. She arrives within the fortnight and I'm dreading it. I haven't seen my sister-in-law in years and we didn't part on good terms. She has never forgiven me for being the reason her sister was cast out of her family. Knowing the things I know now, maybe my sweet Chloe would have been better off if she never married me, she might still be alive.

- 55 -
Adaline

Yesterday was my first day of training and I thought it would be difficult, but difficult doesn't even come close. Every muscle in my body aches. I'm hesitant to get out of bed if the pain is this evident when I'm laying still, it's going to be so much worse when I stand. I turn my head slightly so I can see the clock on my bedside table, I should be ready to leave for school by now and I'm still stuck in bed. There's a tentative knock on the door and I know it's not Jerry because he said goodbye before he left with Aedan an hour ago.

"Adaline are you ready for school?" It's Seth. He slowly opens the door a crack and sees me still lying in bed. "Are you okay? It's almost time to leave," he opens the door all the way and walks over to my side.

"I'm not going today, I can't really move," I say into my blankets and avoid his eyes. When I can't take the silence anymore I look up at his gorgeous face and register his confusion. "My muscles ache so badly I'm frightened to stand up. Is this normal after using the elements, because I didn't feel this pain after what happened in the woods? I felt tired and passed out, but I didn't hurt like this," I say pathetically.

"When you used your powers against Shaylin it was a natural reflex, you didn't have to force it like you did yesterday. It will be more bearable the more you practice. Just rest, I'll be back in a few minutes," he says kindly and scurries out my room. He left my door open a crack and I can hear him talking to someone downstairs and then the front door closing. I'm too exhausted to care, I close my eyes and try to sleep.

I find myself settled between sleep and wakefulness. I'm vaguely aware of the world around me, the birds singing outside my window and the breeze blowing through the trees. Then I hear loud banging and the sound of glass breaking. I sit up quickly and cringe as the pain in my neck and shoulders seizes me in place. Then I hear Seth yell profanities from the kitchen, it sounds like he is fighting the dishwasher. I relax the muscles in my back and lower myself back into my bed. I feel safer knowing Seth's just a few feet away and my body relaxes.

Just as I'm drifting off to sleep I hear footsteps enter my bedroom, my eyes fly open and they meet Seth's deep gaze staring back at me. He stands at the end of my bed for a moment before he approaches me. In his hand is a plate of food. Fresh strawberries, blueberries and some slices of banana and an overly large croissant filled with ham and cheese. In his other hand, he is precariously holding a bottle of juice and a cup of tea. I try to sit up so I can take the plate from him, but as I begin to move my jaw tightens and I can't contain the painful moan that escapes my lips. Seth quickly puts the plate down on the table and gracefully places the tea and juice beside it. He reaches forward and in one swift movement he has placed a pillow behind my back so I'm sitting comfortably upright.

"Thank you. I feel like such a wuss, I can't even sit up without almost crying," I say with a pained smile.

"You will feel better when you eat something, Aedan said the natural sugars help," he says sweetly as he positions the plate of food on my lap.

I pick up a few berries and place them in my mouth. They taste amazing, the strawberries are sickly sweet, which I love and I instantly start feeling better. Seth watches me intently as I finish the fruit on my plate. It's awkward having someone watch you eat, I feel uncomfortable and start to tear delicate ladylike pieces of the croissant and chew them gracefully. The truth is all I want to do is shove the croissant in my mouth and swallow it whole.

"Where did you get the croissant, it's really good?" I ask to fill the silence.

"There is a nice bakery near the hotel, we got breakfast there a few times. Are you feeling better?" He asks not taking his eye off me.

"I am actually, can you pass me the juice please," I ask. He hands it over and I drink it deeply, when I relax for a breath it spills over my lips and down the front of me. He laughs and hands me a tissue. "So much for ladylike," I laugh.

"I like that you're not as delicate as your appearance suggests," he whispers like he's sharing a secret. I smile and feel my cheeks turning red.

"I suppose I should go have a shower," I say. I can smell the remnants of last night's exertion and I was way too tired to shower before bed. Gingerly I swing my legs over the bed and attempt to stand, my legs protest and turn into jelly before I collapse, Seth's arms are supporting me. "Maybe you can just help me to the bathroom until my legs start working," I offer.

We take it slow and eventually my legs start to respond to the movement. I can almost hold my own weight but Seth holds me steady with his firm grip around my waist. When we reach the bathroom he's not sure how to proceed, I release myself from his grasp and support my weight on the vanity. I didn't realise Seth was supporting the majority of my weight until he let go of me.

"I'll wait out here in case you need anything," he says whilst looking intently at his shoes. I close the door between us and start the shower.

It takes me a while to remove my clothing and the room has filled with steam by the time I'm undressed. When I climb into the shower the water feels like tiny daggers slicing into my skin.

I look over my body for some indication of the pain I'm feeling, but my skin is blemish free. I wish I could sit down in the shower, but I know if I sit down I won't be able to get myself back up and there's no way I'm letting Seth carry my naked body out of this bathroom. Eventually, the sensation of the warm water changes from pain to pleasure and my body aches a little less. I don't bother with shampoo or soap, but I do brush my teeth as much as I can manage. I get out of the shower and wrap myself securely in a bath sheet. I look over to the vanity where I usually leave my clean clothes and realise I didn't bring anything to change into.

"Seth, I didn't bring any clothes do you think you could bring me some. Any shirt will do, some pants and underwear," I ask awkwardly.

"Sure," he says and I hear the discomfort in his tone. My god, he's going to be going through my underwear drawer, at least everything inside it is clean.

- 56 -

SETH

I found a t-shirt and some tights easy enough, but as I open and close draws filled with her personal possessions, I begin to feel a little seedy. I feel worse when I find the draw I need. All her delicate items are folded and pressed immaculately, some are wrapped in brown paper and still have the dry-cleaning tags attached. I discovered that her uncle didn't do laundry the first night we moved in. Aedan had asked for laundry detergent and Jerry laughed hysterically in response.

As I sort through her undergarments I realise I have never once considered how many different types of underwear there are, I always assumed that from modern advancements there were only two types of undergarments that women wear, a thong or the full kind.

Adaline's draw contains short ones, long ones that look like shorts and a scarce amount of thongs. I can't even begin to process the different fabrics, some smooth as silk while others are thick with stability. I'm confused what type I should bring her. I feel like I'm crossing a line, I'm delving into her most intimate secrets. I can hear her opening the bathroom door and know I've taken far too long to decide. Although the purple lace pair is the underwear I would like to see her in I settle for a simple black pair. I also grab a bra that matches close enough to the pants. Practical seems the appropriate choice.

Hurriedly, I rush back to the bathroom door and knock. Adaline opens it just enough to retrieve the bundle of clothing. I wait patiently as her intoxicating smell seeps under the bathroom door. The hot shower has intensified her blissful scent and the hallway is perfumed with her. Just when I'm beginning to worry about how long she is taking the bathroom door creeks and opens slightly.

"Um do you think you could help me, I can't do up the bra. I have it on but I can't do the clasp, my shoulder won't bend that way," she asks with a nervous tremor in her voice.

She opens the door further, she's wearing her tights and she has a towel firmly secured over the front of the bra to eliminate any unintentional slips. As she turns her back to me the bra straps hang loosely over her shoulders and the clasp sits open like an invitation to her flawless skin. I clear my throat, I don't remember being nervous with a woman before but I guess there is a first for everything. I reach forward and hold the clasp between my fingers, I fumble at first. I've had plenty of practice removing bras, but none putting them on. Her hair falls between her shoulder blades getting in the way of my task. I tuck the stray hairs over her shoulder, my finger accidentally touching her skin. She shivers in response. Regrettably, I pull my fingers back to finish closing the retched clasp. Once it's secure I turn around so she can finish getting dressed.

"All done," she says and I turn to face her.

Her skin glows in the low light and her eyes are radiant. I reach out my hand and gently stroke her cheek, she closes her eyes and leans her face into my hand.

The skin of my palm begins to warm and I'm worried it's going to turn her cheek to cinders. I begin to pull away, but she pulls my hand back to her face and kisses the base of my palm. I reach down and pull her face to mine. I kiss her forcefully, unleashing all the desire I have been trying desperately to suppress. She ignited something inside me when we kissed at the lookout and it's been a raging inferno ever since. Her lips meld with mine and she matches my passion with her own. I lean into her body, pressing myself against her, fusing us into a single being. Adaline leans back against the vanity and moans loudly. Not a moan of pleasure, but of pain. I pull back abruptly, worried I had hurt her. I take stock of her body and everything seems in place, then she winces and rubs her back.

"Sorry, my muscles still hurt," she whimpers.

"I'm the one who's sorry, I should never have," I admit.

"I'm glad you did. I think I should go back to bed and rest a little while, especially if I have another session this afternoon," she says.

I watch her stumble back to her room on weak legs. Without warning I feel like a part of me has fallen away, a part I never knew existed until she entered my life. A warmth that fades the second she's gone. I'm hollow, a vacant space of darkness and fear. The feelings I have for her are too intense to deny and I'm afraid if I keep trying to refute what I feel for her I'll lose all control and the darkness will consume me. I can still taste her on my lips, my element responds inside me, eager for more. I want her more than I have ever wanted anything.

- 57 -
Adaline

The last week has been challenging, in public, I live the uncomplicated life of a high school student, but behind closed doors, I'm training for my life. In spite of my extracurricular activities, I still need to have my homework and assignments in on time and keep up with domestic chores. Learning to use my earth element has been harder than I expected. Every evening after training I have fallen into bed exhausted and woken up in agony. Last night was my fifth lesson and the last of the week. Deklan has graciously given me the weekends off to recuperate, unfortunately, due to my aching body and fatigue, I have spent my first day of freedom sleeping.

It's early evening when I wake, the sky still holds a glimmer of light as the sun begins to set and a cool breeze settles in the air as it floats through my window.

I have become accustomed to the aches and pains my body suffers each morning. The magic takes its toll and since I haven't transitioned to full fae yet I can only support so much magic at once. Each morning it hurts a little less and I feel myself getting stronger every day.

I'm pleasantly surprised when the usual pain is non-existent, my mind is fresh and alert. I rise from my bed and find my legs hold me contentedly, finally, my body is starting to feel like it belongs to me once more. My nose detects the alluring scent of meat cooking on a barbeque and my stomach rumbles in response. I follow the delectable aroma downstairs and into the backyard. Deklan stands over the barbeque turning thick pieces of steak with one hand and tossing some onions with the other. Jerry and Aedan sit at the table laughing, each relaxing with a beer in their hand. Seth is nowhere to be seen.

"Good evening princess," Jerry beams.

Aedan gives me an exaggerated bow and pulls a chair out for me.

There is a large bowl of salad and some bread rolls on the table, I help myself to a few carrots while we wait for Deklan to finish cooking. I pour myself some iced tea from the pitcher and ease into the chair. It's pleasant sitting here listening to Jerry and Aedan swap stories, the sizzling sounds from the barbeque and the cool breeze blowing through the trees. I could almost forget my life was in constant danger. If Seth was here holding my hand the moment would be perfect.

"Where is Seth?" I ask

"Said he had to run some errands. He should be back any minute," Aedan says.

"He had better, I told him what time dinner was and he said he wouldn't be late," Deklan adds. I've picked up on Deklan's love of punctuality and Seth's incessant need to push against it.

"Jesus papa wolf don't worry I'm here," Seth jokes as he walks through the back door. His smile is genuine and I notice the tone of his mockery toward Deklan has changed from disdain to something that could almost be mistaken as friendship. It's clear to me he likes Deklan more than he's willing to admit.

Dinner is enjoyable, so much so it makes my toes curl up in pleasure. The steak is cooked to perfection and melts like butter on my tongue. Just when I think it can't get any better Seth runs off into the house and emerges with a huge chocolate cake. I've lost some weight this week from all the training and skipping meals, but I'm sure this cake will bring it back with a vengeance. Seth places the cake down in front of me, I'm obsessed by the chocolate curls that adorn the sides and the glazed cherries scattered between. I draw my attention away from the cake in search of a knife and realise everyone is watching me. I glance around the table feeling slightly unnerved, am I missing something?

"What's going on?" I query.

"Well, we know how hard things have been for you lately and you have been working so diligently," Aedan explains.

"So, we thought you needed some normal fun," Seth gestures to the cake. I was so focused on the chocolate itself I didn't notice the writing on top. It reads 'winter formal?'

I look from Seth to the cake in a daze. "Isn't this how human people ask girls to dances these days? Random gestures that make no sense. That tool Chris spray painted the football field asking Barbie," Seth says.

"I don't know if this is how people do it, I haven't been asked to a dance before. I'm not going to lie, it's corny as hell, but I love it,"

I admit.

"At least if you go with Seth we can be assured of your safety and you won't let your dress go to waste," Aedan says with a shrewd grin. He is all too familiar with the recent entanglements Seth and I have found ourselves in.

"I offered to take you, but apparently only students enrolled in the school may attend," Deklan declares. I laugh out loud at the thought of Deklan dancing.

"Yes, I would love to go, thank you," I beam at Seth. He stares at me too intimately for this crowd, so I quickly turn my attention to the others. "Thank you all for everything. I know this seems silly, but this really means a lot to me," I say.

I stand and give each of them a hug, excluding Seth. Suddenly all the concerns I had about the dance are gone. I'm attending my first dance with a handsome man on my arm and a dress to die for. Best of all I didn't have to fight anyone to let me go, all my protectors seem to be on the same page and are happy for me to attend. Maybe this is the start of better things to come.

- 58 -
Adaline

Last night's dinner was the happiest time I have had since losing my mother. The four men downstairs who are running my life feel like home, like my family. I wonder what my mother would think of them, not as a werewolf and two vampires, but as the people they are. Deklan is practical and fiercely protective. Aedan is loyal and loving, a man of peace and wisdom. Seth is everything in between, a wild creature of desire and darkness. His tough exterior is a smokescreen, the real Seth is the man who cared for me when I was weak. He was gentle and kind. He didn't look after me out of duty or obligation, he did it because he cares for me and I feel a connection to him that's too strong to deny.

The weather is darker today and it's finally beginning to feel like winter. The sky is overshadowed with malicious clouds blocking the sun's rays, a storm might be on its way.

I dress in some jeans and a t-shirt and make my way downstairs. Seth and Aedan are in the kitchen drinking their coffee while looking through the paper. Jerry had surgery this morning so he left early with Deklan accompanying him. Both vampires greet me as I enter the kitchen and I give them both a small wave, I'm still riddled with sleep and until I have my cup of tea talking requires more effort than I have. The steam rises from my cup and I sip it slowly, careful not to burn my tongue like I have a million times before. As the cup of heaven warms my body I feel improved.

"So, what's on the agenda today fella's?" I ask happily.

"Actually, I have some things I need to pick up in Dallas so I'll be gone all day. I had better go now or I'll be stuck in traffic," Aedan says scooping up the car keys and heads for the front door. He murmurs something my tired ears can't comprehend and Seth suppresses a grin.

We sit silently for a few minutes. We haven't been alone since the last time we kissed. Thinking of his passionate lips I start to shiver, I'm nervous and excited at all the possibilities our new-found privacy could entail.

If only he was a normal boy and I was a normal girl. If only neither of us had nothing to lose.

"What shall we do then?" Seth asks while he slurps the last of his coffee.

"What do you usually do? When you aren't watching a person's every move," I ask. He glances up from the paper with a confused look on his face. "You know, for fun," I clarify.

"Often, I spend time training or I'm out with Jason looking for rogue vamps who are causing trouble and need to be put down," He smiles like he answered my question.

"Seriously? What about going to the movies or listening to bands, heck what about sports?" I ask. Running is as close as I get to sports, but I can't imagine living for hundreds of years and not having something that makes you happy. Maybe this is why Seth's so tense all the time. "I have an idea. Do you have board shorts?" I ask. Again, he looks puzzled. I raise my eyebrows in frustration.

"Why would I have board shorts?" He questions.

"Forget it. We can pick some up on the way. You get ready and go start the car. I'll be out in five," I say excitedly.

I run upstairs taking them two at a time. The weather's cool, but I don't think Seth will mind too much. I change into my black and green bikini and hurriedly put my clothes back on over the top. On my way downstairs I open the linen closet and retrieve the picnic basket we used when I was little, I also grab two large towels. Seth has reversed the lighter coloured SUV into the driveway, I open the boot and load the towels and basket into the back. When I climb into the front seat he asks what I put in the back. I give him a cheeky grin and tell him he will find out.

We arrive at Kmart and it doesn't take long to find the men's section. I thought finding his shorts would be easy since his usual attire is so relaxed, but he can't find anything he likes. I eventually pull some pale blue ones off the rack and make him try them on. He says they fit but doesn't come out of the change room. I roll my eyes at him as he purchases the shorts, he looks physically pained as he hands over the fifteen dollars to the cashier.

With shorts begrudgingly purchased I ask him to stop at the deli. He waits in the car while I run inside. Unfortunately, when I get out I realise in my haste I forgot my wallet and phone. I ask him if we can go back to the house to get my things, instead, he hands me a hundred-dollar bill and tells me to spend what I want. He doesn't even seem concerned giving me the money, why couldn't he have acted like this when we purchased the shorts.

The deli is run by a sweet older couple, the husband slices some fresh pieces of ham while his wife fills two fresh sourdough rolls with salad and cheese. Her husband comes to her side and kisses her cheek lovingly while he places the ham on the rolls she has prepared. I collect two bottles of water from the fridge, a small tray of mixed fruits and a packet of crisps from the counter. The lady wraps the rolls in brown paper and places all my items into a bag. I hand her the bill Seth had given me and she rings up my balance at the register.

"Going on a date honey?" She asks sweetly as she gestures to Seth waiting in the car out front.

"Something like that," I reply and feel myself blush.

"You just take care darling, make sure that boy treats you right," she says while handing me my change. I give her a warm smile and thank her kindly.

Again, I open the boot and place our lunch into the basket and secure the ribbon tightly. Seth gives me a small smile as I fasten my seat belt and we settle into the drive. It's quiet between us, but it never feels awkward. I give Seth directions when needed and before long we arrive at the lake. The sun has broken through the clouds and the lake glistens under its gentle light. The leaves on the trees have turned to dark golds and browns, but the grass surrounding the lake is still lush and green. I pick a spot under a large oak tree and spread out our towels. Seth wanders over slowly with the picnic basket in hand, he sits it down beside me. I start taking off my shoes and pull my shirt over my head.

"What are you doing?" Seth asks as he turns his back to me. I believe I even saw his cheeks beginning to redden.

"Relax I'm not stripping for you. I have my bathing suit on, put your shorts on. The last one inside has to take out the trash tonight," I tease.

I finish removing my shirt and take off my pants. I walk to the lake and dip my toe in to check the temperature. It's cold but it's not freezing. I turn back and watch Seth remove his shirt, his perfect chest is exposed and it's as breathtaking as I remember. He begins to take off his jeans and before my mind can run away with me I dive into the lake. I swim out a few meters and turn to float on my back. I glide my arms back and forth through the water, my body relaxing with every stroke. I love the sensation of weightlessness you feel when swimming, it's almost like flying.

The lake is serene, the only sound is my own breathing and the trickle of water following the movement of my arms. The colder weather has driven away other swimmers. If it was summer time this place would be packed. For the moment, it belongs to the two of us. I make myself upright and search for my swimming partner, he is sitting on a rock with his feet hanging just above the water. He's watching me carefully so I swim closer.

"Can you swim?" I ask. I never thought to ask if he could. I just assumed everyone can, especially someone who's been alive over a century. Maybe vampires don't like water.

"I can, I just haven't in a very long time. Isn't the water too cold for you?" He asks.

"No, it's lovely, if you came in you could see for yourself. I'll hold your hand if you're scared," I mock.

He smirks and reluctantly dives in. He's awkward at first, he fumbles like he doesn't know if he should float or freestyle. I laugh out loud and splash him. He looks cranky, but then he splashes me back and soon he begins to laugh. He doesn't laugh enough, I wish he did it more often, he has a wonderful laugh. It raises deep from his belly and echo's around the lake like music playing on the water. We swim carelessly for a while and eventually find ourselves just floating on our backs, looking up at the sky. The clouds have hidden the sun once more and the air turns cold. My exposed skin starts to shiver and goosebumps begin to rise. Seth reaches over taking my hand in his, the water around us starts to warm and my body stops shivering.

"Are you doing that?" I ask him.

"Yeah, it's one thing I can do easily, at least with warming the water I don't have to worry about setting everything on fire," he says dispassionately. "It also save's on the hot water bill," He laughs.

We continue to float in the warmer waters for a little while longer until my stomach tells me it's well after lunchtime. Walking out of the lake is harder than diving in, the rocks are slimy and each step is an obstacle. I stop and look down into the muddy water and will the earth to cover over the rocks, constructing a smooth path for me to walk on. The earth obeys immediately to my request, the rocks sink beneath the soil and the earth settles firmly into a sturdy path.

Seth follows behind me and I smile smugly at my progress. When I emerge from the lake I collect a few fallen branches and place them in a pile in front of our towels.

"Can you light them, that way we can dry off quicker?" I ask Seth. He looks concerned but does as I ask.

The branches turn to fire immediately, I settle myself on my towel and draw the warmth into my body. Seth sits beside me but not as closely as I would like.

I hand him a roll and a drink as I collect my own. We eat quietly. It's tranquil here and I feel comfortable. I don't mind him watching me eat this time. I don't care that I have a little extra fat on my hips or that my hair is a mess and I'm wearing no make-up. I'm just blissfully at ease. We finish eating and I lay back on the towel and close my eyes, I listen to our breathing and the crackle of the fire. Our inhalations begin to match breath for breath.

"So, this is mortal dating?" Seth asks.

"What do you mean?" I ask confused. "Are we dating?"

"This is what people do on dates. I know people have dinner and see movies, but this feels like a date too," he says. I look up and he's sitting close to the fire looking deeply at the embers.

"Has dating really changed that much over the last two hundred years?" I query.

"Actually, I haven't really dated before. I have seen women in my time, but I never experienced the event's you do before you sleep with someone," he says it casually and I feel sorry for him. To have lived so long and missed so much.

"You can consider us just friends hanging out if that makes you feel more comfortable," I offer.

"If we are just friends I don't think I would have this urge to kiss you," he says and he leans down to kiss me.

Even though this isn't our first kiss I'm still taken back when his lips touch mine. I wrap my arms around his shoulders. He pulls me into his arms and as our skin connects it's like fuel meeting a flame. The sensation is surreal, his passionate heat combined with mine could easily burn the forest down around us.

- 59 -

SETH

This time when I kissed Adaline it was a conscious decision, I wasn't caught up in the moment. I chose to bring her lips to mine. All week I have had to force myself to maintain my distance, to make sure I didn't look too long or touch her too intimately, but here by the lake with no one around we can be together. Her body is pressed firmly against mine and her heavenly scent clouds all my senses. Her hands are grasping my shoulders while mine are secured around her waist. The small fire I had started responds excitedly to our passion, it begins to blaze. I can feel the heat radiating on my skin and although it won't burn me I fear what other damage it could do. Being with Adaline makes me feel more alive than when I was actually human. Begrudgingly I pull my mouth away from hers, if we don't stop now it's likely I will accidentally set the whole forest on fire and I would hate to have to explain that to Deklan.

"That was unexpected," she simply says between laboured breaths. I smile and kiss her forehead.

I stand and decide it's time to get dressed before my morals lose the battle with my physical desires. Adaline follows suit. Once she's dressed she starts collecting the towels and rolls them to fit inside the picnic basket. I turn my attention to the fire and use my abilities to put it out. It's always easier to start a fire than it is to extinguish it. Same theory goes for life I guess.

"Beautiful isn't it," Adaline says looking out at the pristine lake before us.

"The most beautiful thing I have ever seen," I reply, but I'm not looking at the lake, I'm looking at her.

We walk towards the car hand in hand, when Adaline comes to an abrupt halt. She turns around and starts scanning the tree line, she lingers on a heavily bushed area at the far end of the lake. I use my vampire senses to gauge the area, I don't hear anything and my keen vision picks up no trace of movement.

"I can feel something out there," She says quietly.

I pull her towards me and hurry her to the car. When she is safely inside I join her and start the engine, we leave the lake with no signs we are being followed. Maybe she was just confusing her connection to the earth and she misjudged what she felt. Once we are on the road my anxiety eases, I reduce my speed and drive cautiously.

Adaline starts biting her fingernails nervously. I pull her hand away from her mouth and kiss it. Since meeting Adaline, I have thought of no one else. I don't like the word love, but it's the only thing I can think of to describe the way my heart aches at the thought of her. I instantly feel guilty, remembering my regrettable tryst with Shaylin in a car that closely resembles this one only weeks ago. Nothing had happened between Adaline and me at the time, but it still feels like I betrayed her somehow. Maybe I should say something?

Adaline relaxes and leans over to rest her head on my shoulder. Eventually, I feel her low even breaths and I know she has fallen asleep. I glance down at her perfect features and try to capture this moment in time.

Tomorrow we start her training with the fire elements and soon enough Florence the beast will arrive for further instruction. Before I know it, she will be eighteen and Deklan will whisk her away to court. That's when this dream will end, but it's better to have her in my life for a short time than never at all.

We arrive at the house; the other cars are still nowhere to be seen and the house sits silent. I open Adaline's door and she's sleeping soundly, all the magic she has used lately has taken so much of her energy. I unbuckle her seat belt and cradle her in my arms. Her head falls into the crook of my neck and her hand rests against my heart. I carry her inside and up the stairs to her bedroom. I lay her down on her bed and cover her resting body with a light blanket. I lean down and plant a kiss on her cheek.

"You're going to be the death of me," I whisper.

- 60 -
Adaline

I know Seth doesn't think anyone was watching us yesterday at the lake, but I have my reservations. I felt someone, I felt their distress radiating through the earth. I have tried to be vigilant ever since but I haven't felt anything sinister.

Monday morning homeroom is more eventful than I could have imagined. Apparently, Chris spent the last week telling everyone that I slept with him and apparently it wasn't any good. All the whispers and snide comments I have overheard make it clear whose side everyone believes. I wish it didn't bother me, but it cuts me deeper than it should. I just wish they knew the truth about their golden boy and what a pitiful sexual deviant he really is.

Usually music class is my favourite, but with Chris sitting behind me it's quickly becoming the worst. Just hearing his breathing behind me is making my skin crawl.

Obviously, Seth hasn't heard about my new reputation or Chris would be laid out in a body bag at the morgue by now. Which seems preferable than him sitting behind me laughing with his stupid friends. The bell finally rings and I start putting my notebooks in my bag and one of Chris's friends approaches me.

"If you need some practice I'm willing to take one for the team," he says through fits of moronic laughter. He turns back to another guy from the football team and gives him a high five. I see red.

"Actually, between you and me it's really hard to work with such tiny equipment, maybe the next girl should bring a microscope," I say loud enough for everyone to hear. Chris turns red and the girls in class giggle. Choose my battles I tell myself. It would have been a struggle to convince everyone nothing happened between us, at least I can send some rumours in his direction, maybe then he will know how it feels.

I make my way to the cafeteria and feel a little stronger in myself. Seth is sitting at his usual table and gives me a radiating smile as I approach.

Hailey and the twins whisper and pass judgemental looks in our direction but I don't care. Seth simply smiles and makes me forget all my troubles. I slide into the bench beside him and he gives me a quick kiss.

"I figured since you got lunch yesterday it's my turn," he slides over a chicken salad and a fruit cup.

"You know you paid for lunch yesterday, but thank you," I say. He shrugs his shoulders in response and digs into his mountain of meat and chips.

Lunch is over too quickly and our blissful little bubble is broken by the high-pitched sounds of bells urging us to move on to our final classes. Seth and I share the rest of our classes which I'm thankful for. We walk to class hand in hand, inside the school grounds we are safe to be affectionate and I like that Seth is making the most of it. I notice a few more judgmental glances in our direction as we walk through the halls and I can only imagine what people must be thinking about me.

"Is there something you aren't telling me?" Seth whispers.

"Childish gossip, please don't get involved," I plead. I can feel Seth's body stiffen beside me, his tension sneaking back in, I give him a reassuring smile and drag him into class.

The day doesn't end soon enough and once we pass the school gates we keep a professional distance between us, I don't even know where Deklan's hidden cameras are so he could be watching us at any moment. Deklan is going to pitch a fit when he finds out about Seth and me, but that's a problem for another day.

I change into my workout gear for my first fire training lesson. Seth and Deklan are waiting in the backyard when I arrive. Deklan has three large piles of wood evenly spaced across the yard and he has a small bunch of twigs in front of the patio. Deklan instructs Seth to start burning the twigs. He does it as effortlessly as he did yesterday at the lake. I blush remembering our stolen kisses.

"Adaline, are you paying attention?" shouts Deklan.

"Sorry," I cringe, so much for focus.

"Seth has put the fire out now, you do the same. Start it and extinguish it," Deklan instructs and waits for me to comply.

I stare at the twigs for the longest time and I feel myself becoming weak. I try again focusing all my energy on the heat and flames, a small puff of smoke emerges from the pile but the flames fall short.

Seth comes to my side and takes my hand in his. I freeze immediately worried that Deklan will sense the intimate way Seth touches me.

"You're trying too hard, fire is connected to emotion more than thought," Seth says and raises my hand out towards the pile before me. "Close your eyes and think of something that makes you angry," he says.

When he's touching me like this I can't think of anything negative. I feel safe and warm. I think about the electricity I feel between us, I feel the passion burning under my skin. The pile of twigs bursts into robust flames, Seth releases my hand from his and smiles. I feel depleted and the fire reacts to my body and fades out. I repeat my fire task three more times before Deklan relieves me. With my mind and body drained I take myself straight to bed after dinner and fall asleep with ease.

- 61 -

SETH

Adaline has been practising her fire magic for the past four days and she is gaining confidence. I have always had trouble with my abilities, my anger often overpowers me making me lose my hold on it. Adaline is different, she has much more control than I do. She is smart and learns quickly. She can already create a fireball in her hand after a few days and it's something that took me years to master. She is sleeping soundly upstairs with Aedan and Deklan just down the hall. I decide to go for a run and burn off some of my excess energy.

My foot hits the pavement and I run at human speed until I'm sure no one is around, I feel the power surge in my muscles and push forward. Even running at this inhuman speed, I can feel someone coming towards me, their speed matches my own and before he is upon me I breathe in Jason's scent.

I haven't been alone with him since the Shaylin incident at the hotel, but he has sent me updates about Adaline's location when I haven't been around so I know he's doing his job.

"Hey Seth, can we talk?" He asks. I slow down to a human jog and he follows instep.

"Has Adaline tried to leave?" I ask.

"No, she's still at home. It's actually her I want to talk about" he says. I wait for him to continue. "Who is she? I know we wouldn't be wasting our time on some human. You can trust me, Seth, you know you can," He pleads.

"She needs our protection that's all you need to know," I simply say. I hate lying to Jason he has been nothing but loyal to me since the day I turned him. He's as much my brother as Aedan is.

"Is it because the two of you are involved?" He asks.

"We aren't involved," I reply defensively.

"Seth it's me, I saw you two at the lake. I'm glad you finally found someone you can be happy with. I'm just worried about your safety," he says trying to be supportive.

I'm enraged, not at Jason but at myself, of cause he would do his job efficiently and follow Adaline's every move. I was foolish and let him see us. It was a mistake on my part. How can I deny us kissing at the lake? How can I keep lying to Jason after all he does for me? I decide he deserves the truth. I tell him everything, except the part about Adaline being the princess. He understands why the chosen needs our protection. I tell him that despite myself I find I'm falling for her. Jason gives me his oath that he will protect her with his last breath.

"It's not going to last. I'm trying not to think about it but it's always in the back of my mind. Eventually, it has to end, nothing good ever lasts," I admit.

"I disagree. Things work out the way they are meant to," he says and pats me on the shoulder. I shove him back. "Don't worry so much, you might be pleasantly surprised," he says and shoves me once more before he sprints ahead and we race back to the house.

Tomorrow night is the winter formal. All the other girls are skipping afternoon classes to have their hair and makeup attended. Adaline is skipping the whole day so she can fit in an early training session and have time to rest before the dance. I have attended school hundreds of times, but I always skipped the social events. I tried to avoid getting too close to any humans unless it was so I could make them my next meal. This is going to be a whole new experience for me. Excitement seems like a childish word to use in reference to a dance, but I can't help but look forward to going with Adaline.

By the end of our final session, Adaline has a firm grasp on her fire abilities and I'm feeling more confident that she will be able to protect herself if need be. She will need to continue to practice both her earth and fire magic to ensure her body doesn't drain so easily. In time Adaline will be an unstoppable force.

- 62 -

SETH

Last weekend I tried on a suit for the formal and ordered one of those wrist flowers everyone has been going on about, while Adaline is sleeping off her session I sneak out to pick them up. The last time I wore a suit was at the last peace treaty at court and the only reason I did that was because Aedan had forced me to. I get myself dressed and look at the tie left in the bottom of the bag and groan. I put it on and secure it tightly around my collar. The lady at the florist asked me what colour my date's dress was and I told her I had no idea. She insisted on an off-white orchid on an ivory ribbon. It's beautiful and delicate just like Adaline, I hope she likes it. We are all waiting impatiently downstairs for Adaline to make herself known. Jerry's camera is burning a hole in his hand and Deklan paces back and forth uncomfortably.

"Nervous?" Aedan whispers at my side.

"No, I'm fine," I lie. I have never been more nervous in either of my lives. Everything feels so formal, so significant. I'm worried I'll let her down or somehow ruin her special night.

My nerves are about to get the better of me when I look up and all I see is her. Adaline descends the staircase; more beautiful than any depiction of an angel I have ever seen. Her long creamy gown flows behind her and shows off her feminine figure flawlessly. Her hair is loose, but she has pinned it to one side with a crystal flower. She has minimal makeup, just enough to highlight her natural beauty. I stop breathing. Everyone gushes how beautiful she looks, Jerry is taking photos and she begins to blush. She approaches me and I'm still floored, frozen in place.

"You scrub up nicely," she comments.

"Nothing compared to you," I say honestly. She blushes again and smiles broadly. I love the way she smiles, it's always a fraction crooked which somehow makes it more perfect.

"Okay let's have a photo of you both by the stairs," Jerry asks shattering our intimate gaze. "Come on Seth get closer, she won't bite," Jerry jokes.

"Seth might," Aedan says and nudges me with his shoulder. Everyone laughs, but I'm insanely embarrassed.

"Wait," Adaline asks and she leans forward and laces her fingers through my tie. Swiftly she loosens it and removes it from my neck. She opens the top button of my shirt and fiddles with my collar. "Much better, now you can relax," she says. I may feel better without the tie, but I still can't relax, not when she's looking at me the way she does.

Once Jerry has filled his camera and Deklan is certain we have memorised all the exit strategies, they finally allow us to leave. Released into the cool night air I can breathe again. There's a crescent moon tonight, and it illuminates the sky with a ghostly white haze. Adaline's looking up at the stars, smiling to herself.

"You're beautiful," I tell her.

"Thank you. You're very handsome yourself," she says leaning forward then thinks better of it and pulls back. We still need to be cautious, the front yard is covered with security cameras and Deklan is only a door away.

I escort her to the car and hold the bottom of her dress while she climbs into the SUV, I should have hired another car, but it's too late to do anything about it now. I get into the driver's side and I remember the flower on the back seat. I lean over to collect it and remove it from its plastic casing. Adaline holds out her delicate wrist so I can slip it on for her.

– 63 –
Adaline

We arrive at the school and Seth opens my door and helps me down from the car like a gentleman. He looks so handsome tonight, I'm glad I removed his tie, it was like a noose around his neck, at least now he looks more at ease. The corsage he got me is beautiful and it matches my dress impeccably. The only jewellery I'm wearing is the pendant Seth gave me and a small clutch purse that was my mothers. Tonight, I feel beautiful, I'm comfortable in my own skin and proud to have Seth by my side. It's nice that I can fool myself into thinking I'm not my usual awkward self and if I don't trip over in this gown, I might just be able to fool everyone else too.

The school has gone all out with decorations. They have a red carpet at the front entrance that leads into the school gym. Thanks to some strategically hung fabrics and low lighting the gym looks pretty magical.

We find our seats and I put down my purse. Seth takes my hand and leads me to the dance floor. When he touches me it's distinct, a pulsating electricity that runs through my entire body, I quiver in response. He wraps his arm around my waist and pulls me close. I place my head on his chest and drink him in. He smells of heated spices like cinnamon. I think about his fire element and how fittingly it matches his personality. Seth is a commanding force of nature, he could as easily provide the warmth to sustain life or the destructive burn that could end it. I pull back and look into his coffee coloured eyes. I smile and he releases his hand on my back and spins me out onto the dancefloor. In the same movement, he draws me back into him and holds me tightly. I laugh deeply surprised by his flamboyant dance moves. He laughs along with me as I stumble on my feet, catching me each time I slip. Back in his arms, I'm safe, even from myself.

I feel my skin start to warm. I'm flushed and hot, partly from the dancing, but mostly from being in Seth's embrace. We return to our seats and discover that Chris and Hailey are seated across from us. Chris ignores our arrival, clearly preoccupied with his hand on Hailey's exposed thigh. It reminds me of the night he tried to feel me up and my body tenses. Unlike me, it's clear that Hailey likes his attention, which makes me feel sad for her.

Hailey leans forward and tells me how nice my dress is, with only a mild trace of sarcasm. I thank her and return the forced compliment. She eyes Seth beside me and stares too long for my liking. Chris has a boyish handsomeness that girls flock to, but Seth is a god among men and dressed in his suit he looks like a movie star. Hailey looks from her date to my own and I see the jealousy build in her eyes. She removes Chris's hand from her thigh and leans over the table strategically putting her breasts on display. She asks Seth for a dance and he politely declines. His quick refusal infuriates her, no one says no to Hailey, especially not a man. Then her attention turns to me and she smiles cruelly.

"I'm surprised little Addie can handle a man like you, Seth, from what I hear she finds it hard to keep up," she says. Chris bursts into laughter and Hailey leans back into him looking far too pleased with herself. Seth's hand tightens around mine and I gently stroke it trying to calm him.

"From what I hear the only loose girl around here is you Barbie," Seth replies. He looks at Chris who has become silent. "As for you, I recall the closest you got to Adaline was when she punched you in the balls for putting your hand where it wasn't wanted. I hope Barbie here knows that she is your back up plan," Seth says and pulls me back to the dance floor.

"I can't believe you just said that. My god the look on Hailey's face, you may as well have hit her," I laugh.

"They are both lucky to have their faces still attached to their skulls," he says through clenched teeth.

"They are both assholes and not worth your effort," I say and kiss him before he has time to change his mind. He relaxes into the kiss and I feel the anger leave his body. The touch of his lips and the mellifluous music lull me into a heavenly trance. "I love this song," I whisper as the music shifts.

"I haven't heard it," Seth replies.

"It's called 'Stolen' by Dashboard Confessional. Mum and I used to dance to it in the living room. She is responsible for all my fabulous dance moves," I joke, with an outstretched curtsey.

Seth smiles and spins me once more, my hearts so full, but that's when my happiness is broken. A deafening boom shatters all the windows in the gym making them implode. An invisible force propels us with the power of a hurricane. My ears are ringing and I'm disorientated. I can barely hear the screaming, I watch people's mouths moving in distorted positions as they scream for help. People are lying on the floor in clusters of glass and terror. I look around and see my classmates are all hurt and bleeding, some have large pieces of glass protruding from their bodies. I search for one person in particular. I'm lost in a sea of dark colours and I start to panic. I can't find Seth. I force myself up from the ground. I wince as shards of glass find their way into my hands and knees. I call out for Seth but I don't recognise my own voice, it's croaky and filled with fear.

The first person I recognise is Hailey, she is unconscious beside an upturned table and Chris lays bleeding beside her. I check that she's still breathing, there's a lump on the back of her head but her breaths are steady. I turn her body onto her side and make sure her airways are open. I turn to Chris, he has a huge gash on his forehead, and I rip the bottom of my expensive gown without a second thought. I fold some of the rags into a pad and secure it to his wound with another piece of my dress. I elevate his torso as much as possible and he begins to breathe more steadily. A hand closes on my shoulder and I jump. It's Seth. He looks unharmed aside from the panic in his eyes. I throw myself into his arms and squeeze him so tightly it hurts us both. He holds me firmly for a moment before releasing me.

"We have to get out of here," he screams over the chaos.

He pulls me behind him through a maze of terrified and injured people. No one has been spared from the destruction. Teachers and parents are attending the wounded, a young girl is crying over an unmoving boy whose cradled in her arms. One of the band members is hanging off the stage, I realise he has been impaled by one of the microphone stands and his once white shirt is drenched in blood.

I suppress the trace of nausea rising in my stomach. My hand and fingers are turning numb from Seth's iron grip and I struggle to keep up. We make our way through the doors at the back of the gym and the cold night air washes over me. The sounds are dulled when the heavy doors close behind us, but I can still hear the screaming in the distance.

"What happened?" I ask Seth. He doesn't respond. I open my mouth a second time, but he silences me with his hand clasp firmly over my mouth.

"Don't make a sound. We aren't alone," Seth thrusts me back against a brick wall, shielding me with his body.

Everything's eerily quiet, the only noises I hear are the elevated beating of my own heart and Seth's subdued breathing. He's looking out towards the football field, and at first, I don't see anything. Then three cloaked figures start to emerge from the darkness. As they get closer I realise the two larger figures aren't cloaked like I thought, the moonlight exposes their expansive leathery wings.

They stand at least nine feet tall and have a greenish complexion to their skin. Their ears are pointed like the elves in children's books and their long tails scrape across the grass as they approach. The smaller creature between the two monsters removes their hooded cloak. It's a woman. Tall and elegant looking with pale porcelain skin and golden blonde hair. Seth tenses against me as if bracing for an impact.

"Well, well, well, I never thought I would see you dressed in anything other than the rags you normally attire. Don't you look ravishing and who's this scared little creature you're hiding Seth?"

The woman says politely.

Seth wastes no time with pleasantries and hurls a fireball at her, one of her creatures shields the blast deflecting the fire with his bare skin. Another fireball ricochets from the beasts back like it had hit a stone wall. The wind begins to howl and swirl around us. Seth's body warms, his hands again turning to flames, he reaches forward and propels a wall of fire between us and our attackers. The woman smiles like Seth's fire is a mild amusement and not a threat.

"Seth if you stand aside and give me the girl I'll let you and your brother live. If you fight me you will die, I'm older and stronger than you. Besides I can simply remove the oxygen from the air and your pitiful flames will fizzle out," she says, her voice is firm and unwavering. She says something else, but I can't hear it because of the soaring wind and the sizzle of Seth's flames.

"Touch her and I'll rip your throat out bitch," Seth replies.

"Oh my, that's rather rude," she laughs maliciously.

Seth throws more fire at her and her bodyguards. I feel my own flames growing at my fingertips and the earth vibrates beneath my feet eager to assist. I'm suddenly aware that I have lost my shoes and my toes are cold in the damp soil. Seth turns to me and kisses me fiercely.

"Run," he says.

I turn and start running towards the trees surrounding the school. I trip on my dress pausing only long enough to rip a split in the side that would rival Hailey's. The earth moves beneath my feet clearly a path for me.

I hear Seth scream in the distance and I freeze. I thought he was running behind me. I can't abandon him. I turn and start running back towards his mottled screams. Why didn't he run with me? I enter the clearing in time to see one of the green monsters throw Seth a hundred yards away like he was tossing a pebble from his shoe. I scream out his name as someone grabs me from behind dragging my kicking body into the thick brush.

"Stop screaming they will find us," she says and I recognise her voice immediately. Shaylin. "We need to get out of here before they get a hold of you. Can you run?" She asks while helping me to my feet.

"I'm not leaving Seth. We need to go back. Please help me save him," I say sobbing between my pleas.

"We can't save him it's too late. I need to get you out of here," she says and grabs my arm. Shaylin tries dragging me away. I panic and feel the magic as a force of wind that escapes my body sends her soaring into a nearby tree. It was an accident, I didn't mean to hurt her. I run to her side.

"I'm sorry, I didn't mean it, it just happened," I plead. She stands firmly and cracks her back into place. The sound of her bones breaking makes mine hurt in sympathy. "I'm not leaving without him," I demand.

Shaylin rolls her eyes and sprints towards the football field screaming like a banshee as she runs. I follow as closely as I can, but she's much faster than me. Shaylin has already launched herself on the back of one of the monsters while Seth weakly fights the other one in the distance. The woman is nowhere to be seen. I draw strength from the earth and build balls of fire in my hands, only unlike Seth's golden flames mine burn an electric blue. At least science class taught me one thing, the blue part of the flame is the hottest. I hurdle one at each of the monsters and their attention turns to me. I build more flames and send them back in the same direction.

This time my fire scorches the wings of one beast and burns the face of the other. His face starts to resemble melted play dough by the time my flames die down. The monster screams and releases Seth from his grasp in an attempt to claw away the melted pieces of flesh from his face. Shaylin's expression morphs into something fierce as she forces her elongated fangs into the neck of the other creature. She sinks her nails into the other side and decapitates it with her bare hands. Seth falls weakly to the ground while Shaylin tosses the head of the beast to the ground before me. I run to Seth's aid as the disfigured monster flies away in defeat. Seth is barely breathing and can't hold his own weight. I hold him tightly in my arms, he smiles faintly before passing out.

- 64 -

SETH

My head is pounding when I wake. My thoughts instantly turn to Adaline, where is she? I scream out her name and kind hands caress my forehead, the hands gently sooth me back down onto the bed. My eyes are swollen making it impossible to see, but I can feel her beside me. I hear her heart beating steadily and her heavenly aroma calms my anxiety.

"Just rest, everything's okay," she says as she strokes my temples, lulling me back to sleep.

Sunlight irritates my eyes and I squint to fend it off. I tentatively open my eyes and discover the swelling has gone down and I can see again, it's blurry, but its vision. I don't bruise easily but the gargoyles that Maura used as bodyguards sure packed a wallop. I'm in my bed at Adaline's house. I position myself to stand and feel an intense pain in my left side.

I lift my shirt to find a thick layer of bandages wrapped securely around my waist. There's no blood seeping through so I rise gently. I'm halfway through pulling a shirt over my head when the bedroom door opens and I see Aedan looking dishevelled in a casual t-shirt and jeans. In his hands are two large mugs and I can smell the substance they contain. My body responds to the alluring smell of the blood and I begin to edge closer to him, my fangs emerge a little and pierce my tongue.

"Sit," Aedan gestures to the bed. I follow his instructions and sit back down. I'm too tired to fight. He hands me a mug and I drink eagerly, I snatch the second cup from his hand before I've finished the first. My body already feels stronger and I can feel my muscles beginning to repair themselves. The gash beneath my bandages tightens and starts to granulate. Soon I'll be as good as new.

"How long have I been out?" I ask.

"Two days. No one has made any further attempts on Adaline's life. Maura has abandoned her clan with a small group of followers. Samuel is closing down the Russian stronghold and bringing the remaining vampires home with him," Aedan informs me.

"What do you remember?" He asks.

"The gym exploded, I lost Adaline. When I found her, we tried to escape through the back. Maura was there, she had two gargoyles with her. They attacked and I told Adaline to run. I don't remember much after that. Any sign of Maura?" I ask.

"No, she was gone when we arrived. Adaline put up quite a fight I hear, I'm glad our training proved useful. There is something I should tell you. Are you well enough to keep an open mind?" Aedan asks, waiting for me to agree. I don't, I simply sit there silently until he continues. "Shaylin saved you and Adaline. She killed the other gargoyle and kept her safe until we arrived," he says softly. Apparently, she has been keeping watch of Adaline since she let her go.

"It's a trick. She's lying," I say venomously.

"I don't think she is. She hasn't left Adaline's side since we brought you both home. She seems to genuinely care about her safety and Adaline has forbidden us from harming her," he says.

"She's in the house right now? Get out of my way," I say pushing past him.

I gather some jeans from my drawer and put them on. I will not leave Adaline alone with that treasonous bitch for a second. Downstairs there is a lot of chatter coming from the kitchen. I find Adaline sitting at the breakfast counter with Shaylin at her side. Adaline rises and jumps into my arms hugging me tightly enough that I remember my injuries and wince. Regrettably, she let's go and gently touches where my bandages hide beneath my shirt.

"I'm sorry, I'm just so glad you're okay. I thought we had lost you," she says with watery eyes. My eyes leave Adaline's loving gaze and settle on Shaylin. Adaline positions herself to stand between us. "Shay helped us, Seth, we owe her your life and mine," she pleads.

"Oh, it's Shay, now is it? I owe her nothing," I spit. "The second you do anything that's not in Adaline's best interest I'm going to rip out your throat with my teeth," Shaylin nods in agreement.

I turn my attention to Adaline. She looks unharmed, her skin is blemish free and her cheeks are their usual blushed pink. Her eyes are tired like she hasn't slept in days. I ask her if she's alright and she assures me she is. She points out again that it's thanks to Shaylin that's she's okay. I suppress the urge to scream profanities at Shaylin and her lies. It can wait, I'll have my moment with her soon enough.

Deklan and Aedan fill me in on the details of the attack. Six people died at the high school from injuries sustained in the explosion. The cops are saying it was a freak storm and placing blame on intense wind pressure and lightning. Adaline looks riddled with guilt when we talk about the people that died. Their wretched lives mean nothing to me, but I know they mean something to her and my heart breaks for her sadness.

Jerry's excited to delve into his detailed account of how he removed multiple pieces of splintered wood from my abdomen and stitched me up on the dining room table in under an hour. Simple stabbings would have healed almost instantly but the wood Maura stabbed me with was laced with magic and would require time to heal, I'm just lucky she missed my heart.

I am acutely aware of Shaylin's presence hovering in the corner of the room and it makes me restless. She moves around Adaline like a shadow, following her closely, but never touching. She is constantly scanning the room for signs of a threat or more likely she's looking for an opportunity. I recognise these movements from the training she received at the stronghold. Her body language mimics the story she's told everyone and she would be foolish to attempt anything with all of us here, but I still have reservations.

Adaline goes upstairs to rest but not before she shoots me a warning look and gestures to Shaylin. Once she's satisfied I won't attack the evil bitch she leaves us alone. Jerry and Deklan excuse themselves and Aedan sits idly at the table drinking coffee. Shaylin remains in position at the breakfast bar, glancing every few seconds toward the staircase.

"What's your end game?" I ask her.

"I want to keep her safe, same as you," she says innocently.

"Bullshit, a few weeks ago you wanted her dead and now suddenly you want to be her bodyguard," I say.

She's standing over me before I sense her move. My reflexes are definitely deficient in my injured state.

"She spared me. She had every right to let you kill me, but she let me go. She gave me a choice and I choose to stand by her side," She hisses at me.

"I don't believe you," I admit.

"Maybe you're just worried I'll tell her about our recent history and if that's all that you're concerned about you can forget about it. I won't say a word," she whispers it to me but she and I both know that Aedan can hear. "Excuse me," she says politely and storms outside.

Aedan says nothing beside me, he continues to read his emails and drink his coffee, like he never witnessed the uncomfortable encounter. I drink another two cups of blood before I go back upstairs to rest. As I start to leave the kitchen Aedan calls me back.

"You really scared me, Seth. Adaline's not the only one who thought we were going to lose you," he says, his face stricken with worry.

"No way are you getting rid of me that easily. Now go put one of your stiff shirts on before you make me start to worry," I jest. He laughs wholeheartedly as I climb the mountain of stairs back to my bedroom.

- 65 -
Deklan

The open attack on Adaline was the final straw. The vampire Maura risked exposing us to the humans and almost cost Adaline her life. I should never have let her go to the dance. I shouldn't have let her leave the house period. It's my fault for letting her emotional needs overwhelm me, making me lenient. I know deep down that my growing fondness for the vampire brothers has also clouded my judgement, not anymore. Adaline's too valuable.

My sister-in-law Florence has been in town for the last two days and we were going to start Adaline's training tomorrow. Florence is the top self-defence trainer in court and has been one of the most sought-after private guardians for the last thirty years. Unfortunately, she has restricted her training techniques to royals only and I had to pull some strings to hire her without divulging Adaline's true identity.

Thank god for family. I send her a message and ask her to be ready and waiting for me tonight. She replies with a simple yes and I reserve myself to what needs to be done, I only pray that Adaline can forgive me.

- 66 -
Adaline

I haven't slept more than an hour since Seth was injured. I have spent the last two nights by his bedside waiting for him to wake up. He stirred the first night and I settled him back to sleep to heal. I'm trying not to be too angry with him for his behaviour this afternoon when he saw Shay, I can understand his hesitations, but he doesn't know her like I do.

Shay has been through hell. As she sat by Seth's bedside with me she told me of her past. Her maker used her sexually until he no longer found her amusing. Then he bit her and left her for dead. She awoke a monster, not knowing what she truly was. She killed aimlessly for years, living a life where she never trusted anyone and when she was accepted into the clan she thought she had found her home.

Sadly that wasn't so. She divulged the secrets of the previous clan leader and his horrific mistreatment of his people. I don't even know if Seth and Aedan knew how bad it was before they inherited the clans. Seth was the first person who was kind to her and it broke her heart when he couldn't love her in return. When Shay explained her history with Seth I felt guilty like I had stolen something from her, but Seth's love was never something that belonged to her and she knows that.

If Shay was the monster people thought she was, she wouldn't have held my hand as I cried over Seth's broken body. She shared my sadness and fear. I hugged her tightly when Seth woke that first night and I felt the change within her. Affection had returned to her heart and the fondness she felt for me was genuine. At that moment, I realised what she really needed. She needed a friend, she needed someone she could trust and depend on. I knew that night that I could be that for her.

I cast a look at the bed I have made for her next to mine and I'm pleased with the decision I made. There's a knock on my door and I almost stumble over myself to answer it, but it's only Deklan. He's standing there holding two bottles of water dressed in running gear.

"Princess, would you like to accompany me on a run before bed. You have hardly slept since the attack and I think it will help ease all the worry you have been carrying," he asks.

Even though I'm exhausted I agree and tell him I'll meet him downstairs. I change into my running gear and put on a light jacket, the temperature has dropped rapidly since the night of the attack and I wonder if we will get snow this Christmas. I tie my hair back and tuck my necklace under my shirt.

Deklan is fast, but I can tell he's holding back for my benefit, I urge myself to go faster but my body is too tired to respond the way I want. We've been running at a high speed for half an hour when Deklan stops and hands over a bottle of water. We sit down on a bench so I can catch my breath and I drink eagerly. The cold water is refreshing and my body starts protesting to the vigorous exercise I forced upon it.

"The attack should never have happened princess. I'm sorry I let you down," Deklan says.

"You didn't let me down, I'm okay," I tell him. The pendant under my shirt begins to warm. "Deklan, somethings wrong," I start to tell him.

"I'm not risking your safety anymore princess. Please forgive me," he says.

I try to respond but my tongue starts to tingle and turn numb. My muscles become weak, the drink bottle I'm holding falls from my grasp as my arms turn to jelly. I try again to speak but my mouth won't work. I try to gain control of my limbs but fall short, I try to scream. My body is paralysed and I feel myself falling asleep. I force my eyes to stay open as long as I can, but no matter how hard I try, I can't fight the urge to sleep. The last thing I remember is the destroyed look on Deklan's face as he scoops me into his arms. I focus on the deep blue-black of the night sky behind his head and the twinkling stars floating light-years away, my vision fades. Darkness.

- 67 -
Deklan

The sleeping potion I added to the water bottle worked as quickly as promised. Adaline feels like a small child cradled in my arms, her body is limp, but she is breathing comfortably. She will be asleep for at least eight hours before she needs another dose. I wish I didn't have to drug her, but I know she would never come willingly. She wouldn't leave behind her uncle or Seth, not after how close they have become. The affection she feels for him was written on her face the night we arrived at the high school. She was covered in mud and blood; her dress had been torn and her hair was a wreck. I was dazed with fear at the sight of her and all she cared about was Seth. She nearly died to protect him, we should be dying for her not the other way around. He makes her weak.

Florence pulls up in a non-descript sedan in muted colours, exactly as instructed.

I gently place Adaline in the back seat and secure a belt around her waist, I cover her with a blanket and make sure she is comfortable. She is going to hate me when she wakes up, but I can't burden myself with those worries now.

"So, who's the kid?" Florence asks in a rough voice.

"Not your concern. Drive," I tell her.

Once we are on the interstate I dump my cell phones out the window and open a new one I purchased this morning. I contact Theo to inform him that we have left without incident and our plans remain in order. Even he doesn't know where I plan to take Adaline. I thought it best that only I knew of the location of the island. It takes us three hours to arrive at the secluded airport and we board the jet. My team is waiting for me on board. Theo had them dispatched the evening of the dance. I realised that night I needed more than some luck and vampires to protect Adaline. There are five men on board including myself. Adaline and Florence are the only females. Once Adaline is secured in the small bedroom in the back of the jet I leave her to sleep and address my crew.

It was a struggle to decide who would accompany on this mission. Florence was essential. I selected my right-hand Wren, who has worked alongside me for countless years and his trainee Jackson. Both are loyal to Theo and me. Theo requested that he sent his personal healer along to aid us, an elderly man named Wilber who stands four feet tall and is more wrinkled than my fingers get after a long bath. I welcome each member of the team on my way to the cockpit where the final member of our team waits. He is the person I'm most nervous to greet. He is also the one person I want to see above all else. I open the cockpit door and his back is to me, he has his headset on and is readying the jet for take-off. His golden hair has turned sandy since I last saw him. He has cut it short at the sides but he still has some length on top. His shoulders are broader than I remember and even under his shirt, I can see how toned and filled out they have become. He tenses briefly sensing my presence behind him.

"Son, it's good to see you," I say softly and he turns.

"Deklan. If you give me the coordinates we can take-off before the rain sets in," Tripp says formally.

I can't blame him for being mad at me, last time we spoke we said things we shouldn't have and having him gone from my life these past few years has been difficult. It's made me re-evaluate everything I did wrong raising him. I pushed him too hard, I didn't hug him as often as I should and I never told him I loved him. I was too distant and now I'm forced to suffer for my poor choices. I can't help but hold out hope that maybe this mission will give us a chance to reconnect as father and son, or at the very least start fresh as friends.

We are coming up on the seventh hour of our flight and despite the poor weather the flight has been smooth. Adaline could wake within the hour so I excuse myself to give her a secondary sedative to keep her calm until the plane lands. The last thing I need is her starting a cyclone while we are in the air. The end of the flight is drawing near and my son's silence unnerves me. He was never a quiet child. He always talked back and fought me at every obstacle, defiance that reminded me so much of his mother. He sits beside me now as a stranger, a young man who wants nothing to do with me and I can't help but see his mother in his eyes. The next few months will be tiresome if this silence continues.

- 68 -

SETH

Aedan wakes me in a panic a little after one am. Adaline and Deklan had gone for a run hours ago and still haven't returned. Adaline's phone was in her bedroom and Deklan's number is going straight to voicemail. Jason is nowhere to be found and he's not answering his phone either. I drag my still wounded body out of bed and search for Shaylin. I'm sure she has something to do with this, I knew she couldn't be trusted. Jerry frantically calls the hospitals and the human police looking for any sign they have been in an accident. When Aedan can't find Shaylin or any signs of struggle we begin to fear the worst. Aedan tracks their scents to a small park a few miles away. A bench by the running path is soaked in Adaline's floral scent, it lingers across the street then vanishes into thin air. They must have gotten into a car.

I feel the same hopeless panic arising in me reminding me of the first time Adaline was taken. What if she's died while I've been sleeping, someone could be hurting her right now and there's nothing I can do to stop it. I can't afford to spiral into a panicked depression right now. Adaline needs me and I'm going to find her.

"We need to find Jason and Shaylin," Aedan says. We run back to the house to search Deklan's room. We are almost at the front door when Aedan's phone rings. "Where are you? I see. Was she injured? Okay, remain on course, follow closely but don't let them know you are on their trail. Text the coordinates and we will meet you," he snaps his phone shut. "Deklan has taken her. Shay and Jason followed them and are tracking the vehicle," he explains.

We make it to the interstate in record time, Jason is still following the car, but Aedan and I have trouble catching up. Jason calls us when they arrive at a small airfield and the plane takes off before they get close enough to stop it. By the time Aedan and I arrive at the airfield, the plane and Adaline are long gone. Jason is pacing in a panicked state that I'm familiar with while Shaylin sits carelessly on the bonnet of the car waiting for us.

"Why didn't you call sooner?" I yell at Jason.

"There was no cell service. It's lucky we followed them this far. If I hadn't been following Shay we may not have even found out she had been taken until the morning," Jason explains trying to pacify me.

"You had something to do with this," I turn to Shaylin. My rage is exploding and it demands a victim.

"No, I didn't, I was keeping an eye on Adaline. Your lapdog followed me, we were fighting and that's when Deklan put Adaline in a car. We stole the first vehicle we could and followed," she explains.

"I didn't want to risk crashing the plane with gunfire, but I was able to get one shot off," Jason explains. "I hit the wing with one of our tracking darts. The only problem is that it's small and will only work once their altitude decreases, then we should receive the signal. We just have to wait," Jason says.

I have never truly valued Jason's organised personality until right now. Unfortunately, all any of us can do at this point is wait and waiting has never been a strong suit of mine.

I close my eyes and remember the day at the lake. How Adaline's skin glowed as she floated through the cool waters, the sweet innocent smile on her face when she splashed me. I think of her giggling beneath the mirrored ball at the dance as I spun her round and round. I refuse to allow that to be the last happy memory I have of her, it's not enough. I need more. I'll find her no matter where she is and I'll dismember anyone who gets in my way.

- 69 -
Adaline

My minds swimming through a fog and by the time it finally clears I have no idea how much time has passed. When I'm able to sit up unassisted I'm horrified to discover I am dressed in a long sleeve silk nightdress that falls just below my ankles. This isn't the work out gear I was wearing the last time I was conscious. Suddenly I remember how I became unconscious in the first place. Deklan drugged me, he put something in my water. I vaguely remember him carrying me from the park bench but then nothing. On further inspection, I am relieved to find I'm still wearing the same underwear I had on when I left the house and my body doesn't feel like it's been tampered with. At least whoever took the liberty of changing my clothes has left some things to the imagination.

The wrought iron four poster bed that's encasing me must have once been painted white, now it's chipped and flaking. It's surrounded by velvety red and cream drapes that are skillfully tied to the base of the posts, making me feel like I'm wrapped in a comforting cocoon. The sheets are made of the softest silk and feel weighty against my skin. The thick feather quilt is cream with small scattered roses that match the drapes. If my captives have gone to this much effort to make me feel at ease I hope it's a sign that they don't plan on killing me, at least not straight away.

The large wooden door opens slowly revealing an older man with greying hair and a clean-shaven face, in his hands is a silver tray. My body is still not entirely my own, I press myself against one of the bedposts and ready myself for an attack. The man looks bemused by my stance and gently places the silver tray on an ornate table by the door and gives me a graceful bow.

"Milady, your breakfast is here and Deklan will be up to speak with you soon," he says cordially, he bows low once more before he exits the room. I hear a heavy lock closing on the other side before his footsteps disappear down the hall.

I approach the silver tray cautiously, but it appears to contain nothing sinister. A single serve bone china tea set, a generous serving of mixed berries and other fresh fruits. There's even a gold embellished bowl with a large serving of thick creamy yoghurt. My stomach growls in annoyed anticipation, my stomach might be easily fooled, but my mind will not. I tell my stomach to shut up and ignore the growing hunger pains. The last thing Deklan gave me was laced with something unseemly. How can I possibly trust anything else he has to offer? The only cutlery they have provided me is a spoon, which can hardly be used as a weapon against a werewolf and its gold, not silver.

Distracting my mind and stomach from the delicious offerings I assess my surroundings. The room is large but only contains a bed, a tall closet, an elegant chaise by the window and the table by the door. There's another door at the back of the room, I tentatively turn the handle prepared to find resistance but the handle releases easily. Inside is a claw foot bathtub, a sink and toilet. I notice there is an array of body washes and soaps. A new toothbrush still in its casing and some toothpaste. The small window above the bathtub has bars on the outside and is bolted shut on the inside.

I make my way back into the bedroom, the large windows behind the chaise are locked in the same fashion as the bathroom and have thicker bars. This is my prison, my own gilded cage. I might be able to melt the bars if I could use my powers, but every time I try to access them I hit a wall, no matter how hard I try I can't push past it. They have obviously done something to block my abilities. There's a knock at the door and I recognise the soft rattle as Deklan's, he has a distinct knock, assertive and gentle. He enters with a small smile on his face, he looks aggrieved and I'm glad.

"Adaline I'm so sorry I had to do this, but it wasn't safe for you any longer and I had to get you out of there," he says. He sounds sorry and I can feel the guilt burning in him, but I don't care I'm too angry.

"What about my uncle? What about Seth and Aedan. You just left them there. What if people come looking for me and find them. They could be killed!" I scream. "You drugged and kidnapped me. You were supposed to be my friend."

I forget my bodies weakened state and march toward him as I continue to scream a list of blasphemies that would make my uncle cringe. He steps back as I invade his personal space, I wish I was a foot taller so our eyes would be level. I stare up at him with all the rage and hatred I can muster, he finally nods and leaves.

How could he expect me to be okay with this, he was supposed to be my friend and he lied to me, took me from my family? I will never forgive him if something happens to any of them. I pick up the silver tray and smash it into the bedroom door, I pick up the table it had been resting on and send it the same direction. It shatters into pieces, but I only feel mildly better. The bedroom door unlocks, my ruckus must have attracted some attention. Deklan has returned carrying a cell phone in his hand, he holds it out toward me. I pause a moment careful not to be misled by his games. He places the phone into my hand and says I have three minutes.

"Hello?" I ask unsure who waits at the end of the line.

"You have no idea how long I've wanted to hear your voice. I'm so glad you're safe and soon you will be home with me and our people," the voice babbles. It takes me a moment to register whose speaking. It's him. My father, he's gushing like a fool and I feel nothing towards him. There's no instant connection, just the voice of a stranger, another person who's happy to break my trust at their will.

"I want to go back home and I want you to make it happen. Deklan has no right to hold me prisoner like this. If you ever want me to even consider coming to court you will send me home," I demand.

"I'm sorry, but your life is too precious and I won't risk losing you a second time. Your birthdays not far away and then you can come home to me," he says.

"I am never coming home to you," I reply, hanging up before he can say anymore, the last thing I need is promises from someone I can't trust. The first conversation I have ever had with my father and it was nothing like I had hoped. Deklan reclaims the phone immediately.

"Adaline I'm…" Deklan starts to say, but I cut him off with a wave of my hand.

"Don't you dare speak to me, you are not my friend. You're a liar and I hate you," I scream at him. My words must cut him deeply because he flinches like he has suffered a physical blow.

"Forgive me, princess. There's a guard at the door if you need anything, just ask. I will not lock the door again, but I urge you not to do anything ill-advised or you will force us to restrain you," he says glancing at the destroyed table and the smeared food on the floor and sighs deeply. "You really should eat something. I'll have them send some more food up for you," he says as he closes the door.

I begin to sob angrily, Jerry will be so worried about me and Seth is still recovering. Oh god what if Seth hurts Shay, I just pray that Aedan will be able to hold them together until I get back home.

- 70 -
Tripp

The flight with my father had been agony, the man could freeze a volcano with his personality. I spent almost eight silent hours next to him, if I hadn't been flying the plane I would have jumped out the emergency exit just to get away. The day I turned eighteen was the first time I was able to make my own choices and it didn't matter what my father wanted. I was eligible to enlist in the royal guard and deep down I guess I thought it would finally make him proud of me, instead he just seemed more disappointed than ever. I was a constant reminder that the love of his life was dead and he was left looking after me.

I was surprised when King Theodore asked me personally to be a part of this mission. I only have a month left of training and then I will be dispensed to the royal guard. I could be stationed anywhere. After graduation, I will finally be free of my father and the shadow he casts.

Aside from the fact that the king asked me personally, I only accepted because of what he promised once the missions successfully completed. He promised me first rank in my graduating class and first preference of my posting. There's no way I could pass up an opportunity like that.

The air felt lighter when we'd stepped off the plane. As we walked down the dusty road it was evident the grounds had only recently been tended. The small island is beautiful and the old estate is enchanted and inviting. It reminds me of the boarding houses at the training academy, built of wood and stone, in a time before power tools. The small mansion has character in every corner, I could almost smell the blood, sweat and tears that went into building it. I was pleasantly surprised that the estate has a small stable out back with two strong stallions ready for riding. Horses have been a passion of mine since I was a child. My fondest memories of my mother are the stories she would tell me before bed. The horse spirits that would roam the forests through the night, granting wishes and spreading magic, but always disappearing just before the break of dawn. The lost unicorn was always my favourite.

Sadly, my attention was pulled away from the stables as I watched my father carry a small girl up the front stairs of the house and into a large room that had fewer furnishings than the rest. I assisted him to change her into her nightgown before placing her into bed. His eyes glared red when I lingered too long at her half-naked body. I abruptly changed my line of vision and focused on the number of roses on her bedding. My father probably thinks I'm a pervert as well as a disappointment.

At breakfast this morning we were debriefed. My father informed us that Adaline Thomas was under the court's protection and we are her assigned guards until it is deemed safe for her to be returned to her family. He never said what family she belonged to, but she must be high up to warrant this kind of protection detail. I asked him what type of fae she was and her abilities so we know what we are up against. He was rather vague and said she had powers of the earth and fire. It's not uncommon for our kind to be gifted with two elements and in very rare cases there have been some who could channel three. This girl is hardly eighteen and she already has access to two powers, I could only imagine the problems we would have if she had a third element.

My father's bedroom is next to hers and he has insisted that every member of our team is to make her feel safe and welcome, but it's imperative she not be allowed to leave. The girl has refused her meals all day and I could see the worry start to grow on my father's face. If only he cared for me as much as he does this girl. He always did favour his work over family. After reviewing an excessive amount of safety strategies and wards, my father is finally sleeping soundlessly in his room and I have been put on the night shift.

With everyone sleeping the old house is quiet and I feel lonesome. At the academy, I couldn't throw a stone without hitting one of my classmates. The hour's pass and I find myself more frustrated and start pacing back and forth. I decide to make the most of my shift and meet the girl my father values more than his own son.

- 71 -
Adaline

I refused the supper they delivered a few hours ago and the night is dragging on. My hunger strike seems to only have an effect on my stomach, not my captives and the hunger pains are making me rethink my strategy. The sun has long since set and the night sky is breathtaking. There is a haze of broken clouds I can see through the darkness, I watch as they drift over the golden moon that hangs just above the treetops. I'm transfixed on the stars that burn brighter here than back home, I'm suddenly homesick for the dimly lit galaxy outside my bedroom. I find myself wondering if someone else might be staring at the same sky at this very moment and in a small way we are still connected. Lost in thought and sadness I barely notice the presence appear behind me. The hairs on the back of my neck begin to stand and a nervousness washes over me. I turn slowly to discover a young man standing by the bed.

"Did you want something or are you just watching?" I ask spitefully.

"You seemed upset, I didn't want to intrude. Deklan has sent me to try and convince you to eat something," he says unconvincingly. I can sense his curiosity floating in the space between us.

"You can tell him I said to shove it," I say boldly and he laughs.

"Do as you please it's no bother to me, I can say I've done my job," he replies. His green eyes glisten under the pale moonlight and his golden hair looks angelic. There's something familiar about him that

I just can't put my finger on.

"Can you tell me where I am?" I ask innocently.

"You're on a private island roughly eight hours from Dallas. There are no boats if that's what you're thinking. The only way to leave is by plane, which won't be back to collect us until the New Year," he says. "If you change your mind about something to eat Deklan has gone to bed. We can raid the kitchen and he would never have to know," he says with a small smile.

"Thanks, but I'm sure you would tell him anyway," I say.

"Not likely, I like seeing my old man unnerved. I wish I had that effect on the bastard," he jokes.

"There's no way Deklan's your father, you're practically the same age," I remark. I know it's impossible, but the more I look at this young man the more I see Deklan looking back at me. They have different coloured hair and their eyes aren't the same, but they share a quality. A mannerism I can't name, but it's there.

"Perks of being a werewolf, they can pick and choose when to stop aging, he stopped aging when I was a child. I take after my mum, she was a wood sprite. Our aging slows, but we don't stop aging altogether. At least I look old enough to drink, other fae aren't always as lucky," he admits. I can't help but smile.

"Deklan told me your mother passed, I'm sorry," I tell him. I see the same sadness in his eye's that Deklan had when I found the picture of his wife.

"I'm on watch outside if you change your mind about dinner. Night," his smile vanishes and his face turns cold.

I feel a little less hopeless as I lay down in the silk sheets. Maybe Deklan's golden-haired son could be my way off this island and back to Seth.

- 72 -
Tripp

Four hushed hours pass as I stand by her bedroom. I linger in the silenced corridor, with little to keep my attention. Occasionally I take a seat but then my legs feel restless or my eyes turn tired and protest. Everyone's sleeping, I can hear my father snoring in the next room as he falls deeper into slumber, the sound practically vibrating the estate's foundations. I'm just about to go in search of a radio when I hear the creaking of wooden boards. Someone is tiptoeing across their room, suddenly the large door behind me opens, just a crack. I turn to find Adaline still in her nightgown peeking through the small gap. She appears relieved to see me and opens the door wider.

"Patrick, right?" She asks.

"You can call me Tripp," I say simply.

"Would you really not tell Deklan if I had something to eat, the food on the floor is starting to look appealing," she asks.

I smile and nod, I gesture for her to follow me towards the kitchen. At first, she peers down the long hall like I'm setting her up to fail. When she sees we are alone she leaves the safety of her room and follows me to the kitchen. I open the fridge and pull out some grilled chicken left over from our dinner, I also grab some fresh bread the cook had baked for breakfast, some butter and mayonnaise. I set to work making a sandwich while she sits silently at the old wooden table. The fresh bread smells like heaven and I decide to make myself one as well. When I'm finished preparing our meals I place a plate in front of Adaline and sit across from her. I bite into my food first and then she follows suit. She eats so quickly I begin to worry she will choke and I'll have to administer CPR. Which wouldn't be an unpleasant experience for me, I imagine.

"Should I make you another before you steal mine?" I tease. She slows her bites and swallows the oversized mouthful.

"Sorry," she says as she takes a more delicate bite. I slide the other half of my sandwich over to her and stand to make another. "Is there any tea?" She asks.

I fill a pot with water and put it on the stove, I gather the assortment of teas the cook has purchased and set them on the table with a teacup. Once the pot boils I fill a small teapot and place it in front of her. She studies the impressive collection of teas I have laid out and finally decides on a fruit one. It smells sweetly of pomegranates and strawberries. She blows on her hot beverage allowing the steam to rise around her. She glances up, aware that I'm watching her closely.

"Any chance there's a phone here," she queries.

"Afraid not. He even took everyone's personal cells. Looks like we only have each other to talk to for a while," I say. She smiles uncomfortably and despite her earlier boldness, I can tell she's shy.

"Sorry about that," she sighs. What could this girl have done to be in such danger? She hardly seems the criminal type and I have never heard her name mentioned at court. I find it hard to imagine someone wanting to see her come to harm. "Do you know why I'm here?" She asks as if reading my thoughts.

"For protection," I state simply. It's not my job to know all the details, despite my absurd curiosity.

"Yes, that's what Deklan keeps telling me. They want me to be their queen, but they hold me prisoner. Secretly tucked away because I'm no use to them dead. They don't care what happens to the people I love as long as they get to decide what's right for me," she says and her eyes start to water.

"The only way to be queen is if you marry a Talbot, but King Theodore doesn't even have an heir for you to marry so I don't see you being forced to be queen anytime soon," I say.

"Oh, he has an heir, she's sitting right across the table from you," she sighs, no hint of humour in her voice.

The Talbots have governed the Seelie since the end of the dark ages and every time the royal line changed succession it was a male Talbot heir. When I was a child, the queen gave birth to a daughter, the kingdom threw banquets and balls in celebration, but the princess was murdered in her bed.

I look deeper at the porcelain-skinned girl sitting across from me and I see King Theodore's eyes peering back. Her skin, her hair, everything about her I recognise from either the king or queen. Now that I see it, I can't focus on anything else. Adaline is the princess the kingdom lost all those years ago.

"Holy shit," I say without thinking. The surprise escapes my lips before I can think better of my language. My future queen sits less than a meter away from me and in a nightgown and socks no less. In a hundred years, I never would have predicted this.

"Holy shit sounds about right," she echoes.

- 73 -
Adaline

Maybe I shouldn't have told him my secret, he seemed uncomfortable when he walked me back to my room last night. Perhaps he was just disgusted by the way I swallowed my food whole, he was pretty quick to offer up the rest of his meal to sauté my appetite. There was another man in his place when I peeked out my bedroom door this morning. Tripp's probably sleeping days so he can watch me at night. I can't believe Deklan is Tripp's father. I feel a little bit sad for Deklan. It's clear they don't get along and I remember the way he looked at the photo of his son as a little boy. I shouldn't be feeling sorry for Deklan after the way he has treated me but I can't help myself.

After thoroughly checking the bathroom for hidden cameras and finding nothing unsavoury I take a particularly long bath. Opening the enormous closet, I'm bombarded with heavy gowns of all colours and fabrics.

The type of clothing you would wear to a medieval festival, not something you wear to breakfast with the people holding you prisoner. I tighten my towel to my chest and open my bedroom door boldly. The man at the door seems bewildered by my attire and stands aside to let me pass. I call out for Deklan twice before he appears. His expression is hard as stone and he stares me squarely in the eyes. I return his glare with all the force I can muster.

"Where are some normal clothes? You can't seriously expect me to wear these dresses, I doubt I could even tie them properly," I say.

"Those are appropriate clothing for your station and we don't have any more to offer," he explains. I'm about ready to drop my towel in protest, but luckily it doesn't come to that.

"You can borrow some of my things. I'll get you some t-shirts and I have a few sweatpants that might fit you," Tripp offers as he strides up the hallway toward us.

I simply give Tripp a smile and nod my thanks before returning to my room.

Once I've sifted through a drawer in the cabinet I find some underwear they have supplied which thankfully isn't as old-fashioned as the dresses. They are free of embellishments and plain in colour, but they are comfortable and serve their purpose. There's a knock at the door so I adorn my towel once more. Tripp enters with a small pile of clothes. He glances at me nervously before becoming captivated by my window.

"Thank you. Your dad is seriously outdated in the fashion department. These will be great," I assure him.

"Yeah well you should have seen the stuff he made me wear as a kid," he laughs but doesn't look me in the eyes. "Do you like horses?" He asks.

"I don't know I've never been around horses. Why?" I'm surprised by his question. I have never given horses a second thought. Mum and I always lived in large cities so the closest I have been to a horse was watching black beauty when I was eleven.

"There's a stable here and I thought if you wanted I could take you riding?" He asks. I watch him carefully. Is he asking me to keep me busy or is he trying to be kind? "Since we're both stuck here we might as well have a little fun," he adds.

I agree to his offer and excuse him so I can get dressed. The clothes are baggy, but thanks to the drawstrings in the pants I feel certain they won't fall off and finding my runners in the bottom of the closet is a saving grace. Before I have a chance to head to the kitchen for breakfast someone brings to my room a tray with bacon, eggs and a small pot of the fruit tea I enjoyed last night. I devour every bite, who was I kidding. There's no way my hunger strike would last. By the time I stop to breathe I have made myself sick, overfilling my stomach in the process. Tripp promptly arrives at my door to escort me to the stables. He nods to a guard who disappears into another room. Tripp walks ahead and I follow him closely, making sure I take in all my surroundings.

The house is as impressive outside as it is in, it has a vintage quality that I find agreeable. We walk down a small stone path for a few minutes until we arrive at a wooden barn. It's a little run down and the paint has faded, but the structure is strong. Tripp pushes aside a large sliding door to expose two striking horses. There is a brown coloured beauty and one the colour of sand. I approach the sand coloured one slowly, afraid it might bite. My fingers are about to stroke its head when he bucks toward me and I jump back in shock. Tripp laughs behind me.

"He won't bite, he was just eager for you to pat him," he continues laughing at my unease. Tripp steps forward and takes my hand in his and laces my fingers through the horse's mane. It's coarser than I expected, but as I move my hand along his neck I realise the hair coating his body resembles silk beneath my fingers. The horse leans into me impatient and longing for attention.

"He's beautiful. What's his name?" I ask.

"Apollo," he says.

"Makes sense, the god of the sun. Can I ride him?" I ask excitedly.

He answers with a smile. Tripp teaches me how to saddle Apollo and shows me basic techniques for riding before we take the horses out of the stable. Apollo is so large Tripp has to help me climb onto him. I place my foot between Tripp's hands and he hoists me up, once my leg is over and I'm positioned securely in the saddle Apollo starts his tour of the grounds. Tripp chases after us offering occasional instruction as needed and before midday, I'm galloping alongside Tripp with ease.

- 74 -
Tripp

Riding was more enjoyable than I expected. Adaline wasn't afraid of falling and took to the horses naturally. She was reluctant to stop but I assured her we could ride whenever she wanted. I taught her how to brush down the horses after the ride and it's evident she isn't afraid of hard work. Apollo was as fascinated with Adaline as I am, his steady gaze watched her every movement and I swear I could hear him sigh with sadness as we left. She hugged him tightly and promised she would return. I leave Adaline in Wren's care while I shower and change.

Dressed in a fresh set of clothes I find myself checking my reflection more than once in the mirror as my thoughts drift to Adaline. I'm aware a princess can't date commoners or even members of the royal guard but technically no one knows she is the princess yet, maybe there's a sliver of hope.

I arrive at the kitchen a few minutes before Adaline. As she enters, the cook makes his annoyance at our tardiness known. The stout little man starts to swear in French and complains about timing and preparation. I'm about to lose my temper when Adaline bats her eyelashes at him and places a gentle hand on his shoulder.

"I'm very sorry, it was my fault we were late, I just couldn't resist the horses. You don't have to make us anything extra I know you have been working tirelessly. Why don't you go take a break and we can fend for ourselves," she says. The cook's expression softens and his eyebrows lower a fraction. He glances towards his pristine benches and hesitates. "We will clean up I promise," she offers. The cook smiles charmingly at Adaline before taking his leave. "Sit down I'll make us something," Adaline says to me.

"No, I'll do it, it's not your place to be cooking," I say.

"This may come as a shock to you, but I have been cooking for myself for years. I have also cleaned toilets and done my own laundry. What I would really appreciate is if you would just treat me like a normal person. Don't make me regret telling you who I am," she says, her brow set and determined.

"Of cause Adaline. So, wench, what are we having?" I ask playfully.

"I'll surprise you, can you set the table?" She says smiling brightly as she sets to work.

I start fixing the table, taking my time placing the plates and utensils. Adaline sings to herself absentmindedly and I'm in awe of her, her grace and beauty leaves me speechless. She is wearing no make-up and her hair is tied messily above her head, the clothing I lent her is far too big and it does her figure no justice. Despite her attire, she is the most ravishing creature I have ever seen. She begins to dance while tossing things on the stove and I sit patiently watching her. I know her creation is finished when she ceases dancing. She turns towards me carrying two large plates, I can smell the alluring aroma of garlic and freshly squeezed lemon.

"I hope you're not one of those people who hates carbs," she says and she places the dish in front of me.

"I have no issue with carbs," I say. "I don't think my father would approve of a princess waiting on me, just another disappointing quality he can add to my list I guess," I admit.

"I don't think he's disappointed in you. I think he's hurt," she says while swallowing a mouthful of pasta.

"I never did anything to hurt him," I say coldly.

"I don't claim to know everything between you guys and I'm definitely the last person who would be sticking up for Deklan right now, but I saw the look in his eyes this morning. He loves you and I think he's angry at himself," she offers.

"This really is delicious, who taught you to cook?" I ask to change the uncomfortable subject.

"My mother, my adopted one, was a sensational cook. I would usually only make this for her and I on nights we planned to stay home, because of the massive amount of garlic, but there's no chance of kissing anyone tonight," she laughs.

"Well it's still early, you never know," I say without thinking. I laugh and try to shrug off my flirtatious comment.

"I'm seeing someone," she says softly.

"He's a lucky guy and don't worry I was only joking," I say. We both know I'm lying but it's easier than admitting I just got shot down.

- 75 -
Adaline

The last thing I wanted to do was to hurt Tripp's feelings but saying nothing and leading him on would have been worse. He said he had only been joking but there was an unmistakable hopefulness that swept across the table and I could almost touch it. He insisted on washing up after lunch and I accepted without argument, we both needed some time alone.

On my way back to my room I arrive at Deklan's door, it's slightly ajar. The hallways are unoccupied, so I press my ear to the open door. I listen intently, there are no sounds coming from inside the room. I ease the door open cautiously and call out his name, I wait for a response but it's obvious the room is empty. I tiptoe inside, a floorboard creaks under my weight and I freeze, scared that someone will catch me snooping where I shouldn't be. I quietly shut the heavy door behind me.

Deklan's room has more furnishings than my own but remains free from personal clutter. His suitcase sits by the bed, I remember the guest room at my uncle's house and the way Deklan's suitcase always seems abandoned. His shoes are expertly lined up by the door, I bet if I measured they would be exactly two inches apart. I believe the military would approve.

I hastily open the chest of draws nearest to the door and come up empty-handed. I move on to the bedside dresser and find myself with better luck. In the bottom drawer, I find five cell phones but that's as far as my lucky streak goes. Deklan has removed all the sim cards and batteries that are nowhere to be found. I continue looking through the drawers only to find deodorant and other toiletries until I stumble upon the photo of Tripp and his mother. Deklan had hidden it between two washcloths and in my haste, I almost missed it. I see a happy little boy holding his mother's hand tightly and I think back to the man who sat across from me during lunch. My heart breaks for him, the loss of his mother and his absent father. It's no wonder the light in this little boy's eyes can't be found in the man I know. It must have been hard for him losing her so young, I'm thankful I had as much time with my mother as I did.

"It's rude to go through someone's personal belongings," A gruff voice booms from behind me. I turn to see Deklan's bulky form consuming the entrance, I hadn't even heard the door open. His eyes are nowhere near as angry as his voice suggests.

"I'd say I'm sorry, but it would be a lie. Being abducted seems to make a person lose all sense of propriety," I reply.

"Will you ever forgive me?" He asks as he sits on the bed beside me. "I never did it to hurt you. When Sarah first took you home she would send me messages every day while I was in the mortal realm. She was worried you weren't eating enough, weren't sleeping enough, she even sent me a few photos of your bowel movements when she was distressed by the colour," he laughs and I can't help but laugh alongside him. Mum was always an over-sharer. I loved that about her. "I found it hard not to think of you as part of me. I watched you grow and made sure you were always safe, even if you never knew I was there. After the attack at the school, I couldn't accept the thought of you coming to harm. After your birthday if you decide you don't want this life I will support you," he says.

"I would feel better if you let me call my uncle, he will be worried sick. If you care for me the way you say you do, then you can imagine how he is feeling right now. If you let me call him I promise I won't run. I'll stay here until my birthday, as long as I know they are all safe," I say. As heartbreaking as it is my family is probably safer if I'm not around, it's better if people are looking for me and not them.

I wait patiently for Deklan to decide, I can see the battle inside him and I'm praying his heart will overrule his head. He slides a hand into his pocket and removes a large phone in a rubber casing. I look at it curiously, I hadn't given the phone much thought when I spoke to my father, but looking at it now I realise how different it is. It's bulky with thick buttons and a large antenna sticking out the top.

"It's a satellite phone. One call. Three minutes," he says gruffly.

I hug him tightly and take the phone. I dial my uncle's mobile number and wait an excruciatingly long time for the phone to connect. I almost give up hope that he's going to answer until his weary voice speaks on the other end, he sounds broken.

"Uncle Jerry," I whisper, unexpectedly I'm flooded with love. This is how I should have felt when I spoke to my father, but the truth is Jerry means more to me than any stranger ever could. He begins to cry and makes mumbled noises. It's taking him too long to calm down and I'm running out of time. "Jerry, I only have a minute," I plead.

"Are you safe? Has he hurt you? Where are you?" His questions are a blur and I force myself to focus on the important information.

"I'm safe. No one has hurt me. I love you so much. Please don't be angry, but I've decided to stay here until after my birthday. It's the only way I can keep any of you safe. If anything happened to you I would never forgive myself. Tell Aedan and Seth I'm sorry," I say through a steady stream of tears.

Jerry begs and pleads for me to come home, he tells me he loves me and would rather die than lose me, making me cry harder. Deklan signals that my time is almost up when I hear another voice at the end of the line. Seth shouts my name with urgency.

There is so much sentiment and longing in his voice I can hardly keep myself together. I open my mouth to respond, but the timer disconnects the phone. I collapse and start to weep uncontrollably.

- 76 -
Deklan

Adaline sobs into my shoulder. I pull her a little more tightly into my embrace, letting her expel all her sorrows. Allowing her to make that call went against all my training and better judgement, but the sadness in her eyes broke me. I don't know what I was thinking. I thought it would help her but instead, she's destroyed. The longest time passes before her tears subside, she takes a few deep breaths into my chest and eventually, I feel her erratic breathing beginning to steady.

"Thank you," she whispers.

"Your welcome. I really am sorry about everything," I tell her. Maybe Adaline will forgive me one day. She lifts her head and awards me a small smile. Her smile is all the proof I need to know I made the right choice. As she stands to leave she turns and hands me the photo I keep. I hadn't noticed she still had it cradled in her hand.

"You should make it right with him before you miss your chance," she adds and disappears into the hall.

I glance at the photo of my son and wife. My beautiful bride looks at me knowingly and I know she would be disappointed with how I have behaved. I cannot miss the rest of my son's life, I've already missed too much. I put the photo back in its hidden place where it will remain until I can look at my wife and know she would be proud of me. I make sure Wren is keeping watch of Adaline and I go in search of my son. I find him in the stables grooming one of the horses. The horses start to buck and stamp their hooves as they sense my presence, Tripp offers me a disgruntled glance before returning his gaze to the upset beasts.

"Do you need something Deklan?" He asks coldly.

"I wanted to thank you for doing a good job with Adaline. You convinced her to eat which is something considering how stubborn she is and even the horse activities seem to have improved her mood," I tell him.

"Just doing my job," he says without looking at me.

"Listen, son, I know things between us haven't been good," I start to say.

"That's what happens when your dad is a prick and disappointed that you weren't born a wolf like him. But the truth is dad, I just don't care anymore. I don't care that you hate who I am and I don't care that you hate that I joined the guard. Let's just get this mission done and then we can go another three years without speaking," he yells, storming off before I can say another word.

Can he honestly think I hate him that much? I love him more than anything in the world. When he turned eighteen and his woodland powers emerged I was relieved. I didn't want him to be a wolf like me. Werewolves are lesser beings in the fae community and his mother gave up her noble born station when she married me. I had always hoped my son would have an easier life than I had, maybe his grandparents would have welcomed him into his noble birthright and he would have been protected. He gave up any chance of that when he joined the guard.

The phone in my pocket rings, its annoyingly high-pitched tone penetrates my sensitive ears. A disgruntled Florence is on the line, we dropped her at a nearby port as a potential escape plan until I was sure the island was safe. I give her the location of the island and a list of items I require her to collect. She will arrive tomorrow before midday to start Adaline's training.

- 77 -
Tripp

That stupid smug son of a bitch. My whole childhood he was never around and when he was he was callous and constantly undermining everything I did. I don't even remember the last time he praised something I did. Now I'm an adult and ready to move on with my life and he wants to play happy families. The trees begin to quiver reacting to my fury, the wildflowers wilt and the blossoms close themselves tightly, cowering in fear. I breathe deeply calming the rage inside me. I can't believe I finally stood up to my father. I told him I didn't care what he thinks of me and I wonder how much truth my words actually contained. I reach down to the flowers that have hidden themselves from me and stroke their petals. They glow under my touch and open brightly. I cast my powers over the wilted wildflowers and they grow back in abundance, carpeting the ground in a blanket of blue.

I kick off my shoes and wander towards the wooded area. I feel better here, I'm connected to everything. I feel the trees breathing life into the world and the grass beneath my bare feet absorbs everything it touches. The circle of life flows around me and I'm soothed. I walk the perimeter of the estate and find myself drawn to a window. I peer through the dusty glass and see her sleeping on the bed. Neither of us slept much last night and the riding must have tired her out. Watching her sleep, I'm suddenly aware how prowler like this is, like a villain from fairy tales watching an unsuspecting princess sleep. I linger on the curve of her body and the slight parting of her lips as she breathes. She has made it clear she's not interested in me, but that doesn't lessen my growing attraction toward her. I tear myself away from her window before my imagination runs wild on me.

- 78 -
Adaline

Last night I had worn myself out crying, the only positive part of my mini-breakdown is that I slept like the dead. I woke this morning feeling rested thanks to my unbroken sleep. Knowing that Jerry and the others are safe has lifted a weight of worry from my shoulders. Deklan may be right about this being the safest place for me. A couple of months isn't really that long and if I'm not with my family at least I can be comforted in their safety.

I brush my wild hair and clean my teeth vigorously, I dress in another outfit provided by Tripp. I can smell him on his clothes. His scent is different from Seth's. Tripp smells of raindrops and fresh cut grass, like the morning after a storm. Where Seth radiates warmth and spices. My stomach does a little flip as I take in his fragrance once more, my thoughts turn to Seth and I feel guilty. As I remove Tripp's shirt from my body I shiver as I imagine his hands tracing over my nakedness. I scold myself and my devious thoughts.

I search through the outlandish outfits in the closet until I find the least extravagant dress. It's a soft emerald velvet with small capped sleeves and a sweetheart neckline edged in lace. It clings to my curves highlighting my figure and the small train slithers along the floor like a snake in my shadow. My jade necklace is cool against my skin, I take strength from it and steady myself. I need to be stronger than I am, not just for myself, but for the people I care about.

The kitchen is full when I enter for breakfast. Tripp is laughing loudly with Wren's apprentice, whose name has escaped me. Wren and Deklan talk in hushed tones more out of habit than secrecy. A small chubby man I have not met with petite round glasses sits quietly reading a leather-bound book that looks too large for him to carry comfortably. The cook I met yesterday is hurriedly moving between the stove and oven juggling pots and pans. The room falls silent as everyone's eyes dart toward me. I smile nervously.

"Princess, aren't you looking lovely this morning," the small man says. "I'm Wilber princess, your father's personal healer. I am much honoured to make your acquaintance," he says lowering himself from his chair. He takes my hand in his and kisses it gently.

"Thank you," I reply.

"Please sit by me princess," Wilber offers the empty space between him and Tripp. I lower myself into the seat, careful not to touch Tripp. I feel his body tense beside me. Perhaps he's still upset after yesterday.

"I guess the cats out of the bag," I joke.

"No point hiding your identity when you start divulging your secrets to everyone you meet," he says. I blush feeling stupid. "I see you decided to wear one of the gowns," Deklan remarks.

"I was restricted in my clothing options," I reply.

The cook continues to shuffle around behind us while the table of men talk softly to one another. I sit uncomfortably, unsure what to say. I begin to fidget with my necklace and chew absentmindedly on my fingernail that has chipped. The cook startles us all when he drops a pan on the floor and starts hissing loudly in French. Before anyone else moves I'm out of my chair helping pick up the spilt eggs. The cook appears taken back by my assistance, he's more nervous than he was yesterday with me. I guess being outed as a princess will do that to people.

"Oh, princess don't do that, your hands are not made for cleaning, leave the help to his duties," Wilber says dismissively as he waves a limp hand towards the cook.

"I think I'm capable of deciding what my hands are capable of and I would appreciate you showing a little more respect," I say pointedly. Wilber's expression turns volatile and screams disapproval. I glance to Tripp who is suppressing a smile and then to Deklan who is not attempting to suppress anything as he openly laughs.

"Forgive me, princess," Wilber says reluctantly.

"I'm not the one you owe an apology to," I say turning to the cook who has turned red in the face. "What's your name?" I ask the cook.

"Bach, miss," he answers quietly.

"Lovely, like the musician. Would you mind if I make the eggs and you can handle the rest?" I offer.

"Thank you, princess," he smiles broadly.

I start making a fresh batch of scrambled eggs while the menfolk go about their business. I'm happy to have something to keep my hands busy, but I still feel someone's eyes burning into the back of me and it makes me edgy. I glance over my shoulder and Tripp's eyes hold mine in place. Bach bangs another pot and I'm drawn back to my task.

Breakfast is delicious. Bach has made the most exquisite French pastries I have ever eaten, not to mention the other various hot delicacies he has cooked up, sadly my eggs are dull in comparison. Deklan is discussing plans with Wren about a delivery that is supposed to arrive today. Tripp and Jackson are trading stories from their time spent at the academy and Wilber sits silently stewing, still reeling from my earlier chastising. The chatter begins to die down and people begin stacking plates and getting ready to carry on with their daily duties. I wait patiently as people start to head off to their tasks, but no one has told me what I should be doing today so I turn to Tripp.

"Can we go riding today?" I ask. He looks from me to his father.

"It's fine, but she will need to be back by midday for lunch and her training session will follow after," Deklan says.

"I'll be training again?" I comment.

"Yes, Florence will be here soon and she will be your trainer, be safe on those beasts Adaline," Deklan says with a firm squeeze of my shoulder.

"I will," I reward him with a smile and I feel the warmth return to it. Regardless of my anger at Deklan's deception, I know my own heart and its willingness to forgive him.

Tripp and I walk side by side to the stables, the soft sounds of my dress scraping across the stones is the only sounds we need. Tripp had asked me if I wanted to change but the only other clothes I could have worn were his and I didn't want his scent lingering on me. I insisted I can ride in the dress and I'm confident that I can.

I hear Apollo grunting before we open the door to the barn. When I step inside he rears his head up and starts turning in excited circles, like an overexcited oversized puppy. I reach out and hug his head to me, whispering compliments in his ear.

"I have never seen a horse act so affectionately, he's almost human. He really likes you," Tripp says.

"The feelings mutual. Besides who wouldn't love Apollo, he's the most beautiful thing in the whole world," I say as I scratch behind his ear. He snickers in response.

"Horses have always been a passion of mine, my mother used to tell me the old stories before bed," he says fondly. I smile encouragingly. "The lost unicorn was always my favourite tale. My mother would tell me of a golden-horned mare who would aid travellers in need. She is the mother of all horses, the first of the race. She would heal the wounded if they were worthy and return lost soul's home. She hasn't been seen in centuries. Mortals lusted for her, they tore apart forests, hoping to capture her and use her powers for their own selfish ways. Eventually, she vanished, she was last seen in the Mores in England. That's when the magic in mortal forests died," he says gloomily.

"That's so sad, why on earth is that your favourite story?" I ask.

"Because she's lost not gone, eventually when mankind is worthy of her magic she will find her way back to the forest. Nothing is ever really gone. When I channel the forest I feel everything, life and death, it's all connected and there is still hope," he smiles sweetly and my heart flutters for his romanticism.

I find straddling Apollo easier this time even in the dress. I know the shape of his masculine physique and where to position my weight comfortably. The longer we ride the more my body anticipates his movements. Time goes too fast and before I know it the sun is set high above us and Tripp is signalling to slow down.

"It's time for lunch princess and we can't be late or Deklan will have our heads," he says. Apollo grunts his disapproval at Tripp, echoing my own emotions. We slow down and take our time returning to the stables. "You sure did put Wilber in his place this morning. I don't think that's happened in over a hundred years," Tripp laughs.

"I didn't mean to be rude but he treated Bach like a slave and that doesn't sit well with me," I explain.

"It's clear you didn't grow up in our world. At court, if you're not royal or one of the noble families you may as well be a slave. Not many royals are like you princess," he explains.

"I don't understand that kind of thinking, as far as I'm concerned one life is not worth more than another because of an accident at birth," I add. "Do you know what Florence is like?" I ask, thinking of my upcoming training session, what if she's horrible.

"She's my aunt actually and she's as badass as they come. She is the toughest trainer in the Vale. I haven't really had much to do with her since mum died. She was mom's half-sister so she was an outcast as far as my mother's family was concerned but my mother and she stayed close," he says.

I give Apollo a little tap with my heel and gallop toward the stables. As much as I don't want to leave the beautiful beast I'm excited to start training again. When I had trained with Seth and Aedan I liked how it made me feel. I liked knowing I could defend myself and when the attack happened at the school I wasn't able to help as much as I wanted to. People died because I wasn't strong enough to protect them. I refuse to let that happen again. I won't be a victim and no one else is going to die because of me.

- 79 -
Adaline

Tripp stayed behind to tend the horses so I could have lunch before training. By the time I walk back to the house my legs are brittle. My normally unused muscles have had more exercise than I would have thought from riding. Bach offers me an ample array of lunch selections but I select a small serving of designer fruit salad as I still feel breakfast rolling around inside me. The house is tranquil, a gentle breeze has begun forming outside making the old house creak and moan. I could be happy here, hidden away from the world. I wouldn't have to worry about kings and queens or duty. I could spend my days riding Apollo, swimming in the ocean and eating anything the cook plates up for me. It's a nice dream, but I would miss my family too much. I think of my uncle and the vampire brothers I left behind and my heart aches.

I wonder how they are getting on without me. I hope Seth and Shay aren't biting each other's heads off in my absence. I take comfort knowing Aedan is there keeping them in line and he will be looking out for my uncle as well. Once my birthday has passed I can see them again and hopefully start a new life. Maybe Seth would run away with me, we could have a quiet life in a home like this. An image of Seth forms in my mind, he's smiling at me as he spins me across a dance floor made of gold and candles flicker in the darkness. He doesn't smile often enough but when he does the world around him lights up. Without any provocation on my part, my mind fades to an image of another smile, a smile of a young man with golden hair and evergreen eyes. His smile is warm and open, it needs little encouragement to shine. I sigh deeply and force the images from my mind. It's getting harder to deny that I find myself attracted to Tripp. As if sensing my inner thoughts Tripp enters the kitchen and informs me that his aunt has arrived. I try hard to hide the blush from my cheeks when he looks at me but I sense my body's betrayal. I feel an intense heat growing on my face as he hands me a small bag containing ladies leggings and a few t-shirts. I run to my room and change quickly, glad to be rid of the cumbersome gown.

I'm not sure what I was expecting of Florence, but a warrior goddess wasn't it. She is just as stunning as the photo of Tripp's mother. Tall and blonde with perfect cheekbones. The only visible difference between them is the multitude of pale scars across Florence's body. She is only wearing a pair of denim shorts and a black singlet so her arms and legs are exposed. Even across her chest, I can see faded scar lines along her collarbone. The marks look like someone has taken a cheese grater to her limbs and chest but they never went deep enough to cause major harm. Even with her scarring, she is still glorious to look at. Her figure is well toned and her stance proud. I feel tiny when she takes my delicate hand in hers.

"So Deklan tells me you have fire and earth elements," she says. Straight to the point and I'm grateful that she doesn't address me as a princess. I like her instantly.

"Yes, I also have the use of air," I add remembering my accidental attack on Shay.

"You never told me that," Deklan says.

"We had a lot going on," I reply.

In the chaos after the attack at the school, my fluke use of air elements had escaped my mind. I was too worried about Seth and trying to convince everyone that Shay was an ally. Since being on this island I have found my abilities blocked so I haven't even had a chance to test it. While Deklan and Florence talk about my training regime I decide to test my abilities. I feel that same block I had a few days ago, but its weaker and this time as I push against it until I feel it crack. A switch inside me flicks and I can sense everything. Each element more intense than I remember. I feel the earth vibrating around me, and I can feel the air breathe life into everything like a song. The heat of fire burns inside me brighter than the sun.

I reach out my fingers towards a bare patch of dirt and grass sprouts at my will. I push a little harder and a small rose bush creeps from beneath the soil, elongating until a yellow rose blooms brightly. My earth abilities respond quicker and I feel I have more control. Air is harder to manipulate since my experience is limited. I focus as I did with my other abilities and soon I can feel the pull of it.

The air around me takes on a colour, a golden shimmer floating in and out of focus. I form a gentle breeze, building it slowly. My breeze catches died leaves in its path and they dance before me happy for the attention. The dancing leaves encircle me, the cool wind rushing against my skin. I focus on the passion I felt for Seth, the heat rising from deep within me. The leaves start to smoke before bursting into flames. The air keeps the flames spinning around me like a glowing cocoon of fire. I'm enthralled by my new-found control and can't help but laugh out loud.

"How much training has she had?" Florence asks Deklan as she watches me intently, her eyes bulging.

"Two weeks," Deklan responds with a laugh.

"Girls got talent. Okay, Dek I can take it from here," Florence says dismissively.

Tripp was right about Florence. She is a badass. She doesn't just focus on my abilities either. She has me run laps of the estate until my legs can no longer hold me and then she makes me do more push-ups than I can count.

After hours of her intense training, I'm ready to die, I feel like I could vomit if I cough too deeply. That's when she strikes a hand at unarmed combat. No weapons or magic. She explains that I need to be able to fight when every part of me is broken when I have nothing left to give. When I think everything is lost she demands that I find the will to fight.

At first, my punches are weak and timid but after an hour of her flawless instruction, I feel confident with my throws. It's gotten dark by the time we finish. As we enter the kitchen everyone is sitting ready for dinner. I give them a wave and drag my sorry ass up the never-ending hallway to my bedroom. I barely make it to my bed before passing out.

- 80 -

SETH

I've hardly slept since Adaline was taken. Most nights I have spent walking around her room, flipping through her books, listening to her music, continually looking deeper for something I have missed. Anything to make it feel like she isn't gone. Too often I find myself praying to a god I know doesn't exist just wishing for her safe return. I can't remember the last time I prayed, then again Adaline has made me do many things I never thought I would. I miss her. I miss everything about her. I would gladly have her back fighting every decision I make; if it meant I could see her again. Aedan assures me we are on the right track and Jason is closing in on her location. I hate to admit it but even Shaylin has been diligent in retrieving the information we need to find Adaline. Poor Jerry has spent most of the time in a mild coma, only sleeping and eating when Aedan has forced him to. At first, Aedan had to use compulsion on him just to get him to rest, now we can shuffle him around like a puppet without any magical assistance needed.

When she called the house a few weeks ago I had expected her to tell us she had escaped and was waiting for us to collect her. Instead, she had told Jerry she was staying where she was for our safety. The others thought that her captives forced her to say that so we would stop trying to find her, but I know better. I saw it in her eyes when she came back for me at the dance. Love, it will be her undoing. She loves us all so deeply that in her mind staying away keeps us safe, no matter how much it hurts her. Adaline's selfless and that selflessness will get her killed.

Her absence is making me tense, I'm snapping at everyone who's trying to help. My friends aren't the only ones who have taken a thrashing from my tantrums, Jerry's house has lost multiple cushions and a few lamps to my feverish outbursts. I glance over to one of the mangled teddy bears that usually lives on Adaline's window seat. One of its eyes has melted into a miss-shaped teardrop, an ear has melted completely flat and the once white bears head his blackened and charred. I can feel the fire begging to be released from my fingertips to finish off the stupid stuffed animal and melt its idiotic smile when Jason and Shaylin enter abruptly.

"We have her," Jason says with a sigh of relief.

- 81 -
Tripp

Aunt Florence has never been the type of woman who discriminates and Princess Adaline is no different. I watched her first week of sessions until my aunt decided if I could watch, I could work. Sometimes that has meant physical combat or using my earth element offensively. The hand to hand combat I enjoyed because it often meant Adaline was pressed up against me in positions that sent my imagination wild. The first session I held back constantly afraid I would hurt Adaline by mistake.

This only seemed to piss her off and then I remembered her saying that she wanted to be treated just like anyone else. I didn't hold back after that but I did struggle with my attention. Yesterday I froze when I had her locked against me and my lips were inches from her glistening neck.

My mind was spinning in a million directions but then she elbowed me in the groin and I came hurtling back to reality. I have always believed strongly that a man should never cry in front of a woman especially one they are interested in, but that strategy went out the window when my genitals were embedded in my stomach. Turns out crying in front of a girl isn't bad after all, once she stopped her victory dance and realised I was in actual pain she was by my side hugging me with apologies.

Deklan has agreed to give Adaline a break on weekends which is fair since her sessions with Florence are basically full days now and she's been working harder than I ever have. Before I know it, a month has past and I can hardly remember a time before Adaline was a part of my life. I shudder as I conjure up a world without her in it and I'm filled with dread.

I promised her we would spend the day with the horses and she is already eating breakfast in the kitchen when I arrive. She is wearing one of the outfits Florence brought with her, nothing extravagant, simple dark shorts and a pale blue singlet. Regrettably, the blue singlet draws my attention to the marks on her body. Her perfect fair skin is marred with bruises in various stages of healing.

She has purple and blue fingerprints on her arms and the trace of a fading black eye on her left lid. She smiles broadly when I enter, my breath catching in my chest before I smile back. She radiates power and strength but she's still as delicate as the evening when I watched her sleeping all those weeks ago.

"Morning sunshine," she grins.

"You're happy this morning. Is it the fact you don't have to train or is it just being in my presence that's brightened your mood?" I smirk.

"Actually, Deklan said this evening I could call home, he has even worked out some extra security on the phone so I have more than three minutes. It has felt like a lifetime since I've spoken to them," she says happily and continues fiddling with the strange food in her bowl.

"Do you think Deklan will let you call your boyfriend?" I ask. I've become so comfortable with Adaline I keep forgetting to filter my thoughts, the last thing I want her to think about is her boyfriend.

"I think he is still staying with my uncle, I can't imagine him leaving until I'm home," she adds softly.

"Loyal guy," I say coldly. It's my own fault for asking. Her face dulls, I know it's because she's worried about my feelings and my harsh tone didn't help. How can I be mad at her when she made it clear from the start we would only be friends? "What are you eating?" I ask in a brighter manner. I look down at her bowl and it looks like fruit, but it doesn't smell like fruit.

"It's spiced fruit salad, with a whipped creamy filling all wrapped in puff pastry. I mentioned to Bach the other day how mum and I used to have it at least once a week from this deli in Portland and he surprised me with it. Want some?" She offers me her spoon heaped with pieces of mango and strawberries dripping with whipped cheese and flakes of pastry. I take the fruit in my mouth and I can't help, but wonder if this is as close as I will get to being able to kiss her. There's almost a floral flavour to the fruit puff and I'm positive it's the taste of her lips lingering on the spoon.

Once we clean our breakfast plates we race to the stables. I have always been a quick runner but Adaline's just as fast and I only beat her by a second. Apollo's excitement is seeping through the ground and I can feel the earth tremble with anticipation. I know Adaline can feel it too by the way her face lights up. It's hard to believe she has the power of three elements and she even mentioned being able to sense others emotions. After she told me about that ability I have tried keeping my emotions bound tightly in my chest if I don't keep myself in-check she will know everything I'm feeling for her, and I am not ready to be that forthcoming. Today we are riding out of the estate's grounds and down to the shoreline. I've only been to the shore when supplies have been delivered and Adaline hasn't been down at all. The horses slow as we reach the sand, they enjoy splashing their hooves in the water. Adaline looks out thoughtfully toward the ocean and I wish I could tell what she's thinking. I wish she was thinking about me but I can't have everything. My heart aches for her affections, an indulgence I will never claim as my own.

I look up at the clear blue sky, wishing for a life and a love different than this. The clouds start floating across the ocean, they start out white and welcoming until they settle overhead. They begin to turn dark and ominous, moving at an unnatural speed. The ocean starts to swell and foam with force, as it starts beating down on the sand. Before I can react, a wave rises up as high as the tree line and breaks down on us. The water weighs into my lungs as it consumes me, the pressure trying to crush my chest. I grasp for air but only find sickly salty wetness. I struggle to reach for the surface, kicking feverishly against the brutal waters. I can't hold the pressure at bay any longer my mouth fills with iced water, it cools my throat as it tracks down into my chest, and my lungs turn heavy and cold. The ocean swallows me.

- 82 -

Adaline

The horses are loving the water and I love the sensation as the cool droplets splash against my bare skin. Apollo and I are further out than Tripp who is waiting in the shallows. If I let Apollo have free reign he would have us swimming across the ocean. I can't stop thinking about how wounded Tripp felt at breakfast. Even now his pain is skipping across the ocean's surface like a stone. My ability to sense other people's feelings has been growing stronger and I no longer need to rely on touch to know what's stirring inside of them.

A thought is all it takes and I can pick up a glimmer of what's inside their heart. Tripp's emotions are broadcasting loud and clear. My heart aches with his agony and I feel the guilt building. Guilty for a number of reasons.

Tripp and I have become closer, I feel myself caring for him more than I want to admit and that makes me think of Seth. I hate myself for letting another man enter my mind let alone my heart. There's a war raging inside me and if it keeps building at this speed I'm going to explode. I don't realise I'm crying until I taste the tears on my lips. I also didn't notice how dark the sky has become.

Apollo rears his head as the ocean descends upon us. My abilities react before my mind can process what's happening. Apollo and I are enclosed in an impenetrable sphere. We are able to breathe but the violent waters around us thrash forcefully beating against our unyielding bubble. I wait anxiously for the onslaught to end.

Apollo's panicked breathing is almost lost to the sounds of the thrashing sea, I wrap my arms around his neck and squeeze tightly, settling him under my touch. The ocean begins to calm and we can see the sky once more. As the threat against us fades the sphere dissolves and I look around frantically for Tripp. I spot his horse stumbling further down the shore, but Tripp is nowhere to be seen.

I jump down from Apollo and I use all my abilities to reach out to him. I find nothing in the earth so I reach out further. Fire and air find nothing and I start to sob. I feel the draw of the ocean calling out to me, wanting to soothe my tears. I plead and beg for the ocean to bring him back to me. Another wave starts forming and I prepare myself for the attack, but instead, a limp figure is floating along the wave's peak. The ocean is fast but gentle as it washes Tripp's body onto the sand. I shake him frantically trying to wake him from his slumber, but he's not breathing, his lips have turned blue and his face is void of colour. I draw strength from all the elements around me, willing their power to bring him back but it's not working.

I feel his chest with my hand and I hold my ear to his open mouth, silence. I clear his mouth and tilt his chin to open his airways. I'm alone and no one will hear my cries in time to help me. I hold his tilted head firmly between my thighs and begin compressions on his chest. I hear my mother's training gnawing in the back of my mind, by the time I reach my count my arms and shoulders ache.

I feel the broken bones beneath my palms as I press into his chest. I start compressions again, begging all the gods in the heavens to help me save him. I see water rise into his mouth. I pull back as he coughs and reaches forward. He falls back against the sand weakly. He can hardly keep his eyes open and his face is stricken with fear. I draw him to me hugging him tightly, I'm so thankful he's alive. He pulls back feebly and stares into my eyes. I feel passion erupt in his chest. Lust illuminates my senses, every inch of me tingles, I can't be sure if it's his feelings or mine. I don't know who moves first, but his lips are pressed firmly against mine. A crystal clear calm washes over me as I fall into the kiss until he starts to cough and lowers himself back to the ground.

- 83 -

SETH

It had taken longer than I expected to gather the details of the private islands occupancy. Magic has been useless and we have had to rely on old-fashioned detective skills to determine which one is Adaline's prison. The boat we hired looks more like a luxury yacht, Aedan thought it would give us a better disguise to mingle amongst the rich and famous that rent the local lands. Attached to the side of the boat is a small dinghy with a sturdy motor that can carry us to shore. Aedan orders the anchor to be dropped as we are within range. Once the anchor is in position Aedan and I get ready to board the dinghy. Jason and Shaylin agreed to wait aboard to keep watch over Jerry. Aedan wants us to sneak in and remove Adaline secretly so there's minimal bloodshed. I agree, but I would rather burn the whole island to ashes.

We climb into the tin can and I hope it's safer than it looks. Aedan starts the motor and directs us toward a small overgrown docking area. The motor is louder than I like and I'm worried it will give away our position, but it's soon drowned out by the thundering sound of crashing waves. The sky is filled with darkness and thunder and our little boat begins to rock. Almost as suddenly the sky turns bright again, no trace of clouds in sight. The water is steady and calm. Then I hear it, a painful scream that stabs at my heart. It's the sound I have dreaded, the sound of my nightmares. Adaline's cries have escaped my dreams and entered my reality.

Aedan turns the boat in the direction of the distress. It won't move fast enough and I shuffle to the front, my body is almost hanging in the water desperately inching closer. We pass a thick brush of trees, I see a wounded horse limping away from the shore and another horse the colour of the sun stares down at a figure on the beach. As we edge closer I see it's not just one person, but two.

My heart shatters as I come to terms with the vision before me. Adaline is embraced in another's arms; another's lips are touching hers and everything inside me shatters. The man collapses back onto the beaches sand and her head turns toward us. Her glowing eyes finding mine in a single breath.

- 84 -
Adaline

Seth hasn't been able to look at me since they pulled into shore, his inner voice screams random abuses of hatred and disappointment towards me. How could I have been so callous? Playing games with his feelings like that, after everything he has been through to keep me safe. My emotions are so mixed up, I'm feeling everything and nothing all at once. My powers are out of control, I almost killed Tripp, I let myself get swept away in my worry and it almost cost him his life. The relief keeps playing on my mind, I was so overwhelmed when he woke up and his feelings were so strong. I still can't entirely claim the feelings as my own or if I just reflected his own desire. Deklan was beside himself with distress when he found us on the beach. Tripp was so weak and Deklan put blame on the vampires, convinced they were the cause of his son's harm. I'll never forget the disappointment I saw on his face when he learned the cause had been me.

Deklan agrees that everyone can stay, it's too risky to let them leave in case they are being watched. Seth is quick to volunteer to collect my uncle and the others from their boat. He wants nothing more to do with me, my heart starts drowning in sorrow and my eyes threaten tears.

Aedan hugs me tightly, trying to ease my anguish, but between Deklan's disappointments, Tripp's near death and Seth's hatred I can't help but be consumed by it all. Their feelings are open wounds in my soul and my own guilt is the vulture pecking and tearing at the gaping flesh. Aedan begins introductions and while everyone is busy with the chaos I slip away to my room. I shed my clothes and discard them in the bin. I want nothing to remind me of this day or the damage I have caused. Florence has loaned me more than enough clothes and I'm grateful for some familiar items, even dressed in my jeans and warm jumper I'm still shivering with sorrow.

A bright golden light outside my window catches my eye, I stand to see Apollo peering through the glass, despite my heartache I smile at him.

I creep through the house, my footsteps hidden by the loud voices shuffling into the foyer. By the time I reach Apollo and stroke his beautiful mane I feel less fractured. I walk him back to the stables, carefully checking his stride as we walk.

"At least someone has remained unharmed by my actions," I tell him.

He leans into me, tucking his head over my shoulder. His affection warms me and my heart feels lighter. We take our time making our way back to the stables and I'm thankful for the stillness of the moment. The only person's emotions troubling me right now are my own. I reach the stables and find two empty stalls, I remember Tripp's horse is still roaming around the grounds injured, once Apollo is settled I'll go find him too.

I brush Apollo down briskly after removing his riding gear, he's unhappy when I latch the stable door. He begins circling in his stall, panting wildly. Somethings wrong with him, he starts stamping his hooves into the door, each time harder than the last.

The door begins to splinter and crack until the hinge comes loose and Apollo is free, I back up against the stable frightened what he might do. Apollo pushes me aside as he makes his way out of the stable, he neighs loudly and the sound almost pierces my ears.

A large green figure emerges from the trees, but Apollo is too fast and the creature's disbelief gives Apollo the upper hand. He rears up on his hind legs and tramples his imposing hooves on the creature, the green beast tries to stand, but Apollo keeps him down. Black blood starts seeping from the creature's face and torso as it cowers under the impressive stallion. Unmoving it lays dead among the grass, the hatred and pain it carried absorbing into the earth. I'm frozen in shock. Apollo returns to my side and nudges me, waking me from my paralysing fear. His legs are stained black with the monster's blood, there are twinges of red from scattered gashes and cuts that cover his body.

"We need to warn them," I say distantly. Apollo lowers his head, I hold onto his mane and pull myself onto his back. I wrap my arms tightly around his neck and he gallops toward the house.

- 85 -
Tripp

Wilber's tonic is speeding up my recovery and my connection to the earth can do the rest. No matter how healed my body feels it's hard to forget the sensation of drowning, in my mind I'm still numb and breathless. Adaline saved me. She breathed life into me more than once today. When I open the living room door it's filled with people, the vampire brothers I met on the beach are talking to my father with raised voices and a human man at their side. The dark-haired brother looks like he's trying to kill me with sheer will. Wonder what crawled up his ass? Aedan the blonde brother is friendlier and once he's finished talking to my father he begins introducing Adaline's human uncle to the group.

He ushers in two more vampires, one male and one female who has as many scars on her body as my aunt. I watch quietly as everyone talks amongst themselves.

Adaline's uncle asks where she is, it's obvious that he couldn't care less about pleasantries and he's eager to see her. I look around curiously, but she's nowhere to be seen.

"I'll go get her, she must be in her room," I offer. The brooding vampire snaps his head toward me.

"I'll accompany you," he says aggressively.

As we walk down the hallway I can feel his eyes burning into the back of my skull. I haven't spent much time with vamps but this guy is unreasonably aggressive even for their kind. Aedan seems like a noble fellow and the other two didn't appear too bad. Maybe this guy is just an asshole.

"How long have you known Adaline?" I ask politely.

"Longer than you," he answers. I turn to face him; his fists are tightly clenched at his sides and his jaw is set.

"What's your problem?" I ask.

"Might be the fact you were kissing my girlfriend a short time ago and I'm trying not to snap your neck," he grunts.

"Wow, a vampire. I kind of assumed her boyfriend was human, never thought a princess would slum it that low," I laugh.

His eyes flare red, I've hit a nerve. He slams me into the wall, his hand is pressed against my throat. My neck begins to warm, no, not just warm it's on fucking fire. I can smell my flesh starting to sizzle under his grasp and I struggle to breathe. I punch him in the throat and he releases his grip. My body falls weakly to the floor. I cough wildly trying to expel the aroma of burnt flesh from my nose and throat. My neck stings and throbs viciously, I can feel blisters starting to rise. I lurch forward to fight him, but the window behind me shatters and an enormous gargoyle towers over us both.

The vamp starts throwing fire at our attacker, I call the trees outside into action, and their branches stretch through the window wrapping around the gargoyle. The fiend is losing the fight, the vampire's fire is making him weak and my branches trap him in place. The vampire jumps forward for the final blow. He rips out its throat with his teeth, spitting the black blood and mangled patch of skin to the floor. The gargoyle shrivels as it turns to stone before crumbling in front of our eyes.

I run to Adaline's bedroom with the vamp close at my side, we open the door and find her room empty. Her ocean-soaked clothes sit in the trash bin by the door, her window is open, but the bars are still in place. We call out to her with no response. A roar of screams is unleashed and the sound of breaking glass explodes from the front of the house. The vampire makes it to the foyer first, but I'm close behind. Two more gargoyles stand before destroyed furniture and my wounded friends, my father lays unmoving on the floor by Aedan and the male vampire. The others stand back in defeat. Between the two monsters is a beautiful woman with long blonde hair and blood dripping from her fangs. She has a fist full of Jerry's hair, his neck is bleeding loosely.

"Seth, I'm surprised you're still alive. I thought I had taken care of that," she says to the vampire who attacked me. "Where is our little pet, I'm sure she's not far from your side?" She purrs. Seth forms a fireball in his palm, but the woman draws Adaline's uncle nearer. "Tut, tut Seth. You don't want me to kill your lover's uncle, do you? Now if you hand her over I'll allow all of you to keep your lives," she offers. The woman waits, but the problem is none of us knows where Adaline is. "Very well then," she says.

Her claws elongate and she presses them into the side of Jerry's neck, she sighs ambiguously as she slashes her claws all the way across his neck opening it like a tin can. Blood and tissue spill from his neck, his eyes turn dark and his skin pales instantly. She twists his head free from his body and tosses it to the floor. His headless figure slumps to the ground loudly. The rooms frozen, silent with fear. Adaline's blood-curdling scream shakes the foundations of the house and wakens our instinct to fight. Her eyes are wide and bulging as she stares at her uncle's dead body, she starts running toward her uncle's killer, but Seth intercepts her. She thrashes wildly trying to escape his grasp. This is the moment when we need to attack, while the woman and her beasts are distracted. Aedan and I lock eyes, he nods once and we make our move. The others join in, fighting the gargoyles in pairs.

Adaline falls helplessly to floor consumed with grief, the woman makes her way toward her. I try blocking her path but the floorboards snap into splinters as the earth shakes beneath us. The woman laughs and propels me across the room with a wave of her hand. I push past the stabbing pain in my shoulder, moving forward to attack, but her attention has turned to Seth.

"Take Adaline you fuckwit," Seth screams. I suddenly realize he's been yelling at me. I'm at Adaline's side as the woman dispatches Seth as easily as she did me. Adaline's in shock, she's crying hysterically repeating incoherent words, I gather her in my arms, directing her out through the back. I hear Seth make a disgustingly moist curdled cry behind us. Adaline hears it too, her crying ceases, she squares her shoulders and turns back the way we came.

"Adaline stop, we have to go!" I scream above the chaos. She waves her hand as casually as the blonde who's slaughtering our friends, another gale forced wind sends me flying into another wall.

By the time I regain my strength from the impact, Adaline has the woman on the run. Roots and branches are chasing after her while Adaline hurls fire in her direction. The woman attempts to knock Adaline off her feet with a commanding gust of wind, but Adaline shields herself with her own air element. The blonde looks frightened. Both of Adaline's arms become encased in fire, even her hair has flames dancing along the edges.

The blonde looks around for aid, but all she finds is the pieces of her gargoyles that have been scattered across the foyer. She retreats through a shattered window disappearing into the night. Adaline starts to follow her until a pained moan beside me distracts her.

Her flames vanish from her body and her eyes change from lethal back to kind. Seth lays dying on the floor beside me, a solid piece of wood is protruding through his chest. Vampires can survive almost any mortal wound, but this injury was filled with magic and he's lost so much blood, he won't make it. Adaline attempts to remove the wood but she's too weak and begins to cry. She looks up at me pleading for my help. At this moment, I understand. The love she has for him is stronger than anything she could feel for me. I reach down and grasp the impaled wood, I place my foot on his still bleeding chest and pull. The wood gives way releasing his suffering body to the ground.

- 86 -
Adaline

I wipe the blood and grime from his face, searching for the man beneath the muck. I press my lips tenderly to his forehead. My love is the only thing I have left to offer and it's not enough to save him. He reaches out a cool hand tucking my unruly hair behind my ear, a loving gesture I never truly appreciated until now. I feel the trickle of tears running down my cheek, each one vanishing only to be replaced by another. I kiss his palm and hold it against me firmly. If I hold him tightly enough maybe I can fend off death. His strengths wavering. I can feel the life being stolen from him. Mother Nature forcefully dragging him back into the earth.

"I failed you," he whispers.

"You never failed me," I assure him.

He smiles weakly, his chest rising once more before falling flat. I watch the warmth of his coffee coloured eyes fade as they start rolling behind his lids, leaving a ghostly glimmer of white. I feel Tripp's presence behind me, he tentatively places a hand on my shoulder. A gesture of comfort and nothing more, but I'm repulsed by his touch. I smack away his hand cruelly and collapse onto Seth's lifeless body. I cling to him, refusing to see the truth, unwilling to admit that he's gone.

My eyes sting, abused by the onslaught of endless tears. My breathing has hushed to a murmur, barely audible even to myself.

My eyes search out across the debris of battle looking for some hope to cling onto, they pause on a familiar pair of shoes. My uncles black leather uppers. Attached to his shoes are a smart pair of trousers with a few scuff marks on the knees, my eyes wander further towards his crisp white shirt. A sticky crimson substance traces the neckline and I tell myself it's stained with stewed cherries. But I can't lie when I face the blank space before me.

The emptiness that should be filled with a kind face and a loving smile. I watch in slow motion as my hands begin to shake uncontrollably, my body growing increasingly numb with every vibration. A dark silence consumes me. The others continue to walk through the chaos, assessing our losses. I can see their mouths moving, but I can't make out the sounds. In the back of my mind, a small voice whispers that I need to get up. It tells me I need to keep going.

Aedan's gentle arms lift me away from Seth's body. He draws me in close, holding me in a blood-streaked embrace. I can smell his expensive cologne and it reminds me of a better time. There is a serrated wound on his chest that is still bleeding, but I can see it starting to heal, even a fingernail that has been forcibly removed has started to regenerate. I focus on the smell of him, but the stench of the demon's tar-like blood coats his clothes and hair. Aedan's pain mirrors my own, I know his physical injuries are nothing compared to the heartache he's feeling. Aedan trembles around me, between the two of us we have nothing left. What a tragic pair we make. The sun begins to set and pale moonlight glistens on fragments of broken glass that still hugs the window panes.

"Can we move them outside?" I ask. It doesn't feel right having the two people I love most resting amongst all this misery and destruction. Aedan releases his hold on me, leaning down to look at his brother and the filth that is his bed. He agrees to my request and ushers the others inside.

Jason and Aedan gently lift Seth's body and carry him outside, Tripp and Shaylin follow closely behind with my uncle safely in their arms. Jason's struggling to fight back tears as they place Seth in a shallow grave under a beautiful ash tree. I sit down beside Seth and smooth his hair from his face. I'm grateful when Jason starts shovelling dirt on my uncle's grave, I'm not strong enough to look at his disfigured body. I lean down and press my lips to Seth's once more, our kisses never should have been tainted by such sorrow. I feel the earth quiver beneath my fingertips, the wind sings sadly as it dances picking up the debris of battle.

The water deep within the earth yearns for my tears as they sink into the soil. The ground grumbles beneath me shifting at will, sealing Seth's body in the earth. Blue forget-me-nots grow in abundance, transforming the burial site into a serene garden.

I see the flicker of Tripp's hand and I'm appreciative of his gesture. Seth's connection to fire seeps through the earth attempting to warm the bitterness that's taking root within me. It's too late for that.

Aedan and I are the last to leave. Each of us drowning in guilt. Leaving our loved ones behind in unmarked graves is too much to bear. It's a burial that's inadequate of the love we have for them. But it's no longer safe for any of us to stay. Reluctantly we make our way down to the shore.

- 87 -

SETH

A sandy weight is pressing tightly against me, pinning me in place. A strange sensation that's not entirely unpleasant. It's moist and cool against my skin. It's almost comforting, like the day I spent at the lake with Adaline. I can't remember the last time I felt the cold, but I like the way my skin prickles in response to the change in sensations. I breathe deeply, trying to clear the fog that's shadowing my memory, but I just want to sleep.

Everything's dark, I can't remember where I am. There's a gritty substance encasing me makes its way into my nasal passages, dragging the smell of mildew along with it. I cough trying to expel the foreign bodies before they have a chance to travel any further. My lips part, seeking oxygen to clear my airways. I inhale, but there is only heavy moisture to be found. It fill's my mouth, my taste buds recoil from the sharpness of it. It's familiar but I cannot place it. The word lingers on the tip my tongue.

I open my eyes but they are confused by a veil of darkness. The grainy substance finds its way into my eyes. My hands frantically attempt to fend off the assault on my senses. I fight against the pressure holding me down, I squeeze my fists tightly clawing against the weight, desperate to escape. It dawns on me, the word I couldn't grasp, its soil. My prison is the earth itself, I'm surrounded by it. I'm overwhelmed as I struggle to breathe, I panic. I'm buried alive…

Coming 2018

The second instalment of the Seelie Court Chronicles
Awakened

Sadness and LOSS don't stop the world from spinning, even when it feels like it should. The inevitable is still coming and it's time for Adaline to go home.

With her heart shattered and the world around her caving in, will she be able to embrace new LOVE or will she be lost in the darkness of her past?

When secrets and deception lie around every corner, LOYALTY has never been more important.

The SCC Soundtrack One

1. Monster-Imagine Dragons
2. High Hope- Kodaline
3. Centuries- Fall Out Boy
4. Supermarket Flowers- Ed Sheeran
5. Sweater Weather- The Neighbourhood
6. Fear Of Fear- Passenger
7. Send Them Off- Bastille
8. The Little Things- Danny Elfman
9. Look After You- The Fray
10. Falling- HAIM
11. No Light, No Light- Florence + the Machine
12. No Good For Me- The Corrs
13. Thinking of You- Katy Perry
14. These Final Words- Fractured Light Music
15. Secrets- One Republic
16. Howl- Florence and the Machine
17. Fear- Blue October
18. Feel Again- One Republic
19. Let Her Go- Passenger
20. Put The Gun Down- ZZ Ward
21. Powerful- Major Lazer- Powerful feat. Ellie Goulding & Tarrus Riley
22. Dancing On Quick Sand- Bad Suns
23. Stay In The Dark- The Band Perry
24. Waves-Dean Lewis
25. Bare Naked- Jennifer Love Hewitt
26. Sun Comes Up-Rudimental feat. James Arthur
27. Salt- Bad Suns
28. Jealous- Nick Jonas

29. Uh Huh- Julia Michaels
30. If I Die Young- The Band Perry
31. Distance- Christina Perri ft Jason Mraz
32. Ocean Drive - Duke Dumont
33. Closer- The Chainsmokers Feat Halsey
34. Helium- SIA
35. Why- Sabrina Carpenter
36. Breathe Me- SIA
37. Tenerife Sea- Ed Sheeran
38. Stolen- Dashboard Confessional
39. Somebody To Die For- Hurts
40. Fall Out- Marianas Trench
41. Don't Deserve You- Plum
42. You Don't Know- Katelyn Tarver
43. Where Is My Mind- Maxence Cyrin
44. We Move like the Ocean- Bad Suns
45. I'm Gonna Show You Crazy- Bebe Rexha
46. Heavy- Linkin Park feat Kiiara
47. In the Name Of Love- Bebe Rexha and Martin Garrix
48. Sad Song- We The Kings Feat Elena Coats
49. Worst In Me- Julia Michaels
50. Sing Me To Sleep- Alan Walker

About the Author

Hailing from the suburbs of Sydney Australia Jessica grew up in testosterone-fuelled surroundings, overwhelmed with football, fighting and alpha male prowess. To escape the ferociously masculine world her five brothers created around her she turned to the far-off lands of books for salvation.

When Jessica's own creative thoughts could no longer be contained and the pages of the books she read didn't fulfil her needs she turned her vivid imaginings towards paper and pen. In writing she discovered a kind of freedom she had never known, the euphoria consumed her.

Writing like a woman possessed she beckoned the world of her dreams from the deepest recesses of her mind and thrust them into reality.

Jessica has a unique perspective on the human condition that captivates her readers leaving them on the edge of their seats, begging for more. She brings a relatable down to earth quality to her characters that will make you laugh and cry. Her beguiling world of fantasy, betrayal, and love will have you completely hooked.